S. L. Grey

THE APARTMENT

S. L. Grey is a collaboration between Sarah
Lotz and Louis Greenberg. Sarah Lotz is
an award-winning novelist and screenwriter
with a fondness for the macabre. Her col-
laborative and solo novels have been trans-
lated into more than twenty-five languages.
She currently lives in the United Kingdom
with her family and other animals. Louis is
a Johannesburg-bred fiction writer and edi-
tor. He was a bookseller for several years and
has a master's degree in vampire fiction and a
doctorate in postreligious apocalyptic fiction.

slgrey.com

The Apartment

THE APARTMENT

A Novel

S. L. Grey

BLUM**H**OUSE
BOOKS

Blumhouse Books I Anchor Books
A Division of Penguin Random House LLC
New York

A BLUMHOUSE BOOKS/ANCHOR BOOKS ORIGINAL,
OCTOBER 2016

The Library of Congress Cataloging-in-Publication Data
Names: Grey, S. L., author. | Greenberg, Louis, author. | Lotz, Sarah, author.
Title: The apartment / S. L. Grey.
Description: New York : Blumhouse Books/Anchor, [2016] | "A Blumhouse
original novel."
Identifiers: LCCN 2016002574 (print) | LCCN 2016006398 (ebook) |
ISBN 9781101972946 (softcover) | ISBN 9781101972953 (ebook)
Subjects: LCSH: South African fiction (English) | GSAFD: Suspense fiction. |
Mystery fiction. | Occult fiction.
Classification: LCC PR9369.4.G745 A87 2016 (print) |
LCC PR9369.4.G745 (ebook) | DDC 823/.92—dc23
LC record available at http://lccn.loc.gov/2016002574

Anchor Books Trade Paperback ISBN: 978-1-101-97294-6
eBook ISBN: 978-1-101-97295-3

Book design by Steven E. Walker

www.anchorbooks.com

Printed in the United States of America
10   9   8   7   6   5   4   3   2

The Apartment

Chapter 1

Mark

The wine's gone to my head, I realize, as I sway into the kitchen to get another bottle. I'm at that perfect stage of tipsy when I feel padded and warm, forgetful. Carla's belting out her trademark laugh—that Wiccan cackle that's hearty enough to scare ghosts into corners. And somewhere, softly, tentatively, under Carla's vital bray, Steph is laughing too, a sound I haven't heard for weeks. Since.

Trying to ignore the clot of history under the bottom shelf of the narrow pantry, I grab another bag of chips and reverse out into the kitchen again. Carla's date brought an expensive red wine tonight, telling me as he pressed it into my hand that we shouldn't drink it this evening, that we should save it for an occasion, but I'm sure it will go down just fine now. I open the chips and cram a handful into my mouth, then reach for the bottle on the overloaded counter, just as the new motion-activated floodlight in the backyard flicks on. Glancing up, I misjudge my grasp, and the bottle skittles down, smashing into a clutter of dirty glasses and sending a shatter of knives and forks wheeling off the plate on top of the pile.

For just a second the racket is too much; as it crescendoes and settles, the shards and cutlery landing on my feet and the floor around me, I'm unable to move my eyes from the window, staring into the light, as if a floodlight will keep the monsters away.

But it's more than a second, really, a lot more, because when the floodlight finally flicks off after revealing nothing, there's silence around me until I hear someone shifting in the kitchen doorway behind me.

"Mark?" Steph's voice. "You okay, honey?"

I shake myself out of it. "Yes. Sorry, I just ... dropped something."

Steph approaches me, treading with her bare feet across the hazardous floor.

"Don't," I say. "You'll cut yourself."

She ignores me, tiptoes to my side, and looks out at the nothing in the dark yard. "Did you see something?" she asks softly. "Someone?"

"It must have been a cat."

"You sure you're okay?" she says, squeezing my arm.

"I'm fine," I say. But I'm embarrassed by my reaction, so I grab the wine and guide Steph between the shards back through to the dining room, as if she needs my guidance. But the truth is, right now, next to this firm, strong young woman, I feel blind and vulnerable. "Let's drink this while we still can."

Steph glances at me. "Sounds rather ominous."

"I meant—while we can still appreciate it."

"Yes, you should really leave it for a better time." I've forgotten the name of Carla's latest "friend," who's standing at the music dock, putting in his phone and choosing some smooth, cynical track. "You'll miss that famous chocolate on the palate."

"Famous chocolate?" Carla says from her place at the table, artfully pretending that she hasn't heard the disaster in the kitchen. "You mean notorious? That Duiwelsfontein is a tricksy wine for hipster dilettantes. No offense, Damon darling."

"None taken, Carla pumpkin."

I sit down and watch Damon as he sidles back to the table, wondering what's between him and Carla. Does he know he's the latest in Carla's long series of boy toys? What does she get from him? What does he get from her? He must be twenty-five years younger than she is, but then—I pull myself up and remember—I'm twenty-three years older than Steph. I forget that every day. I don't feel forty-seven; I don't feel middle-aged. I can't allow myself to imagine how she sees me—paunchy, floppy, pathetic, damaged, failed, washed-up, some sort of freakish fetish.

Steph's standing behind me, rubbing my shoulders, and now she leans over, and her hair, fragrant from some herbal shampoo and the spice of the supper, falls across my face and saves me from that line of inquiry.

"Just going to run upstairs and check on Hayden," she says.

"I'm sure she's fine. The monitor's right here. We would have heard."

"Just checking."

"Sure. Okay. Thanks."

"If Carla's laughing hasn't woken her, nothing will," Damon chips in at Steph's back, as if he's ever seen our daughter, as if he knows her. Carla smiles and rolls her eyes. I still don't get it.

I take a gulp of the wine—it doesn't taste anything like chocolate—and listen to the lazy drawl of the singer as I concentrate on getting that soft buzz back.

"How're you doing?" Carla asks me. "I mean, really."

I shrug and sigh, then glance at Damon.

"Don't worry, I know," he says. "And I'm really sorry. Same thing happened to my brother."

Steph comes back in, tips me a look saying that Hayden's fine. "Stop it, Damon," Carla says as Steph sits back down, but Damon blunders on.

"This country's fucked, I'm telling you. It's different in other places, you know. People want to steal something, they don't feel the need to torture and—"

"Look," I say, "I don't want to talk about it."

"But you don't have to shush him on my account, Carla," Steph adds. "I'm a big girl."

"Yes," I tell Carla. "In fact, Steph's handling it brilliantly." Better than I am, I don't admit as I put my hand on Steph's thigh under the table and she grips my fingers.

"*Ag,* I'm sorry," Damon says huffily. "It's none of my business."

"It's okay. It's just that, you know . . ."

"I'm just trying to say that I understand," he says. "This sort of shit happens to so many people here. It's just wrong."

"Yes. Yes, it is."

"Now, Damon darling, if you could kindly shut your empathetic trap for a moment while my friend speaks."

"I'll go outside for a smoke. Help me keep my mouth closed." He stands up and heads to the front door while I repress the urge to tell him not to go out, to leave us all safely locked inside. From her place at the head of the table, Carla nudges her bare toes into my shin, then runs them down to my ankle. I'm not sure what it means. I have to presume it's in lieu of a small hug or a pat on the shoulder that she doesn't feel like getting up for. I have to presume that, because Carla and I haven't been physical since forever. At my side, Steph's noticed nothing.

"Does he mind you talking to him like that?" I ask Carla.

She shrugs. "He'll survive. He should learn some manners."

"I don't get you," I say.

She ignores this. "Are you seeing a therapist at least?"

"Me?" I say.

"Both of you. All of you. This sort of trauma lodges in little ones too. You could send Hayden for art therapy."

"We couldn't afford it," Steph says, "even if we thought it would help."

"But the police offered some trauma counseling, didn't they?"

"Yes," I say. Yes, they did. The day after the attack we dutifully showered and got into the cheap new clothes I'd bought for us at the supermarket and headed to the Woodstock police station. The cops were surprisingly polite and sympathetic, despite the fact that we stood out like aliens in the middle of that miserable mass of broken-headed men and ripped women who cluttered the reception area waiting for attention. We were shown through to a small office down a long corridor. Out of the window and across a courtyard I could see the holding cells, the slatted windows draped with fragments of torn cloth, the walls peeling and cracking like the very building was boiling with spite, being reduced to toxic sludge from the inside. The station's trauma counselor was lovely and warm and enthusiastic, one of those people who just won't be worn down by the onslaught of horrible reality, giving us all the time we wanted. While Hayden piled blocks on the carpet, I wished I'd brought hand sanitizer, and while the counselor talked Steph through a meditative energy-clearing visualization technique, I stared into the dingy little shower cubicle and at the plastic caddy of toys and dolls ready for the next case. I couldn't pull my eyes away, despite how the image sent a cold sweat prickling over my forehead. "I got the feeling they had worse traumas to worry about than some middle-class family being burgled."

"Jesus, Mark. You need to value yourself more."

"Value myself? Why?"

Steph says nothing, turning the stem of her wineglass with those restless fingers. Now Carla leans across me, jangling showily, and places her hand on Steph's arm. "You two should get away. Go somewhere for a break. It will make things better—I know it will."

"Where to?" Steph says.

"Somewhere exotic. Bali. Thailand. Or romantic. Barcelona, the Greek islands . . . Paris."

"Ooh, Paris!" Steph just about squeals. "God, Mark, wouldn't that be brilliant?"

"With a two-year-old? Super-romantic."

Carla looks down at the table. "I could offer to . . . Nah, I couldn't. I wouldn't want to inflict my nonexistent maternal instincts on the child."

"We couldn't afford it anyway. Christ, we can't even afford to repair Steph's car."

Steph sighs and nods. "I suppose," she says, and that momentary flicker of light going out in her eyes kills a little bit of me. She deserves what she wants. She deserves better . . . than me, than what I can provide. Which is basically nothing. Everything I briefly had is spent.

"We'll come up with a plan," Carla says. "It has to happen. You two need—"

When the screaming starts, I'm up and halfway across the room before I even register what it is I'm hearing. It's a car alarm outside, just a car alarm, but my muscles have bypassed my thinking brain, and before I can talk myself down, I've whipped open the front door, eyes wide and scanning the half dark of the street, ears tuned for any scuffle. It's Damon's cigarette smoke that finally brings me back to myself.

"Jeez, Mark. Are you okay?"

"I . . . yes, just checking on that alarm." Which has bleeped off already, the guy from number 17 starting up and driving away. I shout something reassuring through to Steph.

"You're on edge, hey?" Damon says, holding out his cigarette pack.

I take one, knowing it will probably just wire me even more. I don't smoke; it makes me feel sick, but maybe nausea would help me concentrate on something other than the goddamn invisible monsters.

He holds up his lighter and I get the cigarette started, then blow out into the wind, feeling the hot breeze from the mountain in my hair and behind my ears. "Has it ever happened to you?"

"No, thank God, but I guess I'm just waiting my turn. It's happened to so many people I know. It messes you up, hey?"

I nod, exhaling slowly. The counselor at the police station recommended replacing negative energy trapped inside with healing air, breathing the toxic fear out. I'm scared to let go of my fear; it has a purpose: it keeps me ready.

When we stub out in the dead planter and go back inside, Steph's saying, "I've always wanted to see the Musée d'Orsay, but we don't have enough money. Simple as that."

"For what?" Damon asks, catching the tail end of the conversation.

"Carla thinks it's a good idea for us to go on an overseas holiday, that it will heal our trauma," I say. "But we've got no cash."

"What about a house swap?" he says. "My mates and I did it last year. There's a website. You go to someone's house and they come to yours. We went to this great house in Boston and they came to our place—they loved it. You don't pay a cent for accommodation. You can eat cheaply if you try, so it costs you nothing."

"But having strangers in your house?" I say. "What if they trash the place, steal all your stuff?"

"The people on the site are all registered and there's feedback and testimonials. Like, the American couple who came here have done eight house swaps before and all the previous owners rated them as guests. They have a track record, so you know you can trust them."

Steph smiles. "Hmm, sounds interesting. Hey, Mark?" And it's then that I can see her hopes getting raised by this guy. The kindest thing I can do is nip it in the bud.

"We won't pay a cent," I say. "Apart from the small matter of airfares and visas and transport and entry fees and hundred-rand coffees and God knows what else we'd have to cough up for in Paris." I watch in dismay as Steph's face registers her punctured enthusiasm. It's something I do well—dull the eagerness of young people—I do it every day at the college; it's one of my few marketable skills. She nods in deflated agreement and I wish I hadn't said anything. I always underestimate the full force of my depressive cynicism. I forget that she's young, that she has some spirit in her. I should be more careful with her.

"But it does sound interesting," I add lamely. "The most feasible idea we've heard so far." I try to raise that smile again, but it's all too late.

Later, I wake up standing in the hallway, my heart hammering in my throat and my left leg jittering, my phone clutched in my hand. The time on the red display of the alarm console reads 2:18. The Alsatian next door is barking and I swear I hear a *thump*—another *thump?*—on our side of the dividing wall between the properties.

I should look out of the study window to check if there's anything—anyone—in the alley, but the alarm is armed, the passive transponder scanning that room. I don't want to disarm the system—they may be waiting for me to do just that—so I'm stuck standing in the hallway in the middle of the house, turning slowly so the floorboards don't creak too much and wake Hayden, listening and staring around me, as if I've got supersonic hearing, as if I'm Superman with X-ray vision. I'm not; I'm immobile and impotent.

If there is someone down the side alley, the beams will set off the alarm, I tell myself. *We're okay,* I tell myself.

The dog settles down, and I don't hear anything else, the outside beams don't trip, so I finally go back up to bed. Steph's lying on her back, staring at the ceiling in a resigned way.

I remain standing on the carpet next to the bed. "I should really bypass the study, but it'd be easy for them to get in there through the leaded window."

"Yes, better leave it armed."

"But then I can't see outside."

"The beams would pick up anything."

"I suppose." I put my phone back on the nightstand. "You've got to love our midnight conversations. Our sweet nothings." She doesn't say anything, certainly doesn't laugh, but why should she? I glance at the red numbers on our bedside clock. "Try to get some sleep. It's too early to give up."

"What about you?"

I don't tell her that I think one of us should always stay awake, in case they come back, that I shouldn't have fallen asleep in the first place. That wouldn't be helpful. "I'll just decompress a bit, join you in a little while."

"I hate this place sometimes, you know."

"I know."

"Can't you even consider the trip? Don't you think it would be nice?"

"It just doesn't seem possible. It's a luxury we can't afford."

Steph sits up, her pillows rubbing against the headboard, making a low groan. "I'm thinking it's not a luxury; I'm thinking that it's a necessity. I think it would help. You particularly."

"Me?"

"Yes, you." Now she laughs, but it's a dry laugh. "I reckon getting away would give you some perspective, some peace. Who knows? It might even make you happy."

I'm not comfortable getting into this discussion while I stand above her like some authority, so I sit at the foot of the bed, facing away from her, looking at a piece of her through the dresser mirror. "Even if we could pay for it, I wouldn't want it to be because you think I'm ailing. I don't want to be some hospital case, forcing you to make sacrifices, spending money we don't have just so that I feel better, so that I don't have a mental breakdown. I'm not going to. I'm fine. I'm managing."

Steph doesn't even bother to agree or disagree with my self-diagnosis; she knows me too well. "I've been thinking a lot and I'm sure Hayden would be fine. She's been sleeping much better. Carla says you can rent pushchairs and everything. Kids in Paris all go around in prams. Imagine strolling through the parks like a French family."

I know it would never work, but I watch her dreamy, unguarded smile in the mirror and remember this time not to burst her bubble. The trip's not going to happen—it's just a fantasy, one that's getting her to smile again—so I may as well indulge her.

Chapter 2

Steph

I should have made more of a stink when Mark told me Carla had invited herself to dinner that night. He offered to put her off—he knew the only people I could cope with after the break-in were my parents—but I thought we might as well get it over and done with. And it was about time I faced the outside world. My friends had tried to rally round, but I was sick to death of hearing, "Well, at least Hayden slept through it and you weren't raped," and other fucked-up platitudes. Mark begged me not to fuss, but as usual, I spent far too long preparing for that meal. Scrubbing the house like a neurotic 1950s hostess, splurging on top-quality ingredients that we couldn't afford. I did it every time Carla came over.

Carla intimidated me. There, I've said it. A published poet and academic, she was everything I'm not: confident, chic, charismatic, and whipcord thin. Privately, I thought her writing self-indulgent and unreadable, but it had garnered her several local and international awards, whereas my publishing credits back then amounted to a couple of unpaid book reviews on an insignificant literary website. Like a lot of liberals of her generation, she wore her impeccable Struggle credentials on her sleeve, dropping anecdotes about being detained by the security police into conversation whenever she had a chance (although it's hard to find a middle-aged white person these days, apart from my parents, who admits to just sitting back during apartheid). And of course she and Mark had a history together, one that preceded me; one that excluded me.

He denied they'd ever had a fling, but I don't know what to believe anymore.

I'm not being fair. I might not have liked Carla, but she wasn't all bad. She'd been kind to us during Hayden's colicky infancy, when Mark and I were fragile and fractious after months of ruined sleep. She would pop in to check on us and deliver lentil moussakas once a week. We never ate them; they steadily filled the freezer, and for all I know they might still be there.

That night I dutifully served up the spatchcock chicken and baked potatoes, dolloped vastly expensive chocolate mousse into bowls, and smiled like a geisha, occasionally slipping off for some peace on the pretext of checking on Hayden. I went through the motions, tuning out while pretending to listen to the conversation, which was dominated by Carla and that man she'd brought along (it's funny, I can remember that night in detail, but I can't recall his name). But my attention was caught by the mention of a trip overseas: Carla's blithe suggestion that we get away for a while. Mark usually went along with what Carla said, mostly just to humor her, so when he shot her down I was pleased at first, but then . . . Paris. *Paris.*

Into my mind flashed an image of Mark and me strolling down the Champs-Élysées, Hayden sleeping in Mark's arms, chic French people smiling at us fondly as we passed. I imagined us pausing for coffee and croissants, sitting under an umbrella at a charming corner café; I pictured us eating French onion soup and crêpes for supper in a quaint bistro. My mind filled with one cliché after another, but it wasn't just the lure of the destination. I was drawn to the idea of a house swap. Since the break-in, the atmosphere of our house had shifted somehow. It had become darker, as if sunlight could no longer find its way in. The hastily installed new security measures didn't help: the burglar bars cast fingerish shadows on the floor, and the alarm pipped every time someone opened a door, putting us permanently on edge. I suppose I thought that if someone else stayed in the house—someone who wasn't us—perhaps the bad vibes would be vanquished.

While Mark batted opinions about Jacob Zuma back and forth with Carla's boy toy, I slipped out to make coffee, surprised and dismayed when Carla followed me into the kitchen. I suspected she had an agenda. I was right. "Mark needs help," she said the second we were out of earshot. "He must go and see someone. A therapist." There was a note of accusation in her voice, as if I was the one stopping him. As if the whole thing was my fault. As if I'd got off lighter than he had that night, when objectively the opposite was true. I moved to the sink so that she couldn't see my face, and needlessly rinsed the French press. "You're strong, Steph," Carla continued. "You're obviously coping well. Mark's vulnerable to PTSD. It hasn't been that long since Zoë ... well, you know. A thing like this could spark off all kinds of latent trauma ..." Yadda yadda yadda. I didn't reply, just spooned the coffee and concentrated on not letting her see my hands shaking.

After Carla left, it took me hours to fall asleep, only to be woken by Mark leaping out of bed at two thirty. This wasn't unusual. Since the invasion, the slightest sound—a moth batting against the bathroom light, the distant bark of a neighborhood dog—would jolt us awake. I waited numbly in the bedroom while he finished his patrol, my mouth dry as I imagined the worst—a gunshot, a blow to the head, the slam of footsteps heading for the bedroom door ... I knew from experience that I wouldn't drop off again until it began to get light, so I waited until Mark was dozing, then picked up the cheap replacement laptop and headed for Hayden's room, the only place in the house I felt truly safe. As usual, the groans and creaks of the house cooling after a hot day sounded too much like the scratch of a screwdriver in a lock, or footsteps creeping along the corridor. No amount of convincing myself that Mark had double- and triple-checked the locks and alarm helped: the men who'd invaded our home had stained the house with their shadows. As I passed the bathroom, the towel draped over the open door formed itself into a figure with a cruel knife; the carelessly forgotten laundry basket at the top of the stairs was a hunchback waiting to spring. By the time I made it into the safety of Hayden's room my heart was jitterbugging.

She always slept askew—legs twisted across the bed, duvet kicked around her feet—and I carefully tucked her in before squeezing in next to her and balancing the laptop on my knees. Mark might be reluctant to get away, but I wasn't willing to let it go. He was right, we could never pay for it, but I couldn't see the harm in dreaming about it. There were scores of house swap sites—Carla's companion had been right about that at least. I chose one with a photo of an Alpine chalet on its home page and signed up for the thirty-day free trial. I had to put in three desired destinations in order of priority—"Be flexible!" the site's FAQs encouraged. I put in Paris, then Ireland (no need for a visa), and then the United States. We'd need a tourist visa for most of Europe, but it was Paris I was set on. The seed had been planted. As I uploaded the most flattering pics of our house from the ones we'd taken when we'd almost put it on the market the year before, I felt as if I was doing something illicit—like emailing a lover.

Next I typed in the kind of description I hoped would hook a potential Parisian house swapper. *Comfortable, historic house in sunny Cape Town!* "Historic" was an exaggeration, although our house was nestled on a street of mostly Victorian terraces. I added "secure" but then felt guilty and deleted it. To be fair, it wasn't really a lie. Dad had driven down from Montagu the morning after the break-in, armed with his welding torch and a pickup truck full of rebar, and our sash windows now sported heavy steel burglar bars. Mark had mumbled something about aesthetics, but he hadn't stopped Dad from turning the house into Alcatraz. He wouldn't have dared. He'd stayed out of Dad's way that day, avoiding the silent accusation hanging in the air: *You should have protected your family better, asshole.*

Next, I googled flights. Air France was having a special in February as long as we booked within the next three days—all the pieces were slotting into place. I decided not to contact anyone on the house swap site right away. I'd leave it up to fate, wait to hear from them first. I slept for a blissfully deep hour until Hayden woke me at six.

Not wanting to risk a fight, I didn't tell Mark that morning that I'd signed up on the site. Another rough night had made him tetchy, and he left for work without saying much more than "Lock the gate behind me." I gave Hayden her cereal, then sat her in front of Nickelodeon. I wasn't hungry, but I found myself retrieving the half-empty bowl of chocolate mousse from the fridge and spooning it into my mouth while I checked my emails. Two from the bank, advising us that we'd hit our credit limit again; nothing from the house swap site apart from a thank-you message for signing up.

Mom called, checking up on us as she did every morning, and after listening to her usual pleas to bring Hayden to stay with her for a few days, I told her about the house swap idea. She was immediately enthusiastic, mainly because she was desperate for us to get out of Cape Town, which she now thought of as a hostile, dangerous city. "And what does Mark think?"

"He's not keen. And we can't really afford it." I tried not to dwell on the fact that if I'd bothered to find a job, then we probably *would* have the money.

"You must make him go. We can lend you the money for the flights, can't we, Jan?"

Dad mumbled gutturally in the background.

"I can't let you do that, Mom." Their B and B was struggling—had been since they'd bought it two years before.

"We can find the money. It's about time Mark put you first, my girl."

"It's been hard for all of us, Mom. He's doing his best."

She murmured something I couldn't make out, but then she dropped the subject. She hated confrontation.

"How's business, Mom? Any bookings?"

"We have two Dutch people with us for a week. Gays."

"Does Dad know they're gay?"

"*Ag,* Steffie. He's not completely stuck in the Dark Ages. And then we're empty until March." She paused. "If you did go away, we could look after Hayden."

"I'd take Hayden with us, Mom."

"We'd love to have her. You know that."

I let her continue to try to convince me while I googled "top ten things to do in Paris in February," occasionally checking my Gmail. And that's when I saw the email from the house swap site: *Hey, Stef198, Petit08 has sent you a message! Click here to see more . . .* I wrapped up the call and opened the email: *Bonjour Stephanie et Mark! You are place looks nice! See ours we can come anytime you choose it ;) à bientôt!!!! From Mal et Junie Petit.*

I clicked on the link provided, which opened to the Petits' property page and a thumbnail portrait of a thirtyish couple crowded into the shot, selfie-style, sunglasses on their heads, a double dose of white teeth. They were an advertiser's dream: blond and happy. There were six photos of their apartment, taken mostly from the outside—the only interior shot showed a freestanding Victorian bath, a burgundy towel draped over its lip—along with a succinct description: "Stylish luxurious place in fantastic location for City of Love!!! Sleeps 2 or three personnes." The building looked weathered and elegant and typically French, with a large solid wooden door and narrow windows fringed with curlicued metal balustrades. There were no reviews, but so what? We didn't have any reviews either. Perhaps they were first-time house swappers like us.

I didn't hesitate. *Bonjour!* I typed in. *It's lovely to meet you!*

Chapter 3

Mark

The car behind me bleats the second the light changes, shunting me out of another vague vision of masked men shouting orders. I deliberately take my time releasing the hand brake and pulling off. The suit behind me—a guy no older than twenty-five in an open-top Porsche—gesticulates angrily, and I play the part of the doddery oldster. Cape Town used to have a reputation for being mellow and chilled, but now it seems overrun with uptight corporate types who wish they were in L.A.

The guy tails me all the way to the Buitengracht lights and I feel his glare in the rearview mirror. Not long ago, I would have returned it, but today I can hardly bear to glance back. Any more knocks from life right now and I might just dissolve.

I'm so tired. The irony is that Hayden's sleeping better than ever these past couple of weeks. She's been waking only once, or not at all through the whole night, but still I can't—or don't allow myself to—sleep. Rationally, I know that staying awake all night doesn't make us any safer. I know it's not good for me or for Steph and Hayden when every little bit of attention or help they need from me becomes a difficult demand because I'm so drained. I get irritable and I know I shouldn't be. But still, I can't sleep. What if they come back? If I'm awake, they won't get to Steph.

To try to distract myself, I flick the car's iPod player on. The randomizer selects "I'm a Funny Old Bear" and I'm thrown back seven years to Zoë's first-grade awards ceremony. Packed into the school hall with mothers and lost-looking fathers whose own fathers would never have bothered to attend an insignificant occasion like this. The children were singing this song about Winnie-the-Pooh and it struck me: they seemed happy. Somehow my daughter had escaped the dull, sullen neglect of my own childhood, and something about that plain fact twisted my gut. I started crying as they cheered their way through the chorus. It was her last awards ceremony.

It's a relief, really, to be picking at the scab of this comforting old pain rather than our more recent trauma. I look in the rear-view mirror again, imagining Zoë sitting strapped in the back. But of course she wouldn't be sitting there anymore. She'd be fourteen now, up in the passenger seat. Jesus.

It was several months before I could bring myself to take her booster seat out of the car. There are two holes where it wore through the backseat's fabric and still a collage of stains from all the food she spilled as she grew up.

Why're you sad, Daddy? I imagine her saying.

I'm not, sweetie. Just . . . tired.

Is it the new girl? Your Other Daughter?

The guy behind me honks again, interrupting my fantasy. Not just him, but a row of cars behind me. This time, I put my hand up in apology and pull off. I check in the mirror again, and the backseat's still vacant. I change to morning radio to drown out the voices.

When I've squeezed into the tiny underground parking bay, I scan into the Melbourne City Campus elevators. When I was retrenched from the University of Cape Town—"The department is becoming remodularized into more relevant and productive study areas, Mark, and we simply don't need two specialists in Victorian literature. Maeve's lucky enough to hang on to her portfolio, and that's only because she's more senior than you"—I was offered two positions elsewhere. I chose the Melbourne City Campus job because it presented longer, university-style courses. I thought that was important at the time, but I should have taken the CyberSmarts job instead; I would have been able to lead my online, outcomes-based cram tutorials from the comfort of my study and take naps between emails.

I greet Lindi at the reception desk and head down the sixth-floor corridor, following the sign to Communications, Networking and Correspondence toward my slot of an office. This "campus"—really just another anonymous suite of offices and boardrooms—was furnished no more than three years ago, but already the office door droops and the carpet tiles are coming up, so I have to shoulder my way in every morning. There are three shelves bracketed into one wall, sparsely littered with a pile of files and papers. I still haven't bothered to move my books in here, and I know it's because that would imply some sort of commitment. Twenty-five years' worth of arcane Victorian (not to mention Elizabethan and early-modern) expertise still lies dust-caked in its boxes at home.

I go to the kitchenette to fill up my water bottle. I really feel like coffee, but there's only cheap instant and I still haven't got it together to buy myself a coffeemaker for my office. As I'm bent over the slow-running tap, I feel someone coming into the narrow space behind me. The kitchen's so small that the unspoken etiquette is for only one person at a time to enter, but now I feel a hand clamping my arm.

"How are you doing, Mark?"

I turn awkwardly to Lindi, who's now blocking any escape route.

"Fine, thanks, and you?" I say, hoping that she'll leave it there.

But she doesn't. "No, I mean really. It's such a terrible thing that happened to you and your wonderful family." She's never even met Steph or Hayden—of course I would never bring them here.

"Thanks. We're okay." I don't want this conversation. My wonderful families and terrible things seem to go together. Just imagine how Lindi would be acting if she knew about my *first* family. She's just being kind, but when she probes like this, I feel cornered and snappish, and I don't want to be rude to one of my few friends here.

"I want you to be okay," she says.

"Mmm, thanks," I say again, and pointedly turn back to the sink, where my container is full and overflowing pathetically down the drain.

Finally, Lindi gets the hint and moves away.

Trailing down the corridor to Classroom C12, my water bottle in hand, I realize how hunched I've become. I straighten my back and level my shoulders, girding myself for the soul-sucking onslaught of the Level 1 General Literature class. I stride in with a sad, forced "Good morning!" dripping with false cheer. There's only the slightest dip in the volume of conversation as I set up the keywords on the projector. When I start talking, most of the kids look at me with some variation of loathing and distaste, as if I'm the sand in their Vaseline. It's war poetry today, but it could be anything. I used to be interested in this stuff when I was young—I had better teachers than myself, I suppose—but I can't conceive of a way to engage these students, who stare at me, fuming like angry customers who aren't getting what they paid for. I become aware of the drone in my voice, and the more I talk, the more anxious I become.

Somehow, at last, it's ten o'clock. When I get back to my office, I check my emails, ignoring the departmental circulars and clicking open a message from Steph. After all this time, my mood still bumps up every time I see her name in my in-box.

Hi Mark,

Didn't tell you this morning because I wanted to surprise you, but just to let you know that I put in a request for a house swap. Here are the details of the place that responded—they sound v cool and French!

Mom and Dad are happy to lend us the money for the air tickets—so no excuses!

I know you secretly love the idea and you'll come around—we'll all have fun and it will be good for us.

I love you,

S

I'm surprised by a quick rush of indignation. How could she do this when I've already said no? But I can sense the rot in our marriage caused by this fucking break-in and I know I've got to make an extra effort to be positive. I can see how hard Steph's trying—and, besides, she still knows she'll win me over with that "I love you."

I swivel my chair around and stare out the window at the block work of rooftop air conditioners and silvering in the back lots and the mountain beyond them, looming massive in a hot, clear sky. Paris . . . She knows me—I've always wanted to go. I can't blame Steph that we're in such a dire financial position.

Turning back to the screen, I click on the link she sent. It looks like one of those classic Parisian buildings on a narrow road with a little tree-lined square at the end. The suburb sounds pleasant, apparently close to all the attractions but quiet, near Montmartre, where the artists lived and there's that big white church.

In a different life, it *would* be a great idea. But not this life, not now. Even if we could accept money from Steph's parents to go jaunting overseas, hauling Hayden through a foreign city wouldn't be as romantic as it sounds. Wheeling a docile little French girl in a pram through the Parisian parks sounds like fun, but we both know how Hayden gets when she needs to pee, when she's hungry, when she's tired, when she's hot, when she's cold—and not just Hayden. That's natural for any toddler. Steph's not being realistic.

Clicking to the house swappers' profile, I see a buff young couple called the Petits who have put some tourist links into their property description. I read through a list of literary walks in Paris, and before I realize it, twenty minutes have passed. Just imagine strolling the same cobbles as Hemingway and Gauguin and Monet and Balzac and Foucault—and Woody Allen. It wouldn't be quite the same as strolling the prefab indoor cobbles, circa 2008, of the Canal Walk mall. Steph chose well—I *have* always wanted to go, and I've just thought of a way I can make the trip work.

I pick up the phone and dial Steph's parents. I'm relieved when Rina answers; Jan and I don't get along—he's only five years older than me and doesn't trust me with his daughter, despite the fact that I've always treated her with love and respect. As a father of daughters, though, I understand where he's coming from—I'd hate me too.

"How could you, Mark?"

That was quick. I've only just come back with my daily grande from the coffee shop downstairs. Rina must have called Steph straightaway.

"I wanted to surprise you back. I thought you'd be—"

"I'm calling Mom now. I'm telling her—"

"Hang on, Steph. Think about it." I stand up and close my office door, but I'll still have to keep my voice very low to avoid being heard through the cardboard walls. "If you think about it for one minute, you'd know that taking Hayden to Paris with us would be a bad idea. *She'd* hate it."

"You're so distant with her sometimes, Mark. It makes me wonder if—"

"Don't start. Please, honey. You know how I feel." Because I do love Hayden, everything she represents to me. Because even though it was an accident—I assumed Steph was on the Pill and she assumed I'd had the chop—I'll never forget that feeling when Steph told me she was pregnant. My pure joy took me by surprise as much as it did Steph. For a change, my feelings bypassed my doubts and it took me a while to understand why I was so happy. I was so in love with Steph, the world seemed to glow around her. She was my second chance—one I thought I'd never get and one I certainly didn't deserve—and the gift of a baby felt like part of my redemption. Of course, the idea of a new baby was smothered with guilt and sadness, but it did help to think just how much Zoë would have loved a sister.

"It's so hard for you to say it, isn't it? That you love Hayden."

I think of how different the two girls are. Zoë, fair-haired and always sparkly and game for a challenge, just like her mother; and dark little Hayden, whiny, needy, prone to nightmares. I wonder just how much of that darkness I've instilled in her. I was a different man when Zoë was born, with the joyful confidence that would have encouraged a little girl to explore, but with Hayden . . . Still, it all means that when Hayden has one of her magic moments, it cuts like a knife through all the shit. I do love her, but I won't rise to Steph's taunt to be glib, so I plow on. "Your parents want to see Hayden, and Hayden loves it at their place. It's the perfect plan. And, besides, because she's turned two, she'd pay full price for her air ticket if we took her to France. We're saving your parents that."

She pauses, and I can tell she's started to hear me. "You should have discussed it with me first."

"You never would have agreed."

"To abandoning my daughter so that we can go on holiday? You're right, I wouldn't."

"Exactly."

"Well, fuck it. I don't want to go anymore. You thought it was a stupid idea. I don't know why you're suddenly so—"

"The tickets are nonrefundable."

"You already bought *tickets*? What—"

"Well, your mother did. She didn't want you to end up not going. She thinks it's a good idea for us both—for us all. And I agree. Hayden will love her break as much as we will."

"I don't want to go without her, Mark."

"You wanted this trip, Steph. I know you did. And Rina convinced me just how much we need it." It's not fair to blame Rina, I know, but she really was supportive. "Think about it like this: it'll be the honeymoon we never had."

"You're an arsehole," she says, but her tone isn't very angry. She'll come around.

Chapter 4

Steph

I still feel a kernel of guilt—and resentment—when I think back on how easily Mark manipulated me into leaving Hayden behind.

Yeah, I'll admit, a treacherous part of me relished the thought of shedding the daily routine for a few days, sleeping late and visiting restaurants and museums without a toddler in tow. But still the thought burned: *Why don't you* really *want our daughter to come with us, Mark?* It wasn't as if he was ever cold with her exactly, but since the home invasion, I couldn't help but feel that a distance had crept into his relationship with her.

I suppose I was also swayed by Mark's U-turn about the trip. The anticipation of it seemed to awaken something inside him, something that had lain dormant since the night those fuckers invaded our home. I let him take over the arrangements and chat to the Petits—he would read out the most hilarious of their obviously Google-translated messages to me in bed every evening—and he threw himself into making plans: booking visa appointments, downloading maps, trawling TripAdvisor for budget restaurant recommendations. I was desperate not to do or say anything that would dampen his mood; even the house appeared to take on a lighter atmosphere, as if it knew it would soon be hosting a fresh pair of inhabitants who weren't such downers. Slot, slot, slot, everything fell into place seamlessly. The visa interviews went without a hitch, and Mark would be able to squeeze in a week's leave just before the semester started in mid-February.

She may not have been my favorite person, but Carla also came to the party, offering to liaise with the Petits and hand over the keys when they arrived. A couple of days before we were due to leave, she showed up at the house and thrust a plastic garment bag into my arms. I unzipped it to reveal a chocolate-colored cashmere coat. "You can borrow it," she said. "It should fit you; it's a couple of sizes too big for me." Sting in the tail or not, I was grateful for the thought. The coat was beautiful.

I still have it.

But as the days bled away and the departure date neared, I became anxious. I spent two full days frantically preparing the house and typing out pages of instructions for everything from the alarm system to the dishwasher. The day before we left, I bought milk, butter, bread, bacon, and fresh coffee for the Petits—the kind of expensive fair-trade stuff I'd never have dreamed of buying for Mark and me. I splurged on new sheets, pillowcases, and towels. I scrubbed walls, bleached the bathroom, and tidied drawers, trying not to think about the sinister, gloved fingers that had rooted through their contents during the break-in. The floors gleamed and every room was filled with the scent of cedar oil. I was overcompensating, hoping that an immaculate interior would make up for the rowdy student neighbors, the wailing of the homeless people who lived under the highway bridge, and the welded bars on the windows, which hadn't been featured in the photos I'd uploaded to the house swap site. It's ironic now—actually, tragic—but all I could think was: *What if the Petits complain that we misrepresented the house?*

My parents collected Hayden the morning we were due to leave, and as I helped strap her into her car seat, I was filled with the certainty that I would never see her again. I had to will myself not to scream at my parents to stop as they pulled away.

Mark put an arm around me as the car disappeared around the corner. "She'll be fine, Steph."

"Yeah."

I was being irrational. I knew I was. Nothing was going to happen to Hayden. Collectively, Mark and I had been through more than our fair share of hardship: Zoë's death, Hayden's chronic colic, the break-in—surely we were due a run of good luck? To take the edge off, I downed two of the Urbanol tablets the doctor had given me for anxiety after the attack—the visit to the doctor and the tranquilizers were my little secret; knowing about them would only have upset Mark—and, numbed by the meds, I helped Mark pack. I had to remember that the trip was for him as well. *It'll be the honeymoon we never had.* Things had moved so quickly after we met, we hadn't managed to find the time for that sort of romantic gesture.

I first saw Mark on my second day working part-time in the UCT English Department office. A roommate had helped me get the job; I was struggling to pay my rent after moving to Cape Town to do an English honors degree. Xoliswa, the department secretary, and I were about to go to lunch when a man with a rumpled Robert Downey Jr. face and creased trousers blundered into the office to use the printer. I offered to help him and he smiled at me—a warm just-for-you smile.

"Who's that?" I asked Xoliswa the second he was out of earshot.

"Mark. English lecturer. Nice guy."

"And?" I waited for Xoliswa to fill me in. None of the faculty who drifted onto our radar escaped without a gossipy foot-note from her: the senior lecturer who wasn't allowed to have female students in his room without leaving the door open; the tutor who was sleeping with the very married professor of linguistics; the closeted academic who still lived with his mother. Everyone in the department had a scandalous back-story, and she knew them all.

"And what?"

"Come on, Xoliswa. Spill."

She sighed. "I heard his daughter died."

"Oh. Oh God."

"Yes. Very sad. She was seven or something. Destroyed his marriage."

"How did she die?"

"I don't know." She clucked her tongue. I couldn't tell if she was aggrieved that she didn't know the details or felt bad for Mark.

Over the next few days, I found myself keeping an eye out for him, casting around in the cafeteria queue and the department's corridors (I'd learned that he had a temporary office on the top floor). I daydreamed about him; imagined him strolling into the office, where we'd strike up a conversation that would lead to drinks, maybe even dinner. It sounds stalker-ish now, but I googled him, scoured the Web for reviews of his academic work, searched for him on Facebook. I tried to pin down why he'd struck a chord in me. Was it the sadness he must carry around? I wasn't melancholic; I had no edge, no tragic backstory, no grand passion, no heartbreak. My two previous relationships had ended amicably. I thought of myself as boring, level-headed, in control. I was the designated driver, the caretaker. Ms. Reliable.

I next ran into him at a book launch that was being held at a store in town—one of the department heads was launching a tome on Derrida or something and attendance was mandatory. My heart hitched when I saw him in the store's basement collecting a glass of red wine from the makeshift bar. Ignoring the knots of people chatting and laughing too loudly, he wandered over to the poetry section. He was drinking his wine too quickly.

After only a moment's hesitation, I made my excuses to

Xoliswa, who gave me a knowing glance, and then I approached him, although I'd never been that brazen before. "Hi."

It was obvious that he was struggling to place me, and I fought to hide my disappointment. In my fantasy, I'd filled his head as much as he filled mine. He gave me a rueful grin. "Are you one of my students?"

"No. I work in the office."

"Of course. I'm sorry." He gave an embarrassed laugh.

A woman wearing too much jewelry and what looked to be a kimono (Carla, of course) glided up to us. "Mark, there you are. Come and meet Abdul. He's a big fan."

Mark tried to introduce me—which was awkward enough as he didn't yet know my name—but Carla whisked him away before he could finish his sentence. I don't think she was simply being rude. She was perceptive; she must have sensed that something had sparked between us.

During the Q&A, I found a seat at the back of the room, a few rows behind him. He turned to look at me once, as if he could feel my eyes on his back, and gave me a small smile. I made excuses to stay behind while Xoliswa and my friends headed off to Long Street for drinks, but it was hopeless; Mark was sucked into a Carla-clique and I didn't have the nerve to insert myself into the group. After spending far too much money on books I didn't need or want, I left. But my car, the battered Fiat I'd inherited from Mom, was no longer in its parking spot. Stomach hollow, and hoping against hope that I'd misremembered where I'd parked it, I ran up and down the road, scouring side streets. It was gone. I washed up next to a small group of strangers smoking outside the bookshop.

I stood there for more than a minute, my car keys hanging uselessly in my hand.

Someone touched my arm. "Hello again."

It was Mark. I looked at him and burst into tears.

He took me to the police station to make a statement and then gave me a lift home. We sat in the car outside my house talking for hours. Nothing was off-limits that night. I told him about my childhood, about my fear that I wasn't good enough to be a writer, which was all that I'd ever wanted to be, and he told me about his wife's long illness and his divorce. It was the only time that he spoke frankly to me about Zoë. About his guilt, his pain, his struggle to live with the loss and the resentment of a world that just carried on as if nothing had happened. I know now that he opened up to me only because at that stage we were little more than strangers. After that he would mention Zoë only if prompted, but she was there, unspoken, unseen, in our lives, every second of every day.

Two days after that we slept together for the first time. Three weeks after that I moved in with him. In another two months I would be pregnant.

Both of us were lighter the second we stepped onto the plane, and I remember thinking, *We're safe; they can't get us here.* Neither of us slept: we spent the journey drinking too many gin and tonics and talking about what we'd see, where we'd go— I fantasized about strolling along the Champs-Élysées, buying a chic French outfit for Hayden—our plans to sleep late and eat out. We arrived at the train station at Charles de Gaulle exhausted but upbeat. Not even the shivery first sense of the icy winter air or the unexpectedly depressing view from the train window—the cluster of sagging shacks that clung to the side of the train tracks, the bad graffiti, the utilitarian buildings— brought me down. At the first stop, a burly man clutching a microphone and dragging a speaker on a cart clambered on board. He burbled something in French and pressed a button on the speaker, and a synthesized backing track to "Sorry Seems to Be the Hardest Word" blared through the train. I gave Mark a sideways glance as the man began to sing. His voice wasn't bad, but he was having difficulty pronouncing the words—especially "sorry"—and appeared to be making the lyrics up as he went along. Mark leaned toward me, grinned, and whispered, "I'm sowwy, Steph."

And then we were both laughing uncontrollably. Tears ran down my cheeks. It was a good start, a happy start. We came out of the Métro at the busy Place Pigalle and followed the route downhill into a maze of apartment buildings. After a small café-lined square ringed by motorcycles, we turned left into a narrower street that seemed to be more of a thorough-fare than anything else. Most of the buildings here were a uni-form off-white on the outside, with their heavy front doors brightly painted. Many of the windows were shuttered, but here and there we saw a hint of the character and charm that might be hidden inside: bright window boxes, the odd pol-ished brass balustrade, golden light seeping between the slats.

The trip took its first sour turn only when we found our apartment. "We need number 16," Mark said, staring at the numbers stuck next to the intercoms adjacent to each doorway.

We found 15, 17, and 18, but no 16. After retracing our steps, we decided the only option was a huge green door with a faded À LOUER sign nailed to it. I pushed against it, expect-ing it to be locked, but it creaked open, revealing a shadowy courtyard beyond, its brickwork lousy with algae. A row of wooden mailboxes with tags on them lined one wall, and we searched for the Petits' name—according to their last email, the keys would be inside their box. It wasn't hard to find: the other names were washed out and illegible. Keys retrieved, we headed for a pair of smeared glass doors at the far side of the courtyard, and Mark tapped the Petits' combination into the keypad. The doors clicked open, and we stepped into a narrow hallway, a dusty pushchair folded against the wall, climbed a couple of steps tiled in dirty beige, and then reached the foot of a skinny spiraling staircase. I breathed in the specter of ancient cooking and mold.

"Third floor," Mark said, grabbing both suitcases.

I prodded at the light switch, but the stairwell above us stayed pitch-dark. Mark had the sense to use the light on his phone. The only sound was the clump of our footsteps on the wooden stairs. I found myself talking in whispers. "It's a bit grim, isn't it?"

"Communal areas are always like this," Mark panted, the effort of hefting the luggage stealing his breath. We were heading upward, but it felt as if we were descending, as if the air was getting heavier with each step. While I held the phone, Mark wrangled the door lock. After several frustrating minutes, it clicked.

I'd like to say I sensed something was wrong as soon as I walked through the doorway. But really, after we'd fumbled for the light switch—the windows were shuttered and there was no natural light in the apartment—all I felt at first was profound disappointment. The Petits had come across as young and vibrant, and I'd imagined a stylish renovated apartment with white walls, tasteful prints, and hipster-chic minimalist furniture. Instead the place looked like it had been decorated in the seventies and left to rot. The couch was brown corduroy with dirty orange-pine arms, the television a relic from the early nineties; a couple of cardboard boxes sealed with brown tape were shoved against the wall, and a dirty sock lay curled underneath the coffee table, as if the Petits had left in a hurry. At least it was warm—too warm. I shrugged off Carla's coat.

"This can't be the right place. It's a dump." I was still whispering.

"The keys fit. And it said 3B."

"Maybe the apartments all have the same lock?"

"Wait. I'll double-check."

I stood in the center of the room while Mark went back out

into the corridor. A single framed picture on the wall above the couch caught my eye: a photograph of a young woman, freckle-faced, wisps of raven hair blowing across her cheeks. She was smiling, but her eyes were blank. On closer inspection it turned out to be one of those mass-produced frame-filling prints.

"It's definitely the right one." He attempted a smile. "Hey. It's not too bad."

"Seriously?" I grinned to show him I appreciated his stab at reviving the levity between us.

"It's big enough. Most apartments in Paris are the size of shoe boxes."

I scuffed a foot over the floor. "They could have bothered to sweep it."

"Yeah, it wouldn't have taken long." He sat on the couch and pulled out the iPad.

"What are you doing?"

"Setting up the wi-fi. That okay? You need me to do anything for you?"

"I have to pee."

"Okay if you manage that by yourself?" he teased.

"Ha-ha."

The bathroom did, in fact, contain the same claw-foot bathtub I'd seen in the photographs (along with what looked like the same burgundy towel, and a solitary squirl of gray pubic hair next to the plug hole) but was as disappointing as the living room. The walls were covered in white, institutional tiles, the sink's porcelain was chipped and stained with rust spots, and a section of the ceiling was dotted with black mold. The toilet bowl was livid with limescale, and although the seat looked clean enough, I wasn't prepared to come into contact with it until I'd disinfected it myself, so I balanced above the seat, thighs aching. There was a single meager roll of crispy toilet paper, like the kind we used to have at school. With a sting of resentment, I thought of the twelve-pack of three-ply I'd bought for the Petits.

Jet lag had started to get to me: dizziness muddied my vision, and the floor seemed to tip. I walked unsteadily back into the living room. Mark was staring down at the iPad, his brow creased. I tried texting Mom again, but the message wouldn't send.

"I don't get it. I put it on roaming before we got on the plane. Maybe there's no signal here or something."

Mark didn't look up. "We're in the middle of Paris. How can there be no signal?"

"At least there's wi-fi, right?"

"Nope."

"What? There must be. Didn't the Petits send you the code?"

"I've been through the list. Their username isn't on here. The only one with a strong signal is secured. It must belong to one of the other residents."

"Great."

"The modem might need rebooting."

"Where is it?"

"Must be here somewhere."

The shelves around the ancient TV were empty, so I checked the bedroom—the closets were locked—then the kitchen, a space as shabby and neglected as the bathroom: peeling lino-leum, an ancient, grumbling fridge, and cupboards made of dark, brooding wood. The only appliances I unearthed were a broken kettle, an iron, and a coffee machine with a chipped pot.

"No modem, unless it's locked away somewhere. How am I going to call my folks?"

"Let's get ourselves sorted here, take a nap; then we'll make a plan, okay?" Without waiting for me to agree, he kicked off his shoes and padded into the bedroom. I followed.

"But what if there's an emergency? What if Hayden is sick?

What if they need to get hold of us urgently?" The dread was back.

"She's fine, Steph. You know she's being spoiled rotten by your parents." Mark lay back on the bed and thumped the mattress. "It's not too bad. Sheets are clean." He grabbed one of the pillows and sniffed it. "Musty." Then he cracked a huge yawn. Bad move—it infuriated me.

"Mark, can you not just fucking listen to me? I need to call Hayden!" I knew I was being whiny and irrational, but I couldn't stop myself. I hadn't realized how exhausted I'd become by the trip, and Mark telling me how I should feel about my daughter was the last straw. It was as if the fun we'd had on the journey had all been an illusion and this paranoid harridan was the *real* me.

Instead of snapping back at me, he blinked, scrambled to his feet, and put his arms around me. "Hey . . ." He stroked my neck like he used to do when we first met. His shirt stank of sweat and airline food, but I didn't care. "She's fine. Hayden's fine. We'll find a café with wi-fi after we've had a shower and a nap. I promise. I'll get hold of the Petits, find out what the hell is going on, and you can call your parents."

I drew back from him. "I dunno, Mark. This place . . . do we really want to spend a week here?" I glanced at my reflection in the full-length mirror stuck onto the closet door. I looked fatter and shorter than I usually did; my hair greasy, face puffy and pasty. Troll-like. "The building's front door . . . anyone could get in here. It wasn't even locked."

He winced at that. "Steph, come on. Let's rest for a bit. See how we feel after that. We can always go to a hotel." But he knew as well as I did that we couldn't afford that.

He lay back on the bed again and patted the space next to him. "Come on."

I hesitated, then did as he asked. The mattress was comfortable, which was something. Mark fumbled for my hand. Within seconds, he was snoring softly, leaving me to stare up at the stained ceiling.

I don't remember falling asleep, but I remember what woke me up: the sound of a fist slamming on the apartment's door.

Chapter 5

Mark

"It's okay. It's okay," I'm whispering to Steph, pushing my hand down on her hip so she doesn't get up and run into them as they wait in the corridor. "I'll check on Hayden." It's only when I'm halfway across the floor, my shin crashing against the sharp lip of a low coffee table that shouldn't be there, that I remember we're not at home. Still, I can't see anything and I can't exactly remember right now where we are.

"Where is she?" Steph's saying behind me, somewhere in the dead darkness. I hear her fumbling, something clattering onto the floor, and at the same time I'm feeling around the unfamiliar walls, which are tacky with an icy sweat. I find a light switch, but when I push it, nothing happens. My hand bumps into a picture frame and a mantelpiece and then at last Steph's found her phone and the light from it is startling.

We both remember where we are at the same time, and Steph sighs out the breath she's been holding. "Why's it so dark?" she says.

"Lights must've tripped."

I find I've been clutching my own phone like I've done ever since the attack. It's my emergency weapon, as if it's going to save me. It's 11:08 a.m. and inky dark. I rip open one of the heavy curtains, but the windows are shuttered with grim metal slats that let no light in.

"What was that noise?"

"I don't know. Probably just a door slamming, the wind or something." I flick on my phone's little light, approach the front door, and listen. All I hear is my own breathing and the blood shunting in my ears, so I turn back. "Could be anything in a building like this. There's lots of—"

A deep bang freezes me, then another. Not knocking—it's like an animal trying to smash its way through the door. I take three slow steps backward, into the coffee table again, and stand, shining my minuscule light at the door.

For a second something inside me feels brave and validated when Steph slots herself slightly behind my shoulder, but the feeling evaporates as she takes a deep breath and strides to the door, leaving me behind, showing me how it's done. But she's forgotten the second dead bolt at the top of the door and I come over and slide it down and twist the handle for her. The small victories of the middle-aged man. We peer out onto the landing together, and I edge through the door ahead of her. If anyone's going to be a shield, it's me. The stairwell is also windowless and lightless, only the muffled circles from our phones spreading a little way in front of us. For a second there's no motion, no sound, but then there's a tread on the stairs above us and the sound of someone hurrying up them. Emboldened by the fact that the footsteps are going away rather than toward us, I allow my shock to turn to anger. *I didn't come all the way to Paris to be harassed by petty delinquents.*

"Wait there," I say to Steph, and the dissipating fear in my voice must come across as bravery, because she hesitates. "You can't go out like that," I add.

She looks down at herself, in her undies and the socks and sweater she was wearing on the journey here, and then back at me. She assembles an I-can-wear-what-I-like look of defiance, but she doesn't make a move away from the doorjamb. She's probably realized what I have—the footsteps are light and skittering away from us. We're not going to be killed or tortured by the owners of these feet.

I poke my head into the narrow eye of the cramped stairwell and call up. "Wait! *Excusez-moi!*" Summoning the few words

of French I know. I hear the footsteps creaking on the worn
wooden treads another story farther up, and it incites me—
they wake us up; then they run away. If this is some kid playing
a joke, they should know it's not funny. I head up the stairs,
ignoring Steph as she calls, "Mark, don't," behind me. Rounding to the next landing and the next, I press the switch at each
level, but no light comes on and all I have is the phone's weak
spot. I check under each door for light—nothing—stop briefly
to listen for movement in the stagnant, moldy air, and seconds
later I hear a door slamming on the level above me.

The landing on the top floor is even smaller than any of
the others—two three-quarter-size doors squeezed awkwardly
into the angular decline of the ceiling. A rusted bucket filled
with sand stands under an empty bracket for a fire extin-
guisher. The carpet on the floor is completely worn through;
as I approach, the dry wooden boards spike a splinter into my
bare foot. Subdued light oozes from under one of the lopsided
doors, its surface rough with peeling red lacquer. There's no
number, just a small handwritten label reading ROSNER, M.
I knock with the side of my fist—*ba, ba, bang*. I wait. No movement. Then I kick the door—*See how you like it, arsehole*—but
instantly regret it as my cold toes smash against the solid mass.

My stupid bout of anger is quickly spent and I lean back
against the wall, rubbing my toes and inspecting the sole
where the splinter has gone in. By my phone's light I can see
the long black line getting fainter as it digs deeper into my sole,
and now that the effects of the cold and shock are wearing off,
it's starting to ache.

I turn away and go down two steps, the wounded hero
returning from battle, but now I hear a voice on the other side
of the door. Chains clatter and the latch clicks over twice. I'm
hit by a barrage of angry French that I can't understand and
turn to see a short woman with a gray crew cut over a face
that's ashen apart from feverish high red blotches under her

cheekbones. She's backlit by the soft yellow light of candles or lanterns from within. I get a glimpse of canvases stacked against a wall and a table overloaded with containers brimming with brushes and scraps of material and pencils and stacks of colored paper, and a waft of pungent air emerges with the woman, thick with an acrid tang of piss and oil and fish, and some sort of waxy chemical odor. She's wearing a ratty scarf and a coat like an old, ugly carpet, still beaded with melting sleet. Now that I see who my bogeyman is, it's almost funny, but not quite—she's so unpleasant.

I raise my hands and say, "I don't understand what you're saying, so you may as well stop," and turn away. There's no point in being here.

As I'm heading down the first steps, she takes in a breath and says, in a considered, resonant tone, "You must not come inside here, in my home, and disrespect for me."

My temper is shot from interrupted sleep and the sour adrenaline in my veins. I know I should just leave it, but I say, "Disrespect? You're the one bashing on my door for no good reason. Unless you've got a teenage kid in there with an attitude problem."

This shuts her down. Like a switch has tripped, all the fire drains from her face. "No, there is no child."

"Well, can I go now?" I say, aware that I'm the one who chased her up here in the first place.

She backs into her apartment. "You be careful here. It is not for living."

I don't know what she means by that, but I can't criticize—this woman's English is far better than my French. I limp down the stairs, my toes and the splinter throbbing in earnest now. Steph's still in the doorway when I get down to the third floor, but now she's pulled on her jeans and shoes.

"It was just a woman from upstairs," I say, embarrassed. I

must have looked very stupid reacting the way I did, launching off into the darkness in a bite-size rage.

To my relief, Steph smiles tiredly. "I know. I heard. I thought I'd leave you to it. I would have come and rescued you if I'd heard you scream."

I stroke her arm. "Thanks. She was so grumpy!" I laugh. "An artist or something."

"Bound to be crazy, then."

"Of course. Talk about local flavor—we have our own artiste in a garret."

"A madwoman in the attic." Although Steph's joking, the image chills me; it conjures up smoke and death and insanity and blood. I recall that burning tallow smell from the apartment upstairs.

It's only when Steph kicks off her shoes and goes to the couch that I register that the apartment is bathed in safe, sterile electric light. "Hey, you fixed the power."

"Yeah, the board tripped. It's just there." She points at the row of switches behind the open front door. "Useful for future reference."

"Nice one. I'm going to see if there's any coffee. You want some?"

"No, I need to talk to Hayden first."

Not for the first time today, I'm relieved that I stuck to my guns and Hayden's not here. "I'm sure she's fine."

"Yes, but you don't know that." She starts fussing with her phone, muttering under her breath as she tries to find a free signal on the long list of routers it's picking up. By the glaring strip of light in the kitchen, it's easy to locate the cheap and grimy old filter coffee machine in one cluttered corner of the counter. I work out how to plug the thing in and fill it—running the water from the sink for a full minute before it clears and stops spattering—then riffle through the jumble in the cabinet above for a pack of filters and some coffee. There's a patina of mildew on the grounds, so I skim the top layer out of the tin and flick it into the sink before spooning more into the machine. It's going to have to do because there's a knitting needle rammed through my brain that I know is caffeine withdrawal, even though I've never gone cold turkey long enough to suffer it. The hot water will kill whatever mold remains. Besides, I'm not really likely to contract any dire tropical diseases in this cold climate. When the steam starts hissing a smell of coffee into the kitchen, everything begins to feel a lot more homey. I'm actually in a little apartment in Paris. It's seen far better days, but here we are.

I'd be more convinced of our hereness if I could actually see Paris outside, so I raise the blind in the kitchen, but it only reveals another of those thick, slatted metal shutters, swollen with oxidation and thickly painted over. They have to open, though—people live in this apartment and they surely can't live like moles in a cave. I trace the shutter's frame to see where the paint and rust are worn by movement, but I can't see any sign that this one has ever opened. I wriggle the handle, but it doesn't budge. I'm digging at the edge with a bread knife when Steph comes in behind me.

"There're a dozen signals labeled FREE, but I can't connect to any of them. We'll have to go out somewhere for wi-fi." Steph sniffs the air. "Can I get some of that?"

"Of course. There's no milk, though."

"That's okay. Just a quick fix before we go." At least our shared addiction is one way we're sure to bond every day—I could never live with someone who drinks herbal tea. I rinse a mug from the cabinet and pour her a cup of stain. "We must remember to get hold of Carla too," she says.

"Why would you want to talk to Carla?"

"Uh, to find out if the Petits have arrived at our place?"

"Oh, yeah. That."

"Jeez."

"Sorry—my brain's still in transit."

"I'd text her, but the roaming still isn't working."

Steph sips her coffee, sniffs it, then puts it down.

"Not great, huh?" I say.

"We can buy some milk and decent coffee at the grocery."

It's good to hear her say "we." Ever since the attack, we've been tiptoeing around each other, our familiar rhythms disrupted. I've been unsure what to do for Steph, unsure what she expects of me. This morning, it feels like we're doing things as a team again.

"You ready to go?" I say. Even if it's just for coffee and wi-fi, I'm excited by the prospect. I don't want to waste any more of our first day in Paris cooped up in this dingy apartment.

"I'm just going to take a quick shower. I feel disgusting."

Steph pulls off her jeans in the bedroom and heads into the bathroom. I stand by the door, watching her move, tracing the curves of her hips and her shoulders with my eyes, trying to chart the expressive flop of her hair. She labors under a twenty-four-year-old's self-consciousness. She doesn't believe how beautiful she is; she doesn't realize that she's at the height of perfection. That's probably the reason she's here, now, with me, instead of in a five-star hotel suite with some magnate or billionaire soccer star. She could have her pick and she doesn't know it.

I park myself on the couch in the living room and stare at the stain-dappled wall above the TV as I probe idly at the splinter in my foot. The tip's broken off and there's no protrusion to pull on, even if we had tweezers. The wound's developing a red halo. I dig out a fresh pair of socks and tie on my shoes while I wait for Steph to finish.

We've come straight from a Cape Town summer's hot wind to the damp, bracing cold of a Parisian winter. Despite eleven uncomfortable hours on a plane and standing around queuing and waiting for several more, the transition still feels miraculous, like teleporting. After too many lost years of traveling the same suburban route to and from work, this morning I've already been bombarded with a glut of new sights and sounds and smells. Yesterday we were at home; today we're anywhere but.

If only I could work out how to open those bloody shutters. I make for the tall window in the living room, yanking and rattling at the handle, until finally I realize it's a counterweighted sash that opens up and down, not outward. The locking hook at the top of the lower frame is jammed as if it hasn't been opened for years, but I get the bread knife from the kitchen and start bashing at it with the end of the handle, harder as the hook begins to budge.

At last the window's free; a few well-placed thumps seem to loosen some grit in the frame, and it starts to grate upward. I heave, each tug lifting the sash one more grinding inch, bracing myself against the wall so that I won't flip out of the window when it finally opens. Worried about the noise, I take a break, but oddly the keening, shearing noise continues. I jiggle the frame of the closed shutter—it's not the window making the noise anymore. The sound is coming from outside, not far away. It resolves itself into something I was hoping not to hear—the desolate crying of a child.

Chapter 6

Steph

Our search for wi-fi ended at a Starbucks on the boulevard Haussmann. We hadn't planned to walk that far; it had been an almost unconscious decision to head away from Pigalle, taking the narrow, sloping side streets at random. It may not have been the quaint bistro I'd been imagining, but there was something comforting about its familiar, sterile interior after the disappointment of the apartment. And it was warm. There was no hair dryer in the apartment, and despite several minutes of vigorous towel drying, my hair was still damp, the chill air freezing my scalp the second I stepped outside. Mark had been distracted on the walk. He said the splinter in his foot was irritating him, but I could tell there was something else bothering him. He'd barely said a word to me while I dried my hair, and he kept staring at the shuttered window in the living room.

While Mark ordered our coffees, I ignored my emails and logged on to Skype right away, not caring that the cluster of loud American teenagers at the table next to ours would overhear my conversation. My smartphone was secondhand and I still couldn't get the hang of it. My trusty old iPhone and MacBook had disappeared into one of the burglars' backpacks and had no doubt ended up on the black market in Harare or Brazzaville.

Mom was offline, so I had no choice but to call her cell, which would eat the Skype credit. It rang for ages before she picked up. "Yes? This is Rina speaking." She always answered the phone tentatively, as if she was expecting whoever called to unleash a torrent of abuse.

"Mom, hey."

"Stephanie! Are you there safe?"

"Yes, thanks. How's Hayden?"

"Oh, fine. We're out at the moment, at that new petting farm in Barrydale. And don't worry, she's wearing loads of sunscreen. It's so hot today. How is the apartment?"

I told her the apartment was fabulous, better than we'd hoped. The lie made me feel like crying. "Can I talk to Hayden, Mom?"

"'Course you can."

Silence for several seconds, then, "Mumma?"

"Hayden! Mumma misses you. Are you being a good girl?"

She spoke in a rush, talking about the baby animals she'd seen and jumping to what she'd had for lunch.

Mark returned with two lattes. "Hayden, Daddy's here."

"Daddy!"

I caught a blip of dismay in his eyes as he took the cell from me, but I convinced myself that this was because he hated talking on the phone.

"You being good for Nama and Pops, Haydie?" His voice brimmed with artificial joviality. "What's that, chicken? You did what?" Pause. "That's lovely. Be good now." He handed the phone back to me with obvious relief. Mom came back on the line. I explained about the wi-fi issues and she promised to make sure she was home the following morning so that we could use the webcams.

"Hayden seems happy," Mark said after I'd hung up, wincing as coffee burned his tongue.

"Yeah."

I turned to my emails so that I didn't have to look at him. There were a couple from the house swap site, one tagged *Enjoy your trip!*, the other encouraging me to upgrade my membership, and one from Carla, sent half an hour earlier, and also copied in to Mark:

Hello both,

Been texting you. I was outside your house at 9:30 as arranged, but there was no sign of your guests. Not sure what flight they were on so can't check if it was delayed. Stayed until 11. I left them a note with my phone number on it. Let me know if you hear anything.

Hope Paris is magnifique. x

"Mark, Carla's sent us an email."

He was staring out of the window, his eyes following the progress of a slender woman in tuxedo trousers and a tailored coat. It was still raining, but she was wearing sunglasses. The effect was chic rather than pretentious, and I couldn't help but feel puffy and drab in comparison. "Mark!"

He shook himself. "Sorry. Miles away."

"Carla says the Petits haven't shown up."

Now I had his full attention. "What do you mean they haven't turned up?"

"She was waiting for them at our house and they haven't arrived yet. She sent the email just now. It's five hours after they should have arrived."

"Maybe their flight was delayed."

"For five hours?"

"Why not? Happens all the time. For all we know it could have been canceled. Or they could have missed it."

"Without letting us know? That would be a bit thoughtless, wouldn't it?"

He shrugged. "They might have been trying. Your roaming isn't working, is it? And we know they're not exactly reliable.

The apartment is nothing like they described. No wi-fi, for a start."

I nodded, but other, darker explanations for their absence were beginning to form: a crash on the way to the airport, or en route to our house in their rental car. A hijacking. "It was today, right? We didn't get the date wrong?"

"It was definitely today." He took another scalding sip of his coffee. "You know, I bet they don't even live in that apartment."

"You mean it could be a second property or an investment apartment?"

"Yes. It doesn't feel lived in. Not like our house."

"They didn't imply anything like that when you spoke to them, did they?"

"Nah. Although with all the Google translating, there probably were some misunderstandings."

"Did they give you a cell number?"

"No, but they've got ours."

"Send them an email. And ask them where the modem is while you're at it."

I did as he suggested, writing something along the lines of, *Hey, just checking you're okay. We're in the apartment, could you let us know where the modem is, please. Please email me back when you get this. Thanx.*

I kept the tone light, thinking that as pissed off as I was at the Petits for misrepresenting their place, I didn't want to cause any real friction.

"Another coffee?" Mark asked.

"Sure," I said, aware that both of us were postponing leaving the warmth and anonymity of the Starbucks. *What did you do on your trip to Paris? Oh, you know, checked out the global franchises.*

I replied to Carla, apologizing for the hassle. This time Mark returned from the counter with a *pain au chocolat* and a large croissant. We lapsed into silence once more. The rain was petering off, and a teasing sliver of blue sky had appeared in the far distance. I sipped at my latte, immediately regretting ordering it. If I wasn't careful, the caffeine jitters would tip over into a full-on panic attack. I dug my nails into my palms. As usual, the absence of my engagement ring on my left hand gave me a jolt. I've never been a jewelry person—always loathed the bullshit commercialization of the wedding industry—but I loved that ring: an emerald surrounded by a twinkle of delicate diamonds, set on a slender platinum band. I'd even refused to remove it when I was in the hospital giving birth to Hayden, and the nurse had eventually wrapped a piece of sterile tape around it. Mark's mother had given it to him just before she died—it had been her mother's. Was I so attached to it because Mark's first wife never possessed it—as if the heirloom somehow legitimized me; as if it symbolized that I wasn't the despised, weak second wife? It was an embarrassing rationalization that probably stemmed from reading too much Daphne du Maurier.

I forced myself to swallow a piece of croissant, hoping that it would distract my mind, now fixated on the ring, from wandering to places where it shouldn't go.

It didn't.

It's late. Mark and I are on the couch in the living room, an episode of Homeland *on the TV. I'm drifting in and out of consciousness, trying to convince myself to get up and head to bed. Occasionally the baby monitor blips as Hayden giggles to herself in her sleep.*

A bang. A scrape. "You hear that, Mark?"

"No." He's also dropping off.

"We should probably think about—"

The door slams open, and three men, their faces hidden by balaclavas, burst into the room. Metal glints in their hands:

knives—carving knives, like the kind neatly stored in the rack in
the kitchen.

Neither of us screams, but we both leap to our feet. An instant
of disbelief—this isn't happening—followed by a powerful surge
of terror. "They're in the house, Mark," I hear myself say, too late.
Later I will think, Pure fear really is ice cold. *Then,* Hayden,
Hayden, I have to get to Hayden.

I manage a pathetic "Please—"
The shortest man barks, "Don't talk. Where is the safe?"
"There's no safe."
"Where is the safe?"
"We don't have a safe."

Mark doesn't speak. He feels so far away from me now he
could be in another room.

Do what they say, *I think,* don't cause any trouble. *Another*
man leans in so close to me that I can smell the soap on his
skin, the cigarettes on his breath. He roughly checks my ears
for earrings, and then tugs at my left hand. What's he doing?
Then I get it—he's trying to pull the ring off my finger. The knife
in his other hand is serrated; I've heard stories of fingers being
hacked off. I snatch my hand away, babble, "I'll do it." I yank
it off, bruising the knuckle, and hand it to him. I'm patheti-
cally eager to please. Don't rape me, don't hurt my daughter.
Don't rape me, don't hurt my daughter. I will do whatever
you want.

"Safe? Where is the safe?" the short one says again. He has the
most confidence, is less jumpy than the others, and I decide he
must be the leader. I can't look at his eyes.

"There is no safe," I hear myself say. Still Mark doesn't speak.
"Safe? Where is the safe?" His voice is softer now, and I'm
aware that his accent isn't South African.
"There is no safe."
Silent communication passes between the three men.

"Sit." The leader gestures at Mark. He does as he's told, abruptly, his face slack with shock.

"Come." One of the men grabs my wrist, the rough scratch of his woolen glove setting my teeth on edge. He starts pulling me toward the door, a second man close behind him.

"No," I whisper. I try to signal to Mark to do something—to stop them taking me away from him—but he doesn't move or even look in my direction.

The man in the front—he's skinny and seems young and nervous—tugs me forward like a dog, the one behind never more than a pace from my back. We're heading for the stairs, for Hayden, for the bedroom. Another flush of ice-cold panic, followed by a stark decision: if rape looks like it's on the agenda, or they try to hurt Hayden, then I will fight. I will fight to the death. Up the stairs we go, and I steel myself to twist away and lash out as Skinny opens Hayden's door. "Please," I whine. He looks in, hesitates, then mercifully closes the door softly.

The worst is over. The relief is immense, even as they yank me toward my bedroom. Are they going to rape me now? Is this where it's going to happen? Please don't wake up, Hayden. Please don't wake up, sweetheart. One stays glued to my wrist while the other roots through the bedroom drawers, tossing underwear and socks onto the floor. I don't look at their eyes. Not once. Not ever. I study the chipped blue nail polish on my toes. Skinny murmurs something at his companion and he picks up my iPhone, expertly removes the SIM card, and slides the phone into his backpack. My MacBook follows, as does Mark's watch. I don't care. I just want this to be over.

We shuffle back down the stairs, one step at a time. I stumble and the man behind steadies me. I almost thank him. Stupid. Then follows a tedious twenty minutes as they dig through every drawer in the kitchen. I don't think about Mark or what the leader might be doing to him; my senses are all strained for any sign that Hayden is waking up. We dance back along the corridor past the dining room, and here's something curious: I realize I'm bored with it all. Get it over with, I want to scream. The rape, the stabbing, whatever is next.

My pair drag me into the living room, where Mark is still sitting on the couch in the same position, his face ashen.

"You okay?" he croaks.

I nod.

"Hayden?"

"Sleeping."

"Up," the leader says to Mark, who is so wobbly and uncoordinated by fear he has to push himself to his feet with his hands. We're shuffled back into the kitchen and into the pantry. There's a quick exchange among the three intruders in a language I don't understand.

"You stay here until the morning," the leader says softly. He leaves, shutting the pantry door, and we're in darkness. Seconds later, the door flies open. He's testing us.

The door closes once more. There's no lock on it.

I'm shaking now; my mouth tastes like I've been drinking blood. We've got off lightly; we're not tied up, we haven't been blinded, tortured, raped. By South African standards, we're lucky.

Time passes. I can't bear it any longer. I press my ear against the door—have they gone?

"Should we—"

"Shh," Mark says. "They'll hear you."

"But we have to get to Hayden."

"Shh," he says again.

When I leave the pantry to run to my daughter, he stays behind.

"Steph?" Mark's voice snapped me out of reliving that night—
the kind of thinking the police counselor had encouraged
me to avoid. I was still fingering the empty space on my ring
finger. He reached over to touch me, but I snatched my hand
back. "We have to get you another one, Steph. Another ring."

"Yeah. One day." It wasn't as simple as replacing a laptop or
a camera.

"Soon, I promise. Hey, maybe we can buy one here?"

"With the exchange rate like it is? That would be crazy,
Mark." But I smiled at him. "I don't need a ring."

I looked down at my lap. The coat was covered in an ava-
lanche of crumbs, and both the pastries had disappeared. I
didn't remember eating them.

He glanced at his phone. "There's a waxworks museum very
near here. It's supposed to be in an old theater. Feel like doing
something kitschy and fun?"

"Tomorrow, maybe." Right then, it was fresh air I wanted.
"Let's walk for a while."

"Good idea." I could tell he felt bad about his reticence with
Hayden on the phone.

The next few hours were pleasant enough. I pushed the
worry about the Petits out of my head and reminded myself
that Hayden was fine. Sure, the apartment was shoddy, but
it was warm and dry and, let's face it, free. We walked arm
in arm, rambling along the broad boulevards and pausing
to admire the opera house. Next, we window-shopped along
the rue Royale, pretending we were the type of people who
could afford luxury wallets and bespoke chocolates. I let the
city charm me. Women strolled past, swathed in fur and
scarves; slick men streamed around us in shiny shoes that
no one but the most ardent hipster would dare to wear back
at home.

The sky was darkening, and Mark's foot was bothering

him. "Let's head back," he suggested. "Rest for an hour or so, then head to Montmartre for something to eat. Push the boat out. Blow the budget." He drew me to him. "How does that sound?"

We shared a smile, and at that moment I thought, *Yes, this is why we came to Paris.* Using the Sacré-Cœur's domed top as a beacon, we rambled upward through cobbled streets glossy with rain, pausing to read the menus placed outside alluring bistros. A window display caught my eye: child-size mannequins wearing colorful, chic clothes, butterflies dancing around them.

"Oh! Can we go in?"

He hesitated. "Sure."

The elegant brunette behind the counter greeted us warmly. I tried a few words of fledgling French, and she immediately switched to English. Mark hovered by the door while I picked through a pile of handcrafted T-shirts, not daring to look at the price. "Hayden would love this," I called to Mark, holding up one decorated with a quirkily designed dinosaur.

He gave me a tight smile.

"Ah, come on. Let's get it for her."

"Up to you."

The assistant beamed at me as I handed her my credit card, and she began the laborious process of wrapping the shirt in tissue paper. I tried not to feel guilt at the price—fifty-five euros—which was outrageous for something Hayden would outgrow in a couple of months.

I tapped in my PIN, and the assistant frowned. "I am sorry. It does not want to go through."

Flustered, I tried again. It was rejected once more. I called Mark over.

"Perhaps you can call your bank?" the woman said politely. Mark asked her if he could use her wi-fi, and she graciously gave us the security key. He got through to the bank's call center but lost the call almost immediately and had to try again. A smart couple carrying a sleeping toddler entered the shop, and the woman drifted away to deal with them. While Mark whispered into his phone, I checked my emails. There was one from Carla: *Okay. Don't worry. You are there to chill out. I'll make inquiries from here. Probably some mix-up. SIGH. x*

Mark hung up and shook his head. "We were supposed to authorize the card before we left."

"Shit." The couple glanced at us nervously. "But you can sort it out, right?"

"Not from here. I can try phoning our branch tomorrow, but it doesn't sound hopeful."

"How many euros have we got?"

"Around three hundred and fifty."

If we couldn't use the card, then that would be tight for six days. We'd have to be careful. Lavish romantic dinners would be out of the question, and I certainly couldn't buy the T-shirt for Hayden. It was tempting to lash out at him, blame him for the card screw-up, but I bit my tongue. *This wouldn't have happened if you had your own bank account and salary,* the voice of guilt whispered.

Face hot, I approached the shop woman.

"There is still a problem?"

"*Oui.* I am so sorry." And I was. She was charming about it, which somehow made the whole situation worse.

Deflated, we stopped at a supermarket and bought the basics: more coffee, milk, butter, cheese, and a baguette—a meager supper—as well as some adhesive bandages for Mark's foot, neither of us saying anything that wasn't necessary. We found our way back to the apartment with its aura of old food and misery. The woman on the top floor had her music cranked up high, the strains of an eighties pop ballad I couldn't place floating down at us. Duran Duran? David Lee Roth? Something like that. Whatever it was, it didn't suit the building.

Mark kicked his shoes off the second he walked through the door, threw himself on the couch, and peeled off his socks. I wrinkled my nose at the sour foot odor wafting up from his shoes, but he didn't notice. He hauled his left foot onto his knee to inspect the damage. "Shit. That got bad fast."

The only damage to his sole was a tiny black dot. "There's nothing there, Mark."

"It bloody hurts."

I kissed his forehead. "Shame, diddums." I retreated into the kitchen to pack away the groceries. The fridge door screamed as I opened it, releasing a gust of foul air. Homesickness washed through me, taking me by surprise. After the men had broken into our house, it had no longer felt like home.

Again, my mind strayed back to the Petits. What if something *had* happened to them? They might be unreliable and thoughtless, but they probably didn't know anyone in South Africa. Weren't Mark and I in some way responsible for them?

"Mark? Can you check the bedroom, see if there's anything with the Petits' phone number written on it? See if you can find a key to the closet. I'll look in the kitchen."

"Sure."

I started by searching through the top drawer next to the sink, which was crammed with rusty spoons and forks with bent tines. Mark called out that he'd found the key to the wardrobe in one of the drawers next to the bed, but I was too intent on what I was doing to answer him. A piece of paper was scrunched at the back, wedged into a corner. I pulled it out and unwrapped it carefully. It looked like a ripped section from a school essay. The ragged page was scrawled with child-

ish writing in blue ballpoint peppered with red pen correc-
tions. The only word I could understand was *bien*.

"Steph?" Mark stood in the kitchen doorway. There was
something off about his body language.

"What?"

"You'd better come and see."

Chapter 7

Mark

It's some sort of sick joke. Someone's fucking with me.

"What is it?"

Steph's leaning into the bedroom and now I realize I've made a mistake calling her in here. I don't want her in here. I don't want her to touch it—there could be fleas, rabies, mites.

"It's nothing. Don't come in!"

But she takes a step into the room with an impatient frown. "What *is* it, Mark?"

I come up with a lie I know will keep her away. "It's just a dead mouse."

"Ugh, God. I'll leave you to it, okay?" She goes back to the kitchen and I listen until I hear her scrabbling through the drawers again.

I can't believe I almost let Steph see this. I picture her leaning into the closet, titillated, disgusted all at once, wanting to recoil but at the same time unable to help herself from edging nearer to the buckets.

Three white plastic five-gallon buckets, each densely filled with hair. Human hair. Forcing myself to take a longer look than my first glance, I try to reset my eyes, try to trick them into seeing wool or cotton or material swatches, like that woman from upstairs had in her apartment. Perhaps the Petits are artists too. Perhaps the woman upstairs stores her excess material in here. But no—it's hair. Wadded masses of it, from a lot of different heads—curly, straight, black, brown, yellow, and gray, all clumped together like human hair should never be.

What the hell is it for?

I check myself. *For?* I don't care what it's *for.* I've got to throw it out.

But if Steph catches me, I can just imagine her reaction. *We can't. It's not ours. What if they need it?*

I peer down at the matted clumps in the buckets and, drawn by it, I sink down to my knees and bring my face closer, trying not to imagine what could be crawling in the layers, the dander that's circulating as the hair disintegrates. It's pulling my face closer and closer, like the suck of the abyss. My nose almost in it, I breathe in.

Relief clears my mind. It doesn't smell dirty or anything. Perhaps there *is* a good explanation. Perhaps they make dolls. Maybe they're wigmakers.

Surely it's paranoid to think that they—whoever *they* are—know about me, about Odette and Zoë. But I've just been smelling buckets of dead hair in my holiday apartment. I can no longer pretend that this apartment is even halfway livable. We've spent money we don't have to fly all the way here and end up in a filthy shithole. There should be some measure of accountability; there should be a basic bond of decency in this "house swap" scheme. Steph bought these people fresh sheets, for God's sake! In exchange, we get a dingy warren with *buckets of human hair* in the closet.

I want to rail and yell and demand retribution, but nobody cares. *We* blundered into this arrangement sight unseen and it's only our mistake—my mistake for encouraging it. I could have snuffed the idea out when it started.

Could've, should've, would've. Didn't.

I hurry into the kitchen and grab a roll of trash bags from the murk under the sink and dodge out again, but not before Steph can say, "What do you need all those for? It's just a mouse."

I pull a face. "Looks like it's been there for a while. Thought

I'd better wrap a couple of bags over my hands when I scoop it up."

"Yuck. Strange that I didn't smell it." She smiles. "Thanks for clearing it up, Mark."

"Don't worry about it," I say. "It's nothing."

But it's not nothing.

I don't know how I would even begin to explain to Steph what this means without sounding morbid and weird. Of course she knows the basics about what happened to Zoë and Odette, but not the details. How could I even start?

Back in the apartment's bedroom, I fit a bag over the mouth of the first bucket, as carefully as possible so that I don't have to touch any of it, and tip the whole thing over.

Again, I check over my shoulder to see if Steph's going to catch me in the act, but by the sounds of things she's back rooting through the kitchen cupboards.

I carefully empty each of the buckets into the trash bags, tie the tops up, and stack the buckets back in the closet. Despite my care, a few loose strands wisp into my face. My arms and hands tickle where it's touched my skin, long after I've wiped it off. I feel . . . things . . . walking over me. Tiny, invisible things. Microbes. I try not to think of it; thinking too much sends an icy finger trailing down my spine. I'll get these bags out and then have a long shower.

I slip on my shoes, not bothering with a coat, and creep out of the apartment, gruesome cargo bumping softly against my legs. I call out something about heading for the trash cans, then pick my way down the narrow stairs, my phone in my left hand lighting my way and the three black bags in my right fist extended as far away as possible, clutched like three oversize human heads. Out in the courtyard, freezing rain is filtering down from the small rectangle of sulfur sky. There were some green trash cans parked out here earlier, but now they've vanished. I consider taking the bags out to the street and dumping them, but I wouldn't want to have to explain myself if anyone were to challenge me.

Doing what should be done. That's all I ever want to achieve, and the bloody home invasion keeps on cycling through my mind. Did I do the right thing? I let the fuckers take what they wanted without trying to act like a hero. That's what everyone advises. *Don't play the hero. Don't put up a fight.* If they got angry, they could have tipped over into violence. So I sat there as they prowled around our home as if they owned it. I said nothing. I did nothing. Steph blames me for this, I know, but ultimately she and Hayden were unharmed—I did my job. I don't want to ask myself what I would have done if they had tried to hurt Steph and . . . I don't even want to think about it. It didn't happen that way and we all turned out okay.

There's a weathered storeroom door set into the knobbled masonry a few paces along, its once-green wooden slats peeling and flaking. I peer through the low window but can see nothing through its grimy panes. My face is getting numb from the cold already and my muscles are sore from holding the bags at arm's length, so I drop them and don't think quite as much as I should before pushing the door open and entering the room.

A thick, dank, cold miasma of must hits me as I search fruitlessly for a light switch. Casting my phone's pathetic light around the low-vaulted, cellar-like space, I see a clutter of old crates and what seems like stored furniture under dust-caked sheeting. A rough and paint-spattered wooden ladder with rotten rungs leans against the exposed and moldy brickwork of the far wall. I turn to leave, but I almost feel, more than hear, a quiet whimper in the far corner of the space. *It's just a mouse or a rat,* I tell myself, trying to excuse my self-preserving cowardice yet again, but there's something so familiar about the tone of it that I can't just turn to go. It's like the soft, sad crying of a child. I push my feet over the cold, grainy floor, following the sound toward an arched alcove to one side of the room. There's a bare mattress lying in the alcove, covered with a loose knot of sheets brown with aged dirt and spattered with what looks like streaks of mildew. I can still hear the whimpering, closer now, coming from somewhere in this alcove. Heart hammering, I scan my light into the corner, where I see a bundle of soiled clothes that were once bright, trapped for years in a familiar constellation—just thrown to the floor like any kid would do. A pair of still-colorful plastic boots with Scooby-Doo printed on them.

Nobody's here, but still the crying sound, now almost a gasping choke. I have to do it. I bend down and rip away the sheet from the mattress in a flurry of dust and dander. I stumble two paces back, clearing the air in front of me with my arm. Nobody's crying beneath this sheet. *The room is empty,* I tell myself, because I don't want to look too hard at the dark, frenzied stains across the mattress.

Before my mind starts asking too many questions, I hurry to leave, only now remembering to pick up the three bags of hair in my left fist. Finally, as I scurry toward the entrance, I see the two green trash cans in a cranny behind the door. I lift the lid and, not looking inside, dump the bags. The slam of the lid is offensive in the sepulchral space. It chases me out the door into the cold outside air again. Gasping in the night air's freshness and turning toward the lobby, I walk straight into someone emerging from the shadows of the alley.

"Oh, *pardon,*" I say, one of those words you learn quickly here to disguise your shock or dismay.

The madwoman in the attic—the more I tell myself not to think of her like that, the more the phrase lodges in my mind— has dropped her shopping bag and she's kneeling down, huffing and tutting as she gathers her groceries. Two oranges are rolling lopsidedly along the cobbles toward the gutter.

"I'm sorry, let me," I say, hobbling after them as my foot

pierces me with a jab of pain. She stands and opens the grocery bag to let me drop the oranges in. "I'm so sorry."

"What are you looking for in here?" she says, indicating the storeroom door.

For some reason, I feel like a guilty trespasser. It doesn't help that my breath is still jagged. "I was just trying to find a trash can."

She shrugs. At least she's not yelling at me. This might be my one chance to find out some answers about this building, so I try to calm down. I want to know why this building in the middle of this desirable neighborhood is deserted, but as I start to ask, "Do you know . . . ," the night is sliced by a strangled cry of pain and anguish. For a second, the woman shrinks back and cowers, her mask of self-possession shattering and falling, leaving the naked terror of a little girl in its place. Just a flash, like a small cloud whisked across the face of the moon, and then she's back. A cat steps out from a culvert and saunters across our path, flicking its tail in the air and letting out a human-sounding squall as it goes.

"Oh, Lalou," the woman says, and then mutters something to the sauntering cat in French.

I can't ask this woman everything I want to know, and already she's drifting away from me, so I end up rushing to say, "Do you know the Petits well?"

"*Excusez?*"

"The people who live in apartment 3B. Where we are?"

"No. No *petits*," she says.

I don't know if it's my pronunciation or she simply doesn't get what I'm asking, but for the umpteenth time today, I have the frustrating feeling that I'm talking without a tongue. "Never mind," I say. "Thanks."

I turn to the lobby door, but she says behind me, with absolute clarity, "There are no children here. Here is not for living."

I get moving, now picking up my pace, feeling that repeated

phrase chasing me as I go; I am running up the stairs now, despite the ache in my foot, like a little child trying to out-run the darkness in a nighttime corridor. Back to the safety of home, of familiarity. I'm feeling chilled to the bone, to the soul, and right now I need Steph to soothe me.

But when I get to our floor, the landing is dark and the door shut. I pat my pocket once and then remember: I didn't take the keys with me. I knock on the door, my knuckles hurting against its heaviness. If Steph's in the bathroom, she'll never hear me knocking. But then I remember the thumping that woke us up earlier. I hammer the door until I feel a satisfying reverberation in the frame.

"Steph," I call. "Steph."

And now, behind me, the madwoman is coming up the stairs in the darkness, rounding onto our landing with her shopping bag on her arm. I turn my phone light half in her direction and notice her accusing glance as she clumps doggedly on into the blackness above. "You must not be here," she intones into the darkness as she goes, her words trailing toward me like ink in molasses. "There is nothing good here."

I'm not sure what she's talking about, and I'm too exhausted to try to figure it out. My phone light times out and I let it, slumping against the door. If Steph is in the apartment, she will have heard me; if she decided to slip out while I was down in that storeroom, there's nothing for it but to wait for her to return. Now that I've stopped the noise and turned off the phone's light, it's pretty peaceful in the darkness. I've quickly become used to the building's clanks and groans and the sound of faraway music seeping through it like a distant memory.

I close my eyes and there's no difference in what I can see, but my lids are heavy and I let my chin slump to my chest, allowing the stillness to swaddle me. I'm just nodding off when the door behind me disappears and I tumble backward into a glare of light, looking up at Steph's bare legs.

Another day, it would be funny, but she just steps over me and away, tightening the small bath towel around herself. "You're back," she says. "What were you doing out there? You were ages."

"Nothing." I roll myself over and haul myself up, my joints crackling and my muscles pulling.

I stand up and limp to the bedroom doorway, despondently aroused as I watch Steph get dressed in her most shapeless sweater. In my fantasy, she'd have dropped that towel and pushed me onto the bed and we'd be making love in Romantic Paris.

"This place really sucks," I say.

She sits at the end of the bed, looking tired. "What's the matter, Mark? Why are you acting so weird? Please talk to me."

I want to brush her off with another "Nothing," but I can see she's genuinely worried about me. I owe her something, so I try to tell her the truth. "There was just some hair in the bedroom closet. I was chucking it out."

She's incredulous. "*Hair?* You mean like wigs and stuff?"

"No. Cut hair. Like the trimmings you'd find on the floor in a barber's. Buckets of it."

"Hang on, so the closet was full of cut hair as well as a dead mouse?" she says, and for a second I don't know what she's talking about because I've forgotten my lie.

"Uh-huh. A mouse and hair." It sounds ridiculous.

"So why didn't you tell me about this hair when you first found it?"

"I didn't want to worry you. This apartment is disturbing enough as it is."

She snorts but seems to accept this. "You probably shouldn't have thrown it out, Mark. Weird or not, it belongs to them. Hey, what do you think they use it for?"

"How would I know?"

"Maybe they're wigmakers. Or they could actually be hairdressers . . . That's it. They looked stylish in the picture, didn't they? Maybe they need it for . . . for . . ."

"For *what,* Steph? For genetic experiments? Maybe they'll build a clone army of clients so that they—"

"Why are you taking this out on me? What's got into you?"

"Into me? You're the one who thinks we've stumbled upon Vidal Sassoon's secret hair collection."

"Whatever, Mark." She gets up as if to flounce into the bathroom, but I can't let her go. I shouldn't have told her about the hair. The argument is my fault. I need to put it right. "Wait. I'm sorry."

She hesitates, then sits back down.

"I was really looking forward to this trip, Steph."

She places her hand on mine. "I know you were."

"Now I'm sorry I made us come."

"I wanted to come, you know that." Hand retrieved, face slanted away again. "But I wanted to come with Hayden. I still think that would have been happier."

"Maybe you're right." *Seriously?* After all that's gone wrong today? "I'm glad she didn't find that hair, though. Imagine if she'd started playing with it or something."

She shrugs and stands up. "You want some coffee?"

"It's a bit late, don't you think?" Now that things are settled between us, I just want to shower and go to sleep.

"Why? What's the time?" Steph checks her phone. It's nearly eleven p.m. "Jesus," she says. "I've totally lost track of time. It's like we've lost a day."

"And these shutters don't help."

After I've showered until the water's run cold, I get into bed, ignoring the must in the sheets. Half-asleep, Steph pushes her calf into my leg, and it feels good to have my friend back. I know I should just leave well enough alone and let her sleep, but something in me needs to share what I saw down in that storeroom. "You know, when I went down looking for the trash can . . ." I'm just about to tell her everything, but the image of that stained mattress, the children's clothes, closes my throat.

"Mm?" she asks, sleepily. "What?"

"Just that . . . while I was throwing it away, I was really worried that the trash can was for recycling. How bourgeois is that?"

She doesn't answer. I think of something witty to say to make her laugh again. *Maybe the trash can was for organic waste after all . . .* But I don't feel witty. "Not a great start, was it?"

"Mm-mm."

"Tomorrow will be better."

Chapter 8

Steph

On the second day in the apartment I woke abruptly, convinced someone had shaken my shoulder. Groggy and disoriented, I sat up, trying and failing to cling to the last strands of vivid dreams about Hayden. At some point in the night I'd shrugged off my T-shirt, and my body was greasy with sweat, my hair matted. The heat in the room was oppressive, the air almost humid. I'd had two showers the day before, one when we first arrived and one while Mark disposed of the mouse and that hair—unusually obsessive behavior—and I now felt dirty again. I stretched, realizing that Mark's space next to me was empty.

A scratching sound was coming from the living room. *Skrik, skrik, skrik.*

"Mark?"

No response.

I flung off the blankets, pulled on another shirt, and padded into the living room.

Now that he'd managed to open the living room window, he was going at the shutter outside with a knife. "Mark?"

He jumped when I touched his shoulder and let out an embarrassed laugh. "You scared me."

"What time is it?"

"Early. Can't get the bloody shutter open."

"Why are you bothering? It doesn't matter." I squinted through one of the gray metal slats and down into the courtyard. "It's raining again."

He tossed the knife onto the coffee table and wiped his hands on his jeans. "Hey, how about I go get some croissants? And see if I can get hold of the bank again."

"I'll come with. I can call Hayden from the Starbucks. I'll just have a shower."

"You had a rough night. Why don't you relax, and I'll bring you breakfast in bed. We can go out together again later."

"I'll only be a few minutes."

"And I'll only be an hour or so. Come on, let me treat you for once."

I was getting the impression that he wanted some alone time, and decided not to argue. He shrugged on his coat as if he couldn't get out of there fast enough, and leaving the keys on the coffee table "just in case," he hurried out of the apartment. And really, I felt like I could do with some time by myself as well. Mark's behavior the day before had thrown me. He'd been gone far longer than a trip to the trash cans warranted, and when he returned he acted like a man hiding an affair: overcautious, irritable, unsettled. After he left, I toyed with the idea of heading down to the trash cans to see the hair for myself—I knew he was lying about something—but I didn't. I chose to trust him. Stupid. Who knows what I would have found in them?

I took a long shower instead, scrubbing at my body until the skin on my thighs and belly was scarlet. Next, I fiddled with the coffeemaker, giving up when I couldn't get the filthy thing to work. I killed time by wiping down the kitchen counters again, washing the plates, sweeping the floors, and scrubbing the sink. By now, Mark had been gone for more than an hour and I was getting restless. I'd told Mom I would call her at twelve thirty South African time—in less than an hour—and I couldn't leave the apartment: there was only one set of keys, and Mark would be locked out if he returned.

If I wanted wi-fi, there was only one option: a visit to Mark's madwoman in the attic. Someone in close proximity had a private wi-fi network, and it had to be her. I didn't particularly feel like meeting her—Mark had said she was a bona fide weirdo—but it would give me something to do. The worst that could happen, I rationalized, was that she'd tell me to fuck off. Pocketing the keys, I set off to try my luck.

The music wafting down from the top floor that morning was another 1980s greatest hit, and this one I recognized immediately: "99 Red Balloons." (It would weave through my head for the rest of the day.) The higher I walked, my feet clunking on the wooden steps, the louder it became, until I finally reached a narrow hall with two lopsided doors. I headed for the one with the music and knocked.

The door was flung open with force. The woman in the doorway was the sort of person whom Carla would have found interesting: intense, no makeup, dressed in a shapeless smock that was a hybrid between a kimono and a monk's robe, a half-smoked hand-rolled cigarette stuck to her bottom lip. Her hair was shorn to her scalp, and I couldn't help but think perhaps she'd donated it to the Petits' vile collection. She didn't speak, merely peeled the cigarette off her lip and, without taking her eyes from me, crushed it beneath a sandaled foot. Her toenails were long and yellow.

I gave her my best genial smile. "*Bonjour.* Sorry for disturbing you. You speak English—*anglais?*" Mark had told me she spoke fairly good English, but I didn't want to come across as presumptuous.

"What do you want?"

As politely and calmly as I could—although I had to raise my voice above the music—I explained the wi-fi situation and asked her if she'd consider allowing us to use hers. "We would pay you, of course."

She rarely blinked, which contributed to her intense air. She sniffed, said, "*Viens.* Come inside," stepped back, and beckoned me into her apartment, which was really just a single room. The space was dominated by scores of canvases, but I spied a filthy sink piled with dishes in one corner, as well as a futon with a stained Indian spread, and a small camping stove. Was she squatting here? It certainly looked like it. The room reeked of dirty laundry, smoke, and turpentine. I couldn't see a bathroom anywhere and there was nowhere to sit. Self-consciously—she was still staring at me with that intense gaze—I shuffled farther into the room. Most of the canvases were turned to the wall, but the one she was presumably working on was propped on an easel in the center of the room. Through a murky background of heavily applied browns and greens, the half-finished image of a child's face loomed, managing to be both disturbing and kitschy. It reminded me of those paintings of big-eyed children that were so popular in the seventies. "Very interesting," I lied. "You sell your paintings?"

Another sniff. "*Oui.*"

It would be up to me to try to initiate some kind of conversation—that or get the hell out of there. "I'm sorry, I haven't introduced myself. I'm Steph."

"Mireille." A pretty, birdlike name that didn't suit her. The track had changed to "Tainted Love," and I realized the music was coming from a MacBook Pro and speakers balanced on an upturned crate on the far side of the futon, which were at odds with the room's squalor. "You want *café?*" she barked.

I did, but the only mugs appeared to be piled in the sink, a greasy pan leaking oil on top of them. "No, *merci.* I'm fine."

This seemed to please her for some reason. Thankfully she moved to the computer and shut off the music.

"Mireille, can I ask you a question?"

"*Quoi?*"

"Mark—my husband—he said you don't know the Petits, the people in whose apartment we're staying."

She huffed as if she couldn't make sense of what I was saying. "*Quoi?*" she said again.

"The Petits." For the life of me I couldn't remember their first names. "We stay in their apartment. On the third floor." I was aware I was over-enunciating my words like an arsehole tourist.

"*Non.* There is no one who lives here now. Only me."

"But our apartment belongs to someone."

"You should not stay here. I tell this to your husband."

"We don't have a choice."

"Where you from? England?"

"No. South Africa. *Afrique du Sud.*"

A weary nod. "Go to a hotel."

"We don't have the money." Unless we managed to unlock the credit card. Hopefully Mark had been able to sort that out.

She narrowed her eyes, sighed, and then nodded. "*Bien.* Okay for the internet. You give me ten euro a day."

"Sure. Thank you, Mireille," I said, although that would dent our measly budget if we couldn't use the card.

"*D'accord.* I write down the password for you." She rooted around for a pen and piece of paper, giving me an opportunity to check out the room without her noticing. A half-empty bottle of vodka and a pile of Rizla rolling papers were placed next to the bed. An upturned book was half-hidden beneath the grubby sheets. Underwear and clothes were piled on top of the pillows. She handed me the piece of paper, then grabbed my wrist. Her fingernails were grimed with paint—or worse. "Don't stay here. *C'est mal ici.* Sick."

"Sick?" I gently pulled out of her grasp. Strangely, despite her intensity, she didn't intimidate me. There was something beneath the surface that was almost a profound sadness.

She shook her head. "*C'est mal.*"

"Why do you stay?"

"I am like you. I have nowhere to go. Now goodbye. I must work."

She ushered me out, and a few seconds later the music started up again. I wondered—I still wonder—if Mireille played it to try to banish the sickness she thought infested the building, as if early Kylie Minogue and Duran Duran were some kind of cheesy talismans against evil.

Back in the apartment, I logged on, tapped in the key, then Skyped Mom. I was half an hour early, but she'd been waiting for me, Hayden on her lap. "Hey, monkey," I said, feeling a tug in my gut at the sight of her.

"Mumma!"

"Mumma will be home soon, I promise."

She babbled something about a present from Nama, wriggled off my mom's lap, then reappeared, thrusting a Princess Elsa doll at the screen. "Mumma, look!"

I'd planned on buying the doll for her birthday and Mom knew that, but I tried to hide my irritation. Hayden stretched out her arms as if she could touch me through the screen, and again I felt that horrible plummeting feeling that I wouldn't see her again. We spoke for a few minutes about yesterday's trip to see the baby animals; then she said, "Got to go now, bye!" and slithered off. Mom tried to call her back, but with no success. Seeing her so happy without me was somehow worse than if she'd been upset and begging me to come home.

My mother smiled at me sheepishly.

"You've been spoiling her, Mom."

"*Ag*, she's my little princess. Is that the apartment I can see in the background?"

I didn't want Mom to see the true state of it, so I changed the subject, and when it was clear that Hayden wasn't returning to talk to me I hung up, planning to call later, after Hayden's nap time.

I checked my emails. There was nothing from the Petits, but Carla had been in touch again:

Still no sign of your guests. Took it upon myself to check flight arrivals. No delays on any planes from Paris to Joburg. Ditto local flights from Joburg to C Town. Also called local hospitals just in case. No French tourists admitted. Do you want me to get on to the cops, see if they can check the passenger lists? Hope all is well with you two. x

I replied to Carla, thanking her for everything she was doing and asking her to try the cops, although I doubted they'd be prepared to help. Next, I sent an email to the house swap site explaining our situation with the Petits and asking them if they had an emergency phone number on record. Just where the bloody hell were they? The last email I'd sent to them was way too polite. I fired off another one, a sharp one-liner insisting they get back to me ASAP. I ran through the possible explanations again, but paranoia was creeping in. Was this some kind of practical joke designed to freak out some random couple? Exhibit A was the hair Mark saw in the closet. I eyed the cardboard boxes in the corner of the living room, wondering if there was something equally bizarre inside them: a jack-in-the-box maybe. A porcelain clown curled up and waiting to spring. A pile of dolls with broken faces. A human skull or a collection of outlandish sex toys. I went so far as to consider that they could be filming us for some kinky online reality channel, and I even looked around the room for the telltale signs of any hidden cameras, until I snapped out of it and told myself to stop being so stupid.

It was now almost two hours since Mark had left to try to contact the bank, and I was starting to worry. Killing time again, I googled "uses for human hair," coming up with everything from wigmaking to witchcraft. I tried to write but couldn't concentrate. I returned to the kitchen, retrieved the piece of paper I'd unearthed from the drawer, and typed the words on it into a translation app. The app messed up some of the passage's structure, but it was definitely a scrap from a school essay:

> which we do on Sunday. I like going to the house of my grandmother because there it is calm and the noises and the cries of my father are not heard. He is always very sad. He says that mama became very ill after I caught a malady from Luc at school and she was infected also because her chest is not strong.

(The spelling of "calm"—*tranquille*—had been corrected on the original by whoever had marked it.)

> I would like to live at the house of my grandmother the time continuous but I can't because it is not the area where my school is positioned. This is all I have to say about my family now. The end.

It didn't seem likely that a child had lived in the Petits' apartment—for a start, there was only one bedroom.

A *thunk* came from outside the front door, making me start. Assuming it was Mark returning, I jumped up and flung open the door. The hallway was empty and dark, and the only sign of life was the muted sound of "Do They Know It's Christmas?" from Mireille's floor.

"Is anyone there?"

I strained to hear the sound of footsteps running up or down the stairs.

Nothing.

I could have sworn that someone had knocked on the door. Was the rest of the building really unoccupied? We had only Mireille's word that we were the sole inhabitants. Maybe it was time to find out. I slipped out of the apartment, remembering at the last moment to take the keys with me, and scurried to the apartment opposite, which was logically the only place the phantom knocker could have reached before I'd stepped into the hallway. I pressed my ear against its door. Silence. I knocked, waited, knocked again. Recalling something I'd seen in a movie, I tickled my fingers across the top of the lintel, and my fingertips brushed against metal—a rusty key. I stared at it dumbly for a few seconds; I hadn't expected to actually find anything.

Then, before I could change my mind, I slotted it into the keyhole and opened the door, calling out a tentative "hello," although God knows what I would have done if anyone had been in there. My first impression—probably because of the stench of must—was that I'd just entered a mausoleum. It was larger than the Petits' apartment, with an open-plan living room and kitchen area, but it had that same dated feel to it. A set of matching flowery living room furniture lurked at a skewed angle in the center of the room, and a table was laid with dusty plates and a salad bowl containing a desiccated black substance—the remains of dinner perhaps? A *Le Monde* dating from 1995 was crumpled on the coffee table next to the couch. I peered into the master bedroom. The sheets were still on the bed and a pair of men's shoes lay toe to toe near the door. The other bedroom was empty of all personal belongings except for two bare single mattresses and scores of plastic glow-in-the-dark stars stuck on the ceiling. Despite the sunlight coming through the dusty windows, every nerve ending was screaming at me to get the fuck out of there. I couldn't shake the sense that I'd stumbled into some kind of crime scene.

I fled, returning the key to its place, for once grateful to be inside the relative normality of the Petits' stark apartment. Blood roaring in my ears, I was about to slug back another Urbanol tablet when I heard Mark's voice, followed by a *thump* on the door. I raced to let him in, so full of what I'd seen that I didn't notice his demeanor until he'd pushed past me and slumped onto the couch. His eyes were unable to settle and he kept licking his lips. "Mark . . . what's happened?"

"Nothing." He tried to smile—an unconvincing display. "Nothing. Really. I'm just pissed off with the bank. They won't unlock the card."

But there was more to it than that. He looked shell-shocked. I tried again to get him to tell me what had spooked him, but he continued to insist that there was nothing wrong. Eventually, I gave up.

I still don't know what affected him that day. He never told me, not even when he had nothing left to lose.

Chapter 9

Mark

The moment I step onto the street, I feel lighter. I'd like to say it's just because I'm out of that oppressive building and that stifling apartment, but I wonder if I'm also relieved to have some time away from Steph. It feels disloyal to think that way, but it's been ages since we've spent so much time together, just the two of us—there's always been work or Hayden interrupting, and I guess we've become used to that; an hour's absence will only make the heart grow fonder.

I'm in Paris at last; it's so familiar and so overwhelmingly exotic all at once. This ordinary little street with its gray, tagged walls and narrow sidewalks littered with cigarette butts and dog crap and scraped gum is a wonderland to me. Every ten paces there's something new: the entrance to an apartment or a hotel or a school; a greengrocer, a bakery, a bistro, a designer clothing shop, a café, a shop that sells only honey, a shop that sells only Iberian ham, a shop for pâté; look at the seafood on trays of ice in the fishmonger, scalloped shells and blue lobsters, glossy fresh pinkfish; here are strings of giant garlic and red onions and salamis and chorizo. I could walk for miles in the suburbs of Cape Town without seeing anything new, but here, fifty yards is crammed with a lifetime of sensations. This little street, with its jaunty angles and walls of pretty balconied windows and the crisp, refreshing wind coming up from the river, must seem mundane to its residents, but for me it's a joyous celebration of flavor and life.

I smile and nod and say *bonjour* to the shopkeepers and the serious women striding along the sidewalk and the retirees pulling shopping carts and the immaculately dressed children with their coats and scarves and boots and their calm, contained manner. God, Zoë would have loved it here. Already, at the age of seven, Zoë was turning out to be just as much an obsessive geek as me. Once, when we took the train down to Simonstown, she kept asking me to show her my watch, and I wondered why until I noticed her writing every station name down in her diary, along with the time we stopped there. That sweet, brave, inquisitive girl was meant to have a life filled with travel. For months, her favorite bedtime stories were pages from the atlas and the *World Fact File*. She not only knew most of the world's flags by heart but drew her own flags for Zoëland and all the other countries in her mind. I taught her how to say hello and goodbye in twelve languages, and she took ownership of Odette's foreign coin collection as soon as she was tall enough to nab it from the cabinet in her study. We'd find her muttering capitals and greetings to herself on her carpet, the coins all lined up in front of her. Zoë was just getting old enough for Odette and me to consider saving up to take her overseas. Odette got sick and Zoë never made it out of the country.

Odette and I would have had our bloody credit cards working, and we would have splurged on designer outfits for her, sauntered into our boutique hotel, and thrown our shopping bags on the plush bed like they do in the movies. But that was another life; I shove the memories into their well-worn corner.

The fact that I was making such an issue about money before we came here just shows what a cramped rut I've got myself into. We're in Paris for one week and we can afford to get into a little bit of debt to enjoy ourselves properly. I feel like I've immediately gained perspective; all the shit at home seems so faraway. As I make my way down the hill toward the Starbucks, I peer into the windows of the hotels I pass. There are some lovely-looking two- and three-star places that are fairly reasonable. It's not too late to rescue this trip.

In the coffee shop, I order a giant Americano and a Danish, willfully not converting euros into rands. I put in my earphones, sign into the wi-fi, and Skype the bank's credit card helpline. As I hear the tinny waiting music, my heart clenches and I understand that those hotels, the shopping, a pleasant meal or two—Steph and me having a good time this week—are all riding on this call.

Once I've entered my account number, I'm put through to an agent. "Good morning, this is Jeandra speaking. Can you confirm your name and ID number and physical address for me?"

I rattle off my details, bracing myself for a fight, but to my surprise, the agent sounds smart and keen. "Good morning, Dr. Sebastian. How can I help you?"

"I'm overseas now, and I need my credit card unblocked to use here."

"Which country are you in, sir?"

"I'm in France."

"You're aware that you need to pre-authorize your card for use out of the country?"

I consider lying—if I told her that I didn't know, she might take pity on me—but I can't bring myself to. "Yes, I was, actually. But I forgot."

"I'm sorry to hear that, sir. It happens quite a lot."

I'm still suspicious of this woman's tone. She's probably instructed to placate the customer while still not doing a thing to solve the problem. "So, is there anything you can do? Can you authorize it now?"

"You know, sir, we're not really supposed to, but I can understand when you're on a trip, you need your card to work."

"That's right," I say, guarded.

"What we can probably do is just authorize you as if you're arriving today, and it should be fine."

Okay. This is not my normal experience of bank call centers. "Great, thanks so much."

"But I need my supervisor to override that transaction, and he's in a meeting now."

"Oh."

"But he's logged to be back at twelve o'clock. That's eleven your time."

I check my watch: just over an hour.

"If you call back then, we'll get it done. Here's my direct number: it's Jeandra F." I scratch the number into my napkin with the end of my plastic spoon.

"Thank you, Jeandra, you've been really helpful."

"A great pleasure, sir. Speak to you soon, and enjoy your trip further."

I take out the earphones and sit back and take a long, relieved draft of my coffee. What a nice, helpful person. It's good to remember sometimes that the whole world isn't against you.

I click on Steph's name in Skype and then remember: she won't have wi-fi up there. I can't let her know I'll be longer than expected, but it's hardly worth walking all the way up to the apartment and then coming straight down again to finalize the credit card. She'll just have to wait—or she can take a walk of her own if she wants; she's got the keys. What did people do before everyone had cell phones? They relaxed and trusted each other to be grown-ups, that's what. Steph'll be fine; instead of fussing and worrying, I should see her as an adult who can take care of herself. Besides, she's probably fast asleep, catching up on two years' worth of rest. Meanwhile, I'm on a Parisian boulevard and can certainly find something to keep me occupied for an hour.

Pocketing my phone, I take my coffee outside, strolling along the broad sidewalk and staring unashamedly like a tourist at the fingers of the bare trees pointing up at the intricate balconies of plush apartments, the chauffeured sedans cruising the wide road, the subtle neon and opulent façades of designer shops. Joggers and workers and children on their way to school pass brasseries with somehow familiar names and sprawling sidewalk enclosures packed with those famous little round tables. A short way up the road, I pass an ornate marble-tiled and vaulted shopping arcade and reach a doorway advertising the waxworks museum. The poster shows that they've got a Michael Jackson and a George Clooney, a Gandhi and an Einstein—and even a Hemingway and a Sartre. That'll be a good way to kill an hour.

I'm expecting a cluttered little curiosity shop, but the corridor is long and narrow, with glitzy mirrored walls and a bright red carpet. It's five past ten and the museum's just opened, but there's already a small queue ahead of me: a chic designer pair and a venerable couple escorting a small red-haired boy. An Italian-sounding family bustles in from the boulevard on gales of laughter, swapping jokes as we approach the security checkpoint. I smile down at the child, and he clings to his grandmother's leg. As I surrender my pockets' contents under a blast of hot air and I'm scanned by a security wand, I'm numbed by the foreign languages around me, peripheral and strange like an alien hermetically sealed in a space suit.

Once I'm through the entranceway, the corridor widens out into a plush red lobby with a low, dark ceiling. I check my coat and only then notice how expensive the entrance ticket is. But the truth is, I'm intrigued by the red room and the promise of what lies beyond, so I pay up; the credit card will be working when I'm out of here.

I follow the others through a cramped tunnel lined with curved funhouse mirrors and totems made of wax faces and glance ahead at the little boy—I'm sure Hayden or Zoë would find this creepy, but he's laughing and skipping ahead with his grandparents; no doubt they've been here before. I tell myself to stop worrying and try to enjoy this for myself.

Around the next turn, we enter a surprisingly lofty, bright room, like a small version of a grand opera's lobby. The walls are covered with frescoes and baroque gilt-framed mirrors. We're ushered up a sweeping marble staircase to a black door lit with a sign: LE PALAIS DES MIRAGES. The chatter in the group has died down and we file into the darkened room. It's a square about the size of our bedroom at home, with a double-high ceiling and walls glinting with mirrors. I crush down an itchy sense of panic. What if these people are conning us? What if they're planning to rob us? Surely we're perfect marks—blithe tourists with too much money and too much trust. We've herded in here so obediently, like animals to the slaughter.

Don't be stupid, Mark. It's not Steph's voice my mind conjures to berate me; it's a mixture of Odette's and Carla's disapproval—ancient, deeply rooted, formative. *It's just a show. What's happened to you?*

I was attacked, in my home, in the darkness, I want to say to them. *That's what happened to me!* But I know that whatever's been eroding me has been happening since long before the invasion.

In the darkness, the little boy whispers and his grandmother returns a comforting response. He giggles. An announcement comes on in English and French, asking us to turn off our cell phones and not to take photos. The usher leads another group inside, signals for us all to stand against the side of the room, then retreats, closing the door behind her.

Bulbs set into the domed ceiling start to flicker; then tubes of colored lights arrayed around the walls flash on and off in time to an urgent drumming. A crash of lightning is timed to a bright strobe that illuminates four figures set on pedestals high up on the wall in each quadrant of the room, reflected count-lessly in the opposite mirrors. Instantly, the music changes to a sensual bolero as the figures are bathed in undulating light from spots placed in hidden crevices in the ceiling. It looks like they're moving, although they're nothing but wax models. Three women in tribal outfits—African, Polynesian, and Indian—are presided over by the glowering eyes of a malignant swami.

I'm constructing a mental critique of the inherent sexism and racism in the portrayals of these figures—the colonial-ist penchant for exoticizing the "primitive" body—when the lights shut off with a resounding crash and a whole different set of lights comes on. There are green snakes and tendrils and the ceiling has somehow been quilted with a layer of patterned silk that ripples to hidden currents of air in time to the urgent susurration of jungle insects. A roar of a tiger, and I glance over to where the little boy is standing, fearing for him, but he's smiling, rapt, up at the leaves of the canopy.

The lights go off, and now the ceiling is a star-spangled night sky. The tribal figures have disappeared and been replaced on their pedestals by revelers at a masked ball. The stars twinkle over them as they dance motionlessly to a waltz. Gradually the lights come up, rose and orange, as if dawn is ending the party. Another announcement invites the group to continue through the far door and enjoy the rest of the museum.

As the other visitors file out, I linger, studying the room, wondering how they achieved their effects. It's clearly an antique exhibit, but it's still very impressive and clever. They must have used a rotating base on each pedestal that swaps the figures around while the lights are down. I'm scanning the ceiling to trace where the ropes of lights are laid and where the fans and spots must be housed when the lights flick out. My eyes have been narrowed by the brightness of the false dawn, and now I can't see a thing. Muttering something meaningless to indicate that there's still someone in here, I feel my way around the wall toward the exit. But I can't find the door. There's not a seam in the surface, just the feel of slightly tacky velvet. I trail farther around, sure that I've circled way beyond where the door was. It's a small room and the door was just to my right. Even if it was—

A *thump* somewhere above me, answered by a groan from the other side.

"Hello?"

They're in the house, Mark.

They can't be. They're . . . it's probably just . . .

Thump. Thump.

They're inside. Oh fuck.

Steph, don't.

My throat stops working and my chest starts to ache. Trying to suck in some breath, I feel my way urgently around the room toward the entrance side, but I can't . . . I still can't find . . .

The lights blare on, the mirrors jagging the beams around the room. I'm alone in here.

But that groan again, behind me.

I turn and look up at the pedestal. No tribeswoman, no dancer, but a tall teenage girl with long blond hair. She's not part of the old display; she's wearing jeans and a red T-shirt and sneakers with Scooby-Doo on them. She's lean and striking, a lot like Odette, but not exactly. *Look again, force yourself. It's a wax model, and she's looking at you. Look into her eyes.*

Zoë. Fourteen years old. As if she'd never died.

And now she's smiling. I step closer. She opens her mouth . . .

"*Oh, monsieur! Pardonnez!*" An usher hurries through the door and directs me toward the exit, which is set neatly in the velvet wall. I glance back over my shoulder as the woman assists me, back up at the pedestal, but the figure isn't even a girl; it's a dancing man with a tuxedo and a monocle. *Jesus, Mark, get a grip.*

Now there's Elton John at the piano, the young couple taking a selfie with Michael Jackson, a woman in a burqa posing with a peace sign next to Barack Obama for her husband's camera, a comedian in a garish golfing outfit, and I can't wrap my mind around the disjuncture between the smiling visitors and the creepiness of these not-quite-dead effigies. I'm sure it's just a post-traumatic effect of the darkness and the strangeness—perhaps the flashing lights have triggered some sort of recall—but I can't help feeling that their glass eyes are watching me as I meander through the intricate succession of rooms trying to relax, forcing my heart back to its place and my breathing back to normal.

In the theater set, a famous French actress sits on a red velvet seat. Her crisp black bob has been pushed askew by one of the visitors, and as I pass, one of her false eyelashes detaches itself and flutters down into her lap. I can't help thinking that the hair they've used is still alive. Although I'm alone at the moment, the room still thrums with presence.

Zoë was six, grown up into a smart, gorgeous, funny little girl, and Odette and I had started sleeping properly, and our lives seemed settled and happy, and we were just beginning to dream, to make plans as a family, something you can do only once the crisis years of baby care and toddlerhood are past. Then Odette started getting the pains. The doctor found that she was already in stage two and she had to have an immediate hysterectomy and start chemotherapy.

Zoë was so patient when her mommy was tired and listless and nauseous. She'd help Odette with her makeup and come up with quiet games to play while Odette lay on the new couch in the sun. She learned to make sandwiches and tea. But it was the hair loss that frightened Zoë most—and me, to be honest. If someone's looking pale and weak, it's bad enough, but everyone's seen ill people before, and they usually get better. But when clumps of hair fall from their heads, it's like they're dead already. It's like their bodies are giving up on their souls.

It was during Odette's third course of chemotherapy that Zoë's behavior started to become more worrying. It was one night when I was bathing her while we were alone and Odette was overnighting at the hospital that I noticed the purplish weals on Zoë's hands. It wasn't the first time; the first two times, even though I knew better, I'd just written them off as scratches any active kid might get. But this time there were two sets of deep puncture wounds, the skin around them puckered and blue.

"What happened here, sweetie?"

Zoë shrugged. "A dog bit me."

"What? When? What dog?"

"That ice-cream dog from across the road."

"The collie?"

"Yes." Zoë was splashing with her plastic sharks as if nothing had happened.

"Why? What were you doing there?" And when? When the *fuck* had my daughter wandered across the road by herself? Or perhaps Odette had taken her for a walk . . . but she'd surely tell me if Zoë'd been bitten.

"Princess Ariel says the hair has to be living; that's why Mommy's not getting better. The ice-cream dog has nice hair."

I should have taken Zoë to the clinic for tetanus and rabies shots, I should have asked Zoë what else she'd been chatting to Princess Ariel about, but instead I put her to bed and drank myself to sleep beside her.

I've got to get a grip on myself; the past is past. You can't change it by thinking about it. Think about now, here. Deliberately rechanneling my thoughts, as I've learned to do, I inspect the models unemotionally, try to see them as craft works, and

I can start to enjoy the care the museum's taken with each of the sets and the outfits and the figures themselves. They are incredibly realistic—the only thing that gives them away is the static sheen over their wax skin, but you have to look closely to notice that. In each new room, figures are posed in dynamic ways—a rock concert, a theater show, a nightclub bustling with French celebrities, a photo call with sports heroes, and a bar with writers and actors sharing a drink. I use my phone to take a self-portrait with Hemingway, embarrassed when one of the figures I took for a venerable author stands up from the banquette next to me: the grandfather taking a break.

Now the trail leads through the museum shop and I studiously avoid looking at the shelves, considering myself too canny to be taken in by tourist rip-off centers, but as I go to the far door, I'm caught by the glint of a rough-hewn, chunky emerald ring I just know Steph would love. It's tasteful, not emblazoned with any logos, and I idly flick over the price tag. It's really not all that expensive, not for something that will be a wonderful surprise for her. If I could just unblock my card. I check my watch; the bank supervisor should be back by now and there's free wi-fi in the museum, so I smile at the woman behind the shop's counter and retreat to a corner to make the call to Jeandra's direct line.

"Yes, Dr. Sebastian, Kurt's here. I've filled him in. Let me put you through."

Twenty seconds of the waiting music. "Hello, sir. Hang on, please." This man's bored tone is more what I expected from the bank. For half a minute, I hear the rattle of computer keys, a sigh, and then, "No, I'm afraid we're not able to authorize your card."

"But Jeandra said there was a way she could help."

"Uh, right . . . She's not entitled to. There are procedures."

"But she explained it quite clearly. You can just mark me down as having arrived today; then there's no problem."

"Yeah, even if we could, uh, we couldn't. There are already two foreign transactions from yesterday."

"But they didn't go through. They were declined."

"Uh, yes, sir," he says, enunciating like he's talking to an idiot. "But the system has logged the declines as originating from France, so there's no way to predate the authorization."

"What does that mean? That you won't help?"

"We'd love to help you, sir. But it's clear in the Ts and Cs that you should pre-authorize your card when you go outside the borders. You signed the Ts and Cs. You could use another card."

"I don't have another card. What do you . . ." I realize my voice is too loud for the low-ceilinged room and the cashier is looking at me. "Okay, never mind." I cut the call, seething. But there's no point raging against the machine. This is my fuckup; I have only myself to blame.

I stalk out of the shop, trying to find the quickest route to the exit. How am I going to explain this to Steph? When she finds out how much I've wasted getting in here . . . I storm past Brad Pitt and Madonna and a set full of fashion models and an apocalyptic TV-watching couple and into a kids' fiction section, past Obélix and some creature from a Disney movie, swearing under my breath. But when I see the little red-haired boy standing next to the Little Prince, his grandmother aiming a camera at him, I force myself to calm down. These French people are so elegant, so contained. That civility and urbanity is precisely what I've been enjoying about this trip, how different it is from the angry rush at home. Civil, urbane people don't march though museums cursing under their breath.

Besides, I'm here now and it's going to be the last luxury I have, so I'd better enjoy it. I take a deep breath and slow down in the French history and literature section, gleaning from the signs what each scene is about: papist and revolutionary history, great moments in art and science—and quite a lot of bloodshed: Joan of Arc and Marat, the Hunchback of Notre-Dame, a Medici massacre, and here, after I've trailed through an asylum accompanied by a soundtrack of moaning and clanking chains, the plague. I'm shocked to see a dark-coated figure bearing away a plainly dead blue-gray baby from a snow-clogged sewer. Hayden would be terrified by these scenes, and understandably so. Will the little boy's guardians hustle him past this section with his eyes closed?

And look at this horse in the middle of this dark room, its flaring nostrils and terrified eyes wide and glaring, a knight on its back. I round the beast and see that the knight is a skeleton, slashing with a sword. Bizarre: Mickey Mouse in one room, a horseman of the apocalypse and a plague baby in the next.

Something smells odd in this room, and the air is stagnant. I haven't seen anyone coming past me for a while. Despite myself, I'm drawn to the holes in the skull's eyes. There's a soft glow of light inside them. Wondering how they achieve this startling effect, I stand on my tiptoes and crane up to the horse-man, trying to avoid touching the horse, and the light sputters inside, glowing from pale white to orange to red, when there's a glancing yellow motion in my peripheral vision, like some of the flame has dislodged and become whole in the shadows of the room.

I turn my head slowly, as if the air has stalled and thickened. A frigid breeze blows from the fake snow in the sewer, and a stench of rot from deep in the horse's throat. I don't want to look at the glowing shape.

At her. Because I know.

I lock eyes with her. It's Zoë, and she's tall and beautiful like her mother. As if she never died.

She opens her mouth, and before she can speak, I use all my energy to wrench my eyes away from her and drag myself though the last hallway, feeling her following me. I can't walk fast enough.

At last, thank God, I see the exit sign. I push through the door, into a room that's suddenly bright and clinically tiled. There's a red vending machine and a rack of pamphlets. No ghosts can come out here, surely. In there, with horror and death and illusions perhaps, but not out here in the real, mundane, dutiful world.

I scrabble at the handle of the final exit, painted white, normal, thinking if I see the grandparents, the lovers, the Italians, Parisian people going about their day, I'll be free, but the door behind me slams. And she has followed me here.

She's as tall as me now, and the Scooby-Doo sneakers squeak against the tiles on the floor as she approaches. She smiles and her eyes haven't changed. I open my arms and she comes to me and I hold her and she smells like she always did, and like her mother too. And I put my hand into her yellow hair and hold her against me, breathing her in.

She pushes me against the vending machine with a clatter that surely means this is real. I feel the jab of the coin slot in my spine. She grabs my fingers in hers and, like we used to do, she rubs the tip of her nose on mine. She opens her mouth and talks. "You killed me, Papa. *Tu m'as tué. Pourquoi, Papa?*" she says, her breath like sweet rot. And then she kisses me; like Odette used to, she sucks my bottom lip into her mouth and bites down.

Chapter 10

Steph

"Uh-huh. Thanks for doing that, Carla." Mark paced up and down the living room, the phone glued to his ear.

Worried that he'd use up all the Skype credit calling Carla's cell, I mouthed, "Hurry up," but he pretended not to notice. At least he'd recovered from whatever had spooked him during his outing to call the bank—he'd perked up the second I shared the news that we now had wi-fi in the apartment, and immediately decided to Skype Carla, probably as an excuse to prevent me from questioning him further.

"And the cops said they couldn't help? Uh-huh. Right, I understand."

From the one-way conversation it was clear that Carla still hadn't heard anything from the Petits and my assumption that the police wouldn't get involved was correct. With no indication of foul play, the Petits' no-show would be low on the cops' list of priorities. I listened, my irritation growing, as Mark filled Carla in on the disappointing state of the apartment before launching into a description of the hair in the closet. He made it sound like a lark, an amusing eccentricity he'd stumbled upon, rather than the gruesome discovery that had him sniping at me and fleeing for the trash cans. She said something that made him laugh. That was it.

"*Enough*, Mark. Fucking hang up already." I didn't care if Carla could hear me. He frowned at me and held up a hand, as if I were a naughty child who needed admonishing for interrupting the adults.

"*Mark!*"

"Got to go. Uh-huh, I know. She's just stressed. Thanks again." He hung up. "Happy now, Steph? What the hell was that about?"

"We need to conserve the Skype credit. What if we can't recharge the account from here?"

"You don't need credit to talk to Hayden. It's free from computer to computer."

"I know that, but what if Mom's out and I need to call her cell?"

"You're blowing this out of proportion, Steph."

"Oh right, so I shouldn't worry that I might not be able to talk to my daughter now? That I won't be able to because you've wasted all our airtime talking to that bloody woman?"

"Carla's trying to help us, Steph."

"Whatever."

He put his hands up in mock defeat. "Okay, okay. I'm sorry, okay?" He stalked into the kitchen.

Shaky from the fight, I checked my emails, desperate to distract myself. The house swap site had sent a tepid message saying that they were looking into the situation, and I was about to respond to it when another, wholly unexpected, email pinged into my in-box.

Months ago, and without telling Mark, I'd sent query letters to several overseas literary agents, asking them if they'd be interested in representing the young-adult novel I'd written for an online writing course I'd taken last year. I hadn't heard back from any of them, and after a couple of weeks of obsessively checking their Twitter feeds, I'd pushed it out of my mind. The email was from one of the agents, a Canadian woman who specialized in children's fiction, and she'd asked to see the full manuscript.

I had to read it several times before it sank in. "Oh my God. Mark!"

"What is it now?" He emerged from the kitchen, still irritated. Taking my amazed expression for shock, he softened his tone. "What is it?"

I showed him the email, watching him carefully. His face clouded for a second, and then he let out a bark of joy. "Christ, Steph, this is fantastic. Why didn't you tell me you were submitting to agents?"

Yes, why hadn't I? "I don't know. I suppose I didn't want you to see me fail. She might still turn it down."

"Nonsense. She'll love it. It's a great little book. We need to celebrate."

Fingers shaking, I replied to the agent, attaching the full manuscript. A flush of warmth was growing inside me. The news could be the answer to the guilt I felt for not earning my keep. After Hayden's difficult early months, Mark and I decided it was best if I stayed home with her until she turned two and could go to playgroup, but when her second birthday came and went, I let the weeks roll by without so much as looking on the internet for work. Was it fear that held me back? Fear of getting into a rut like Mark had with his career? Or was it a simple lack of ambition? Sure, I was bored to death of staying home—which was why I'd signed up for the cheap course in the first place—but it was easier that way. I knew I was a good mother; I wasn't failing at that. And to be fair to Mark, he'd never once nagged me about it.

Mark handed me my coat and ushered me out of the building—his spirits were restored, either by my news or his chat with Carla. Right then, I didn't care which.

It hurts now to think about the rest of that day. We headed to Notre-Dame, and while we mingled with the tourists flocking around the entrance, all I could think was, *I am good enough, after all.* I barely felt the bite of the air or cared that the skies were gray and drizzly. Everything was charming and beautiful, from the architecture to the slow-moving crowds, which I would normally have found irritating and oppressive.

We squeezed into the Shakespeare and Company bookstore and browsed for an hour or so, then bought crêpes from a vendor and ate them as we strolled across the Seine and on toward the Pompidou Centre. Mindful of our budget, we decided not to splurge on tickets for the art galleries that day. On the way home we bought a couple of bottles of cheap wine from the Monoprix and some more bread and cold meat.

We stayed up talking until midnight—I drunkenly confessed my foray into the neighboring apartment—then lazily padded off to bed.

We didn't make love that night—we were too tired, I suppose—but for the first time since those men had broken into our house, I was almost happy.

I woke around ten from a dreamless sleep with a mild hangover. Mark wasn't next to me, nor was he anywhere in the apartment. I was scouring the kitchen to see if he'd left me a note, when he burst through the front door.

"Steph?"

"Where have you been?"

"In the apartment across the hallway. Christ, you were right about it being creepy. Look." He thrust a battered business card into my hand. His cheeks were flushed and he kept tugging at his bottom lip. I was beginning to regret telling him about my spot of breaking and entering; I should have known he'd want to see the apartment for himself.

"What's this?"

"A business card for a real estate agent, Le Ciel Bleu. *Agence immobilière.* That's what it means, right? It was in one of the kitchen drawers. Could be a lead. For all we know, they might represent the place and be in touch with the Petits."

"You searched through their stuff?"

"Whose stuff? Whoever lived there is long gone. There wasn't much there. A few old clothes in the closet, not much else. It's no big deal. It's a lead, Steph," he said again.

"So we're going to be detectives now?"

"Yes. It's worth talking to them, isn't it?"

"The card looks pretty old."

Ignoring me, he turned on the iPad and asked me to read out the address printed in faded script on the card. "Let's see if they're still around."

I did as he asked, spelling it out letter by letter, and he typed it into Google. "Bingo! It still exists. And it looks like it's not too far from here—we can walk it."

Following the directions Mark had downloaded, we found the Ciel Bleu agency easily, nestled on a side street between a Moroccan restaurant and a high-end unisex hairdresser's.

A smart-suited man of about my age greeted us warmly as we stepped through the door. His blond hair was slicked back, his skin was flawless, and his blue tie was the exact shade of his eyes. He was as well put together as a store mannequin, and I squirmed with self-consciousness at my own disheveled state. I hadn't showered, my hair was all over the place, and I hadn't bothered with makeup.

"*Parlez-vous anglais?*" Mark asked.

"Yes. How may I help you?" His English was as polished as his appearance.

I waited for Mark to explain our errand. He showed the man the business card, told him the building's address, and said that we were desperate to get in touch with the owners of our apartment. I expected the agent to lose interest the second he learned we weren't potential customers, but instead he listened politely and then said, "We do not represent this building, but it is possible that my boss might know something. He has owned the agency for many, many years. You want me to call him and see what it is he has to say?"

"That would be incredible of you," I said, blushing as he smiled back at me. I glanced at Mark to see if he'd noticed—he hadn't, or if he had, he didn't care.

"*D'accord.* He is *en vacances* at the moment, but he will not mind if I call him, I think. Perhaps he can help you."

While he rang his boss, I gazed at the photographs of the properties available for rent and sale. The prices of the tiniest apartments were astounding.

The conversation appeared to be getting quite involved, and his tone had turned serious, but all I could understand were the agent's frequent "*d'accord*s" and "*vraiment?*"

After five minutes or so he hung up and folded his manicured hands together. "This is a very interesting situation. Monsieur le Croix says that he used to represent the building for many years but stopped doing so sometime in the nineties."

"Did he say why?"

"It became too much trouble. The people who would rent there did not stay. They would move in and then leave and would be reluctant to pay. He says many of the agencies have the same problem, so no one is willing to take it on."

"Did he say why they didn't want to stay?"

"*Non.* He was unclear on this matter."

"Did he say who owns the building or anything about the Petits?"

"*Non.* He did not know that name."

Mark's feverish expression was back. "Could we talk to him?"

"*Oui.* I will give you his email address. But I can't guarantee that he will choose to help you. He will be *en vacances* for two more weeks."

We thanked him profusely and headed out into the chill morning.

Mark led the way up to Montmartre, where we stopped for a snack and a cup of coffee at the cheapest place we could find. His growing excitement about getting to the bottom of the Petits' whereabouts and the reason behind the building's abandonment was contagious. Perhaps I should have known then that something was beginning to warp inside him. The overly enthusiastic behavior was at odds with his usual considered approach to life, but I was still lit up by yesterday's book news, so I let it go. As we sipped at lukewarm cappuccinos, we bounced ideas back and forth. For a couple of hours the mystery enthralled us. It would be a story we'd be able to tell people when we got home. *You'll never guess what . . .* It was invigorating.

When we arrived back, Mireille was waiting for us outside our apartment, slumped on a step. The light on the landing was working for a change and we could see the hideous woolen cape she was wearing that day billowing around her like a filthy parachute. There was a smudge of blue paint on her cheek, and she stank of body odor and nicotine.

She ignored Mark and acknowledged me with a nod. "You are still here?"

"Looks that way," I said as lightly as I could manage.

She gave me a pitying look. "The others did not stay as long here."

Mark and I exchanged glances.

"What others?" he asked. "The Petits?"

She finally deigned to look in his direction. "I tell you I do not know those people. *Non.* I am speaking of *les autres visiteurs.* Like you. One family from England or America—they only stay for one night. I see them as they are leaving. They are very angry. You must go too. It is better here after they go, but it is still bad."

"Hang on. When was this?"

She shrugged. "I don't know. I am not good with time."

"Why did they leave? Why were they angry?" Mark was staring at her with as much intensity as she usually exuded, and I couldn't help but think, *If only he'd been this forceful when those men invaded our home,* which made me feel both disloyal and guilty. We'd escaped unscathed; if we'd fought back, who knows what might have happened?

She sighed. "You have my money for wi-fi?" She pronounced it *wee-fee.*

"Why did they leave? Were they staying in this apartment?" His voice was getting more strident.

"Calm down, Mark," I whispered.

Mireille held out a hand, palm upward. "Money."

Mark opened his wallet and fumbled for a ten-euro note.

Mireille gasped, shot to her feet, and grabbed the wallet out of his hand.

"Hey!" Mark tried to snatch it back, but she held it out of his reach.

She was staring intently at the photograph of Hayden in the wallet's see-through pouch. Behind it, I knew, were two folded photographs of Zoë. "Why you not tell me before?"

"Give it back."

She said something to herself in French. Her hand went limp and she almost dropped the wallet. Mark retrieved it from her.

She nodded to herself, then looked straight at me once more. "I see you tonight."

"Excuse me?"

"I see you tonight. We have a drink. I will come here." She whirled around to thunk her way up the stairs.

We should have called after her, told her no, but we were both too blindsided.

"Has she really just invited herself over?" I said to Mark when she was out of earshot.

"Looks like it."

"Shall we pretend to be out if she shows up?"

He ignored me. "You think the Petits have done this before? Invited people to stay in their shithole of an apartment?"

"Why, though? What's the motive? We're not paying them." Somewhat reluctantly, I explained my outlandish theory that the Petits were playing some sort of elaborate trick on us, hoping he would reject it. He didn't.

"And why would she be so surprised that we have a child?"

Mark shrugged. "Maybe it's because of our age difference."

"You think?"

"Who cares. Come on, let's get inside."

While Mark showered, I tried to Skype Mom, but she wasn't online, nor was she answering her cell phone. I left her a message and logged on to Facebook. I'd been avoiding it, and there were several messages from friends asking how our trip was going. Facebook was my only real link to my old crowd. Most of my college friends had drifted away shortly after I'd gotten pregnant and dropped out. I'd tried to keep in touch at first, inviting them over several times, but our get-togethers were awkward and they never stayed long. They tended to treat Mark with cautious respect, as if he was a parent rather than my husband. I thought about sharing my news about the book agent but decided against it in case I jinxed it. In the end, I logged out without posting any updates.

After his shower, Mark disappeared into the kitchen and returned brandishing a knife. "Time to see what's in the boxes."

"You think we should?"

"Who's going to stop us? The Petits—if they even exist— have lost the right to privacy as far as I'm concerned." He stabbed the knife into the edge of the first box and ripped through the tape sealing the flaps down. Bemused, Mark dragged out a white wedding dress that stank of mildew and had been shoved in there with little care. It didn't look expensive: an off-the-rack meringue-style dress made out of shiny polyester and acres of cheap net underskirt that looked dangerously flammable. Nothing else.

"Try the next one."

The second contained nothing but a jumbled pile of French cookbooks from the seventies and rusty DIY tools. Mark chucked the knife on the table. "Shit."

"We should be relieved they aren't full of more of that horrible hair. Or worse, body parts or something."

Dejected, Mark started shoving the books and tools back in the box and wandered to the bathroom.

My computer blipped, signaling that I'd received an email. Heart leaping—was it from the book agent?—I clicked on it immediately.

It wasn't from the agent.

Chapter 11

Mark

The bruise in the small of my back I can explain—I may have bumped into something unaware—but not this cut on the inside of my lip. I peer at my face in the bathroom mirror, fingering my mouth where she bit me. The wisps of the incident cling to me like the remnants of a dream, but it was real; I press my nail into the raw sliver and it stings in confirmation. I shouldn't dwell on it.

That girl *was not Zoë*, I repeat to myself for the umpteenth time, because that's simply not possible. For one thing, Zoë didn't speak French, an unconvincing and panicked voice wheedles in my mind. That girl was probably older than fourteen; perhaps she was drunk or high or something. That would make more sense, make me feel less branded.

She said I killed her. She'll never forgive me. My rational brain reminds me that I made that up: *I'll* never forgive *myself,* and I never should. The death of a child's not something you forgive yourself for; forgiveness is not even offered for that.

"Mark?"

"Yes?" I call.

"You'll never believe it," Steph says from the living room.

I wash my hands and splash some water on my face, then go out to join her. "What's the matter?"

She glances up from the iPad. "Nothing's the matter. The Petits wrote back."

"Oh, good. At last. What did they say?"

She points to the message on the screen. It's just two lines in reply to the last of Steph's urgent emails to them: *We excuser for delay. We were set aside a minute. We hoping you are enjoying our jolie appartement.*

"Weird, huh?" Steph says as she stands and goes to plug the iPad charger into the socket.

"Their English isn't very good, remember? I suppose if I had to write to someone in French, I'd keep it short myself."

"Yeah, but after all this time. Surely they can see we've been worried."

I shrug. "Maybe it's just Gallic laissez-faire. Who knows? But it's great that they're all right. We don't have to worry anymore."

"I don't think you were ever that worried."

"I knew it would be okay."

"Do you think they still intend to stay at our place? The email is so vague."

"Good point. Maybe you should ask them."

"On it." She's already tapping at the screen. "I'll also let Carla know that they're okay and might turn up after all."

I look at her as she bends over the computer, her sweater hanging low, revealing beautifully packed cleavage. *I'm married to her,* I think. *The girl with that cleavage chose to be with me.* She catches me looking, then smiles as she stands. "Let's cook something nice for supper," I say, embarrassed to be caught ogling. "The madwoman's joining us, after all."

"Mireille. She only invited herself for a drink."

"But we can get some great fresh ingredients down the road for cheap. When have we ever had the chance to cook a French-market meal? We can celebrate your book news some more. It'll be like we're living on the Travel Channel."

Steph nods. "Sure, okay." Then she kisses me on the cheek and leans into me, and then we're hugging each other, tight and warm. I don't know when last we've held each other like this, and, God, it feels good.

Within an hour, we've managed to point our fingers and smile through the language barrier and collect a chorizo, some fat black olives, a pack of pasta, some of those amazing giant ribbed tomatoes they call oxheart, a head of garlic, a bunch of parsley that smells sandy, like it came off the farm this morning, a baguette and some Comté cheese, some fresh pears and mandarins, and, of course, four bottles of wine, all for not much more than we'd pay for the same selection at home.

We push through the street-side door into the building's courtyard, Steph chatting about the leather jacket she saw a pug dog wearing, and I want the mood to last. Passing the ragged door of the ground-floor storeroom, I willfully push away any dark residue from my mind—of ghosts, of victims, of death. This, right now, having a happy time with my wife, is more important than any gloomy fancy, and they're not going to mess it up.

Who're "they," Mark?

All of them, all of the dead.

We stump up the inky stairwell in the shallow wash of my phone's light, familiar now, and unlock and push through the heavy door. I work open the small kitchen window while Steph sets up some music—happy lounge grooves that conjure up images of hip, carefree young girls dancing on some dawn-lit beach; that's who Steph was to me when I met her, so exotic in her youth and lightness. I would never have imagined I stood a chance, that I deserved a chance, that I could walk the same dream-beach as her, that with all my scars and regrets and sadness I could inhabit the same planet as she did. But here she is, in a Parisian kitchen with me, swaying her hips as she unpacks the shopping bag.

Steph gasps. "Oh shit."

A stab of ice. "What's wrong, Steph?"

"We didn't get olive oil."

"Christ, you gave me a heart attack."

"Sorry. Should I go back down?"

"Nah. We'll just slice up some of this sausage and we can rub it on the hot pan. That'll lube it up enough."

"Ooh, good idea. I like it when you get all *MasterChef*."

I uncork a bottle of wine—an Argentinean Malbec was more affordable in the capital of France—and pour a glass for each of us. Steph takes a swig and hums along to the tune as she rinses a dinner plate and starts chopping the tomatoes. I cozy in next to her and start mincing the massive, fresh cloves of garlic.

"Listen, Steph. I want to say sorry."

She doesn't say anything, just slows her knife.

"You know, just being here these last few days has really made me see some things. About myself. I've really struggled after the burglary. I haven't known how to react, how to provide what you and Hayden need. I don't think I've been behaving like the person I was when you met me. Like the person you . . ." I trail off.

She stops and turns to face me. "Like the man I fell in love with," she says. "You can say it." "Love" and "man"—two words I've had difficulty applying to myself since the home invasion. "I do love you, Mark. And I know you've had a hard time lately."

I nod and smile, because it takes a while to find my voice. "Thank you. Well, I'm sorry. You and Carla were right that we needed this."

She flinches minutely at Carla's name and I wish I could stuff it back in my mouth. But she surprises me by flashing me a cheeky smile. "Now that we're on that subject, what is it between you and Carla? I've tried to get to the bottom of it ever since I've known you. That first time we went out together to that concert at Kirstenbosch, I honestly thought you two were going out. I was so interested in you and I felt like you were flirting with me, but Carla was always there, mirroring you so blatantly. I went home and told my roommate you were swingers."

"Swingers?" I blurt. "Jesus. If I had known that, I would never have brought her. She's always just been part of the group." Not strictly true. There was the one-night stand just after Odette left. A mistake; I was drunk and in pain and Carla was there. Afterward, we agreed to pretend it never happened, and I've left it too late to come clean with Steph. She won't understand.

"So what is it? Is she in love with you? Is she jealous of us?"

"No!" I've never been asked these exact questions so directly. I've never had to consider them. They just haven't been relevant. "No. She knows how much I love you. You rescued me. You're the second chance I never thought I'd have. I've had some . . ." I stop speaking. She knows enough about Zoë, my heaviest baggage, and Zoë doesn't belong here, tonight.

"That's good to hear. I always feel like I'm— like Hayden and I are competing with everyone else in your life, that we're never as real, never as important."

"Well, then, I'm glad that you know how I feel. I love Hayden. She gives me a reason to, you know, do everything I do. To keep trying. And you're the most important person in my life."

I kiss her on the cheek and she leans into it, a sign that everything is good, so I work my hand up the back of her shirt. Again, she presses into me and murmurs, "Hold that thought," into my ear before turning back to the tomatoes. Trying to repress my excitement—I feel like a teenage boy—I top up our wine and move on to the parsley, and Steph scrapes out tomato seeds beside me.

"I'm sorry too," she says after a while. "I wasn't happy to leave Hayden, you know that. But she's totally fine at Mom's—

having a ball, in fact—and I'm not sure she would've enjoyed it here. It's been a bit of a disaster, hasn't it?"

"Not entirely. Sure, this apartment is a shithole. But the city is as wonderful as we expected, isn't it?" Steph nods. "And I've had real insights that years of therapy couldn't buy. It's amazing how a change of scene can give you instant perspective. It's such a cliché, but it's true—a holiday is as good as a . . ." That's not right.

"Isn't the cliché that a change is as good as a holiday?"

"Yeah, well, that one's bullshit. I'd take the holiday anytime." She laughs. "I'm glad we're here."

She thinks about it, then says, "Me too."

Those three men with their knives are still shadowing my thoughts, but we're far away from that house; Hayden's far away from it. We're all safe. For the first time since the attack, those men are cocooned away so deeply that I can't smell their stink, that I can't hear their barking, unintelligible voices, that I can't hear Steph's stifled whimpering. So faraway that I'm able to bury the emasculating sense of helplessness and shame I'd felt as Steph was dragged away from me and I was forced to remain behind in the living room, too incapacitated by fear to even plead for my family's lives. For the first time since that dreadful night, I think we're going to be okay.

Close to eight, Mireille announces her presence with a sustained rattle on the door handle. She seems to have neatened up for the occasion, wearing a smart red coat over a floral-print dress that's utterly at odds with the grubby knits and shawls and shapeless trousers I've seen her in before. She's carrying an almost-full bottle of Armagnac in her right hand.

"Come in. Welcome," Steph says, ramping up the genteel hostess act. "Let me take your coat."

Mireille dumps the brandy on the coffee table, shucks her

coat off into Steph's hands, and paces around the living room. "It smells nice in here," she says. "It's long since we have good food cooking here." She wanders over to the window, where I've finally worked the shutters open with some implements from the kitchen, then peers down to the courtyard below, her face so close to the window that her breath mists the glass. "It's open now."

"Yes." Steph says, glancing at me. That "now" confirms that Mireille has been in here before. The air through the gap in the sash is cold and fresh and mingles nicely with the cooking aroma to dispel the mustiness and stagnant atmosphere from the apartment. I wonder if Mireille approves—somehow that seems to matter—but she doesn't say anything more, just flaps the heavy brown curtain, pulling it closed a little, then gathering it again.

"Can I get you something to drink?" I take the bottle of brandy from the coffee table. "Would you like some of this? With water? Ice?"

She grimaces in something I take to be a smile. "That you have later maybe."

"Some wine?" Steph asks, holding up a bottle in the kitchen doorway.

"Wine. Yes."

I didn't know what to expect from her, but if this stiff, peculiar formality carries on, it's going to be a long evening; I hope she loosens up soon. She sits at the small, square dining table and I join her. When Steph brings her glass she takes a sip and silently looks out the window at the dark outlines of the buildings and the shaded night sky beyond them. She's almost demure and totally isolated, like some lonely woman in a Hopper painting or a Bresson photo. There's none of that angry defensiveness or rudeness she's shown us so far. Some fire in her seems to have gone out.

I'm about to stand and go check on the pasta water, beg

Steph to trade places with me and try to forge some conversation, when Mireille turns back to me and talks. "I'm not always nice, I know. It's because I am afraid, and I am the only person who can look after myself, yes? It is good you are cooking family food, like there used to be here, long time ago."

Tell me about your family, I want to say. *Who lived here with you? Why does nobody live here now, and what the hell is the story behind all the stuff in the storeroom?* But somehow, now, I don't want to know. Now that we know the Petits are alive at least, we can just get through this week and go home. Everyone's being pleasant to one another—Mireille, Steph, and me—and I want to protect that fine balance.

But Steph's leaning in the kitchen doorway, dishcloth in her hand. "Where's your family from?"

"I always live in Paris."

"Did you stay here with a family? You said you had no children?"

I glance at Steph. "Nobody expects an inquisition, honey."

"Why don't you put the pasta in?" she chirps through a fake smile, tossing the cloth at me and taking my place opposite Mireille. With some relief, I duck into the kitchen and listen as they talk.

"You have only one child, yes?" Mireille asks.

"Yes, one daughter. She's two."

"I think you have two girls," Mireille says.

Steph doesn't stop to consider before she speaks. "Mark also had a—" she starts. *Jesus, Steph.* I cough loudly and she veers off. "Can I top up your wine?"

"Thank you."

There's an awkward pause, so I call out, "Your English is very good, madame."

"I studied one year in London."

"What did you study?" Steph asks.

"I start with accountancy, but soon I come back here to make art."

"How long have you been in this building?"

I glance through the doorway at Steph, clattering my spoon to catch her attention. This is starting to sound like a police interview.

But Mireille continues answering the questions obediently, part of this pensive mood she's in tonight. Perhaps her uppers have stopped working. "A long time. This is why I cannot leave so easy. My whole life is here, even though they want me to go."

"Who? Who wants you to go?"

If Steph keeps grilling Mireille, she'll clam up and we'll never find out the background to this building. I stir the pot one last time and come out and sit down and begin to blabber about our holiday. Everyone likes to hear a visitor praising their city, so I rattle on about how we're enjoying the architecture and the ancient roads and the fresh produce, but Mireille interrupts me. "I now know you. I know about your family, your little girl. Tonight I decide finally. I will leave."

"Leave where?" Steph asks. "Here you mean?"

"*Oui.*"

"Why?"

"You cannot run away from your history." She looks at me as she says this. "It was always with me. I think maybe it will go with the last people. *Mais, non.* Now I must take it with me, or it is with you."

"It? What—" I say, as Steph overrides my question with her own.

"Enough!" Mireille says. Then, softer, "Like I say, I thought *qu'il était parti*, that it had left—with the last people. They had pain, but not enough, I think. I was wrong. I am sorry for you. I am sorry for your child."

Okay, this is getting ridiculous and creepy and really spoiling the atmosphere we've managed to create in this place today. This woman's insane, that's all, and we shouldn't have expected any information from her. I stand up and tap Steph on the arm. "A little help in the kitchen, please. Excuse us, madame."

Steph pushes back from the table and trails me into the kitchen.

"Now it is with you," I mock, clattering the plates and pasta spoon to disguise my voice. "She's crazy. We're not going to get any information from her."

"She's struggling to express herself; that's all. Let's just allow her to speak. We can match what she tells us with what the real estate agent says, and then we'll know."

"Know what? Why is it important? It feels like we're digging in stuff that doesn't concern us. We should just leave it alone."

"I want to know," she says, splatting sauce over the portions of pasta.

I shake my head. I'm not going to dissuade Steph, and I don't want to fight, so I'm just going to shut up and drink wine. This dinner party was a stupid mistake. I chop the baguette into chunks and as I lay them on a board with some of the cheese, I hear the grind of the window sash going up. Steph's carrying two plates of pasta through and I hear them thump and clatter as she shouts, "Mireille! Don't!"

There's only time to turn and glance out of the kitchen window, where I see Mireille perched outside, on the window ledge, pushing off against the rusty brackets that once held a window box, saulting up and gracefully diving headfirst. The floral dress ripples luminously as she goes.

Chapter 12

Steph

I was within lunging distance of Mireille when she threw herself out of the window, but I didn't hear her body crumpling onto the cobblestoned courtyard below. Or maybe I did and I've blocked out the memory. White noise filled my ears; the plates I was carrying crashed to the floor; I was dimly aware that my legs buckled. But I didn't scream—I'm sure of that.

"Steph, Steph, what's she done?" Mark shouted. Still I couldn't move. I felt him bash against my shoulder as he ran for the window and looked down. "Oh fuck," he said. "Oh shit, oh Jesus." He turned to face me. "She's alive. She's trying to move, Steph. She's breathing."

A jolt of adrenaline as swift and vicious as an electric shock rocked through me, and I came back to myself. "Call an ambulance, Mark. Call the police." I sounded absolutely calm. I *felt* absolutely calm. I knew this wasn't rational. By rights I should have been a mess—witnessing Mireille's suicide attempt should have reignited the PTSD that festered inside me after the home invasion.

"What's the number? *Fuck* . . ."

"Google it, Mark."

"Okay . . . good. Yes."

I stepped over the pasta mess on the floor, collected a cushion and the throw from the couch, and made for the door.

"Steph—what are you doing?"

"Getting to Mireille. She needs help."

"Wait. I'll come with, just let me—"

"No time, Mark." And then I left the room.

———————

There was very little blood. She'd thrown herself out headfirst, but she must have twisted as she fell, and she lay on her side, her left arm cruelly angled beneath her, her shoulder dislocated. The left side of her face was pressed into the cobbles, but her right eye was open. Her floral dress was rucked up, revealing pasty, scarred thighs furred with dark hair.

I dropped to my haunches next to her and gently covered her with the throw. "Mireille."

She was breathing in short, whistling gasps. *"Huh, huh, huh, huh."*

"Mireille. Don't move, okay? Help is on its way."

"Uh."

Tiny white flecks haloed her head. *Tooth shards, those are tooth shards,* I thought with that same chilling calm. Her right eye flitted crazily in its socket.

I considered lifting her head to slot the cushion beneath it, but I didn't dare risk further injury. I stared up at the window. She shouldn't have been able to fit through it so easily. A shadow appeared behind the frame.

"Mark!"

"They're on their way," he called. "I'm coming down."

I turned back to Mireille and took her right hand in mine. It was freezing and limp and peppered with blue oil paint. Rain began to fall, and I gently wiped away the drops that threatened to run into her eyes.

She groaned, drawing in a rattling, broken breath. She was trying to lift her head.

"No. Don't move, Mireille. The ambulance is coming. You're going to be fine."

She was trying to speak.

I looked into her eye but could detect no sign that she knew who I was or understood what was happening to her. "Shh. Try and keep calm. They'll be here soon."

"*Je . . . Je pense . . .*"

I had to strain to hear her. "Shh."

And then she hissed, as clear as day, "*Je suis désolée.*" An apology, but it somehow sounded like a threat.

I dropped her hand and skittered away from her on my haunches. Something sharp dug into my palm—a fleck of broken tooth. I scrambled to my feet, rubbing my hands on my jeans to dislodge it. Seconds later I heard the slap of running feet, and then voices and light filled the courtyard. Mark took me to one side as a trio of overalled paramedics fussed around Mireille.

The calm clarity receded then. It had done its job. I started to shake. My memories of the next couple of hours are fragmented, but this I know for sure: Mark and I were there when a young paramedic with a tattoo of a star on his wrist pronounced her dead. It was 8:45 exactly.

While Mark took a pair of grim-faced gendarmes up to the apartment, I waited next to the mailboxes, my back turned to the courtyard. When he returned, a polite but serious policewoman asked us to collect our identity documents and then drove us to the nearest police station. After handing over our passports and numbly giving our statements separately to uniformed officers, we were ushered into an anonymous room that smelled of coffee and paint. The French cops I'd seen wandering around the city had intimidated me with their automatic weapons and steely demeanors, but without exception everyone we encountered that night was sympathetic and spoke good English.

Mark held tightly to my hand throughout. It was his turn

to take over. I don't know how long we were left in that room, but it felt like hours. We barely spoke. Every so often, when he sensed I needed reassurance, he squeezed my fingers.

Finally, a slender woman with tiny hands and pronounced crow's-feet clomped her way into the room and gave us a tired smile. "I am very sorry for keeping you waiting. I am Capitaine Claire Miske. You must be very tired. We have informed the consulate of your country of the events tonight, which is necessary when a foreign national is involved in a suspicious death."

"It wasn't suspicious," I blurted. "We told you, she jumped."

The policewoman nodded. Her eyes were bloodshot and her nails were bitten to the quick. "I know this. But it is still, ah, known as suspicious. That is the terminology."

"Sorry."

"It is no problem. I know that you have had a shock. It is bad for your holiday, *non*?"

Mark shot me a glance. The understatement of the year.

"Is the South African embassy going to send someone to assist us?" he asked.

"*Ce n'est pas nécessaire, monsieur.* We have assured them that we will not detain you for much longer. It is likely in this circumstance that the *procureur* will ask for a full investigation, but we are satisfy that—"

A uniformed officer stuck his head through the door, glanced at us, and then said something in French to the policewoman.

"Ah," she said to us. "Excuse me. I will not be long. I can bring you some *café*? Water?"

"Thank you," Mark said.

A fresh ribbon of anxiety coiled through my gut. "What if there's an inquest and they want us to stay here in Paris, Mark? . . . Christ, what if they think we had something to do with her death?"

"They don't. It won't come to that."

"How do you know?"

"That captain seemed nice, didn't she? And if we were in any trouble, someone from the embassy would have turned up, I'm sure of it."

"Yeah?"

"Really, Steph."

"Did you tell them what Mireille said to us before she jumped? All that crazy stuff she was babbling about?"

"I told them she was talking nonsense," he said, cutting me off. "I said we had no warning that she was about to do what she did. I said we hardly knew her at all."

"Do you think she might have overheard us—"

"I told the police everything they needed to know, Steph." His voice turned cold. "She was out of her mind. You mustn't dwell on anything she said. We didn't know her at all. And she didn't know us. It's the truth. Why complicate it?"

A pretty, dark-haired woman appeared then and handed us each a plastic cup of surprisingly good black coffee.

When she left, Mark sighed and took my hand again. "I'm sorry if I sounded harsh. It'll be fine, Steph. We've been through worse."

I let my head droop onto Mark's shoulder. I dozed, but I didn't dream.

The captain with the crinkly eyes finally returned, apologizing again for keeping us waiting. I was relieved to see our passports were in the file she placed on the table in front of her. "*D'accord.* I think I should tell you that the woman who you know as Mireille is known to us. She has a history."

Mark disengaged his hand from mine. I hadn't realized how sweaty it had become. "What do you mean 'the woman who you know as Mireille'? Is Mireille not her real name?"

"*Oui,* my apologies. It is just, ah, my turn of phrase. This woman has been in many institutions. We are trying to contact her family, but we have spoken to her doctor, and he say she was often talking of ending her life and has tried this before. It seems this time she succeeded."

"Shame," I breathed, although to be honest, I was too drained to feel pity for Mireille right then. Mark took my hand again.

The policewoman picked through the file. "I have read, of course, your statements. You say that it was she who invited herself to come to dinner at the place where you stay?"

"Yes."

"And you saw no sign before that she was, ah, intent on hurting herself?"

"No," Mark said. "Like I said, we hardly knew her. I'd run into her on the stairs a couple of times, and I'd only really thought she was eccentric. Harmless."

She nodded. "*D'accord.* Yet it seems this was her plan. To die in front of you. To jump from the window."

I felt Mark tense next to me. He was the one who'd opened that window. He was the one who'd obsessively hacked at the shutters. If he hadn't opened it, would she still be alive, or would she have found another way to do it?

I found my voice. "Why us? We were strangers."

"Who can say? This woman. She was . . . ah, how you say . . . damaged. She was sick. We are still investigating, but we think that she was living in the building illegally. She was not renting her studio."

"She was squatting?"

"*Oui.*"

"Will we have to return for an inquest?"

"If the *procureur* want a full investigation, it can take many months to complete. We will be in contact with the embassy in your country and inform you if it is *nécessaire*. We have all your details. For now, we are satisfy that you have no part in this situation."

"We can go?"

"*Oui.* We are trying to contact the owners of your apartment to inform them of what has occurred."

"Good luck with that," Mark murmured.

"*Pardon?*"

"They're not the most communicative of people." Mark briefly filled her in about our dealings with the Petits: their no-show at our house; the cryptic email they'd eventually sent us.

"Ah. I see. But for now, my boss, he say it is fine for you to return there."

I started. "Wait—*what*? Isn't it a crime scene?"

"We have what we need from there. Of course, if you prefer to stay at an *hôtel,* that is your choice."

"We . . . that's not an option," Mark said.

"Do you need help to return to your apartment?"

"*Non, merci.*"

She handed us our passports and accompanied us to the door. With a brisk handshake, she strode away.

"I can't go back there, Mark," I said the second she was out of earshot.

"I know. Of course not."

"We can't stay there," I said again. "I *won't* stay there. I want to go home, Mark. I want to go home *today.*"

He put his arm around me and kissed my hair. "I know. Come on. Let's get out of here and we'll make a plan."

It was sunny when we stepped outside. We'd been at the station for more than ten hours, but I'd assumed it would still be dark and rainy when we left, as if time had stopped for us. My body was beginning to ache as if I had the flu, ravaged by lack of sleep and the aftereffects of the anxiety and adrenaline. And I was cold. Freezing. Carla's coat was draped over the couch back in the apartment. I hadn't thought to collect it before we were ferried to the police station. I tugged my cardigan around my body, feeling naked compared to the tourists and commuters swathed in their wool and fleece, and let Mark steer me toward a Métro station. I clung to him, not caring what anyone thought, as he shepherded us onto a train, through a bewildering warren of Métro tunnels, and then out onto the familiar boulevard and along to our Starbucks. Again I was grateful for its bland warmth.

Mark bought us cappuccinos and a couple of croissants (which neither of us touched), and we discussed our options. First prize was changing our tickets. I sipped at my coffee, barely tasting it, as Mark dialed the Air France helpline and was passed from consultant to consultant.

He hung up and sighed. "Unless we buy a new ticket, which is out of the question, the best they can do is put us on standby tomorrow night."

"I don't want to leave tomorrow. I want to leave now."

"I know." He sighed again. "I tried my best, Steph."

"Sorry. I know you did. Okay. Clearly we don't have enough cash for a hotel. Shouldn't we go to the South African embassy, tell them we're in trouble and need help?"

Mark gave me a half smile. "We've got somewhere to stay, Steph. Our embassy of all embassies is unlikely to shell out for a hotel room. Do you think your parents could wire us some money or book us a room for the duration?"

A lurch—I hadn't thought about Hayden for hours. "I don't want to worry them. And besides, they bought our air tickets; they must be strapped."

Mark nodded in agreement. "Okay. I'm going to ask Carla. She can book us something online. We can pay her back when we get home."

Great, Carla to the rescue. She'd love that. But he was right. There was no one else.

While he called Carla, I headed into the ladies'. I was reluctant to glance in the mirror, but in fact I didn't look too bad. My mascara was still intact, and the skin around my eyes was only slightly puffy. I didn't look like I'd had a terrible shock at all.

Mark was smiling when I returned to the table. "She's booking us a place in Pigalle. I caught her just in time. She was about to leave for the countryside—she's headlining a poetry festival there." As usual, talking to Carla had pepped him up like nothing else seemed to do.

"Did you tell her what happened?"

"Yes. She sends her love."

"Great." I smiled tightly.

"We should get our stuff from the apartment. Do you want to stay here while I go?"

I loved him for that. He was as exhausted as I was. "No." I reached inside myself, searching for the calm, controlled Stephanie who had appeared last night. I couldn't let him do it alone. "Let's get it over with."

I tried not to look too closely at the spot where she'd died, but my gaze went there of its own accord. Thankfully, the rain in the night had washed away the blood.

I didn't look up at the window, and neither did Mark.

I kept as close to him as I could get as we thumped up the stairs. The air was too still, as if the building was holding its breath. "Talk to me, Mark."

"What about?"

"Anything. It's too quiet."

"Okay. Do you think the police have managed to contact the Petits yet?"

"I doubt it. They seemed efficient but I don't think they have superpowers."

Mark chuckled, and the tense atmosphere eased.

"You ready?" Mark asked when we reached the third-floor landing.

I nodded but hung back while Mark fiddled with the keys. The sharp odor of spoiled tomato sauce greeted us as we walked in. I was reluctant to breathe in too deeply, as if the air was poisonous. *Je suis désolée,* Mireille's voice ghosted into my head. What was she sorry for? That she'd killed herself in front of us? Or was there something else?

Stop it, I told myself, *don't go there.*

Someone—presumably one of the cops—had stood in the spilled pasta and sauce, and I could make out the tread of his boot in forensic clarity. The window was still wide-open. The rain in the night had slanted in, spattering the wooden floors. I caught Mark glancing at it, but I couldn't read his expression. I knew we'd have to talk about the window at some stage. *It wasn't your fault,* I wanted to say, but I didn't.

"Can you pack?" he asked. "I need to check to see if Carla has forwarded the booking."

I ran into the bathroom to gather up my makeup and shampoo, then threw our clothes in the suitcases, mixing dirty and clean, not bothering to fold Mark's shirts. I couldn't smother the sensation that if we didn't leave the apartment *right that second,* then we'd never get out of there. I slammed the lids closed and dragged the cases into the living room.

"Got it!" Mark grinned. "She's forwarded the reservation."

"Is it far?"

"No. I've downloaded the directions. You ready?"

"Yeah."

"Come on." He took his wheelie bag from me and made for the door.

We were halfway down the stairs when I realized I'd left Carla's coat behind. "Fuck."

"What?"

"Carla's coat. I left it on the couch."

"You take my suitcase; I'll get it for you."

"No. I'll go."

I needed to go. Before we left for good I needed to assure myself that there was nothing to fear in the apartment. A crazy woman had selfishly decided to kill herself in front of us. That was all. I was strong. I didn't need Mark to baby me.

But still, I held my breath as I unlocked the door and grabbed the coat, not daring to look at the window. Because I knew in my heart that if I looked over at it I'd see her standing there, opening and closing her blood-filled mouth, cracking her broken teeth together, and telling me she was sorry in a tone that sounded like a threat. Terror snaked up through my legs and into my gut and I ran, slamming the door behind me. The fear ebbed only when I caught sight of the sunlight filtering into the hallway below.

"Everything okay?" Mark asked when I joined him in the courtyard.

I couldn't find my voice. I nodded and took my time buttoning up the coat. Stupid. I was just letting my imagination play tricks on me—I'd barely slept; my mind was ragged from shock and exhaustion. That was all it was. I palmed a couple of Urbanols and popped them into my mouth. The woolliness kicked in just as we arrived outside the hotel—a tiny boutiquey place with a grubby burgundy awning over its door. The reception area was clad in fake marble; the desk's veneer was bubbled and cracked.

"Looks okay," Mark said.

I managed a smile.

The concierge, a middle-aged Arabic man, greeted us warmly and Mark explained that we had a booking.

"*D'accord.* You cannot to check in until two, but you can leave your luggage here."

We shared a glance. Three and a half hours to kill. We could do that. We'd been through far worse. "That's fine." Mark gave his name and the concierge turned to the computer. "*Non.* I am sorry. There is nothing in that name."

Mark explained that a friend of ours had booked the room for us and asked him to see if it was under Carla's name.

"*Non.* I am sorry."

"This is the Hôtel Trois Oiseaux, right?"

"*Oui.*"

I could tell that Mark was fighting to keep his composure. The pills I'd taken were gently dampening my own anxiety.

"Hang on." Mark took out his phone and scrolled through to Carla's email containing the forwarded confirmation. He handed it to the concierge. "Look."

The man sighed and shot me a sympathetic glance. "Ah. Now I see what has happened. You see, your friend, she has made the booking for March. It is February now. A mistake, I think."

"Can you change it?"

The man shrugged apologetically. "*Mais, non.* It was booked through a discount site. Your friend, she must change it."

"Is there nothing you can do from your side?"

"I am very sorry, *monsieur, mais, non.* What can happen is that you can pay now and book a room if you have a credit card. We have a vacancy."

Mark slapped the counter in frustration, but the concierge didn't lose his sympathetic demeanor. "Not possible. Can I use your wi-fi?"

"Of course."

I sat on a chair next to a dusty plastic hibiscus, the Starbucks coffee churning in my gut, while Mark tried to get hold of Carla.

"No answer. She must have left for the festival already."

"Keep trying."

"I've left three voice mails, Steph. *Fuck.*" He scrabbled a hand through his hair. He badly needed a shave.

"So, what now?" I asked. But I knew what the answer was.

Chapter 13

Mark

We're huddled together in the Tuileries, on a wet bench so cold that the patina of dew is turning to frost on the metal as we watch. It's late, as dark as central Paris can ever be; there are lights everywhere—shining from the ornate lampposts and the headlights of the luxury black sedans growling along rue de Rivoli; there is a rich, warm glow coming from the stately buildings lining the gravel park; the fountains are lit up, the glass pyramids too; and then there is the constant bursts of tourists' camera flashes and phone glows.

It would be beautiful, it would be romantic, but I'm freezing and tired and my feet are aching, the splinter wound in my sole throbbing more than ever, and Steph is crying into my collar, not because she's taking comfort from me, but because she's so bloody cold and tired too. The icy drizzle has become heavier and is starting to turn into sleet blown about by a rising wind off the river.

"We have to go back," I tell her. "We can't stay here anymore."

"I know," she mutters into my jacket with numb lips.

I push myself up, my muscles and bones protesting. When I promised the man at the Hôtel Trois Oiseaux that we'd sort out the booking and come back, he let us store our luggage in their lobby and we set out. As we walked, I figured we're in Paris, there's enough to see and do all night—perhaps we'd make it until tomorrow, have a final, redemptive evening in the City of Love. I didn't share this thought with Steph because she was still stressing about Mireille's death and I knew she'd think it insensitive if I hoped that we could still enjoy ourselves. It wasn't that I didn't care about Mireille, but to my shame I was angry with her too. Things had just started to be good between Steph and me—the trip was working the way it was meant to: it was bringing us closer for the first time since the attack; it was making us smile. And then . . . that.

Petulantly, I resisted wasting any more time thinking about Mireille, but I couldn't convince Steph to forget about her. I hoped that our final walk through the city might gradually make her feel better. Perhaps we'd walk all night and be transformed by the experience like those young lovers in *Before Sunrise.*

That was thirteen hours ago, and now I'm broken. We've tramped around in the freezing rain, with no sense of where we were going. We first stumbled back to the Pompidou Centre, where we sheltered in their vast, warm lobby and even managed to hook up to their free wi-fi. I tried Carla again to satisfy Steph, but as expected there was still no answer—when she's out of town, she never even switches her phone on. We wandered through the obscenely wealthy Place Vendôme, all the luxury brands arrayed in shops scaled to massive height to make normal people who are not driving double-size Rollses and Bentleys feel utterly insignificant. Steph and I felt like hobos under the gaze of the Armani-suited doormen. From there we wandered over the river and along the boulevard Saint-Germain and then down to the Luxembourg Garden; it would have all been dreamlike on another day, but we were just shambling along, getting more and more exhausted and hungry. I began to feel genuine sympathy for refugees on a death march. I even made the mistake of saying so to Steph, thinking she'd understand what I meant and how I meant it, that I wasn't being flippant, but she immediately stepped away from me and grunted, "Jesus, Mark. Nice and sensitive as always." It took several more long blocks and a dip in the temperature to get her back to my side. When my bladder started to ache—inexplicably, since we'd had nothing but a mouthful of water from a public fountain to drink since the morning—I followed the signs to the Louvre, knowing we'd find a bathroom in the lobby. And here we are now in this monumental park, and we've been sitting on this bench, freezing solid, for the last half hour.

We'd walk all night and be transformed by the experience. Yeah, right. The lovers in *Before Sunrise* were *both* young and their all-nighter was in summer. In the end, Steph and I couldn't outrun the Petits' apartment.

"*Before Sunrise* was in Vienna," Steph states.

I stare at her. I didn't even realize I was talking aloud. And why would she say something contrarian like that? "Uh, I'm quite sure it was Paris. It even starts with a reading at Shakespeare and Company. I've watched those films several times, so . . ." But as I'm talking, I realize she's right.

"Paris is the second one, when they're tireder and sadder and older."

"Shit, you're right. Sorry." I was so sure I was right, until I realized I was wrong: my life in a fucking nutshell.

Steph uses my arm to pull herself up and I brace myself and feel useful. "That's what went wrong, then. We should have gone to Vienna." I hold my coat open and she snuggles into it and we stagger a few paces that way until we realize it's not really working. My coat's not big enough for both of us and our bumping thighs make it awkward to walk. We disengage, but I'm glad when she hooks her arm around mine and pulls me close to her. Probably just for warmth, I remind myself, but perhaps not.

Though it's late, the concourse is still busy with tourists and pedestrians, and I eye the steam rising off the carts selling pancakes and hot chocolate.

"I'm starving," I say. "Let's get some of those."

"How much money have we got?"

I know we don't have enough to eat properly until tomorrow and still buy our train tickets to the airport. "We're still doing fine," I lie, stubbornly ignoring the facts and leaving tomorrow's problems for tomorrow. If I can enjoy a Nutella pancake and a cup of hot chocolate with my warm wife in Paris right now, it will go a long way toward erasing the awfulness of this week.

So when the snack is twice as expensive as the same thing up in the ninth arrondissement, I have to swallow down a burst of panic and guilt and hand over the money because we're already committed and the man's already spread batter on his griddle and I don't have the French to say, *Oh, actually, cancel that,* or *Make it just one instead.* There are people behind us in the queue.

The crêpe and hot chocolate are delicious and all regret vanishes—right now I'd sell my house for this, and for the look on Steph's face. She's smiling for the first time today. I take the risk of touching her cheek and wiping off a smear of Nutella. I'm wondering what to do with my chocolatey fingertip, thinking I should lick it off, but Steph surprises me by nudging forward and taking my finger in her mouth, and next thing we're holding each other tight and kissing. I concentrate on enjoying the moment, but I also can't help looking at us from a distance—we're lovers in Paris, indistinguishable from every other flawed and fractious couple here who are all suffering their trials and have managed to put them aside for one moment because they love each other. This is what I wanted this week to bring us. It makes me feel like the weight of my life is lifted, like I'm saved.

"I'm so sorry," Steph's saying into my cheek. "I've been all over the place today. It's just . . . it's been . . ."

"I know. And there's nothing to be sorry for. I'm sorry too." She curls her mouth in that pragmatic way, and I know I'd better not say too much more, not cram her ears with my romantic nonsense. I do want to mark the moment somehow, though. "We're halfway there, Steph. We'll be okay."

"Mm," she says. She pauses. "I'm cold."

"Let's go back. It'll be fine. I'm not sure that apartment has anything else to throw at us."

We find the nearest Métro station—my body won't take walking to the apartment, despite the few euros we'd save— and within fifteen minutes, we're climbing up the steps at Pigalle. After a few false turns, we find the Trois Oiseaux hotel, hoping to get our luggage back, but the front door is locked and the lobby is dim, lit only by a single desk lamp. There's nobody behind the counter.

When I ring the bell outside, I can't hear any responding sound inside. I knock and peer in.

"It's obviously closed," Steph says.

"There's no sign or anything. They should list their times somewhere."

Steph just tuts and turns and starts walking. I hustle up after her, my joints crying out at the effort. "Let's just get inside," she says. Then she mumbles something like, "You can't always bend the world to your will," but I'm not sure.

"What's that?"

She doesn't repeat herself but just stalks away, me limping to keep up, until she's led us to the street door of the building. My heart sinks the moment we step over the threshold into that dank courtyard, my phone's soupy glow so different from the bright cheer down at the Tuileries. I deliberately avoid shining it over the cobbles, and we trudge up those worn stairs we thought we'd never have to see again. There's a difference about the building; we can feel Mireille's absence in the silence—we can almost imagine the lack of cigarette smoke and brandy and paint fumes, but that can only be fancy.

Steph turns on the lights the instant I push the front door open, and we're hit by the smell of last night's cooking. There's a tinge of rot to it, but it's not too bad. At least it smells of something, of life recently lived, rather than the musty void that shrouds the rest of the building.

Without a word Steph shucks off her boots and goes to the bathroom, leaving me to wrestle my way out of my wet jeans and sweater with numb fingers and get into bed. It does feel good—I haven't been in bed for nearly two days and my body melts in relief.

My eyes are sliding closed when Steph hurries in, rubbing herself vigorously with a towel. "There's no fucking hot water," she says.

Another version of me, on a good day, might offer to warm her up some other way, but I can't bring myself to suggest that right now and know she won't appreciate it, so I try to make myself useful by getting out of bed and looking at the electrical board at the front door. I don't know what I'm looking for, but Steph comes up behind me, wrapped in a blanket. "All the switches are up," she said. "I checked. Let's just try to sleep. I'm so tired." So we get into bed and press against each other and again I have the sense that we're just borrowing each other's animal warmth, just clinging on to get through the night.

Soon Steph's snoring in jagged bursts, her breathing shallow and choppy, and I try to go to sleep too, knowing that if we can just fast-forward to the morning we'll be out of here forever. But despite my exhaustion, or maybe because of it, I can't settle, repetitive thoughts tracking graven spirals in my mind. I flash through the jumble of images from the police station, the interminable hours of institutional walls and soft voices and strong coffee, of the vast loop of streets we've walked and the cold and tiredness and hunger. You'd think that would be enough for my bones and muscles to take solace in the relative comfort of this warm and lumpy bed and relax, but instead they tense as I recall Mireille casting herself off from the windowsill. That image is flushed by a memory of the girl in the museum, her firm, tall body and her fragrant hair. *It was Zoë, you fool,* someone is saying, and it's a leering wax-faced actor, smiling endlessly. I must be asleep because now I'm in the building's low storage cellar, picking through a pile of discarded clothes, now scrabbling through them desperately, throwing them out behind me, onto a bloodstained mattress, each item making someone behind me cry out in pain. Now I turn and try to remove the sheet from over the crying, bleeding girl, desperately ripping at the shroud that won't come away, no matter how hard I tug, clawing at the sheet because it's Zoë, the Zoë I know, seven-year-old Zoë, and she's buried under that pile of dusty cloth, buried at the bottom, her crying muffled and desperate, struggling to breathe. *Hack, hack, gasp.*

I startle awake and Steph rolls over onto her side and keeps sleeping. I breathe deeply to try to calm my heart, to take in the air that Zoë needs, skin clammy and cold, flushed with adrenaline. As the images recede, one part of the dream remains: the sound of sobbing, a hitching moan interspersed with jags of high-pitched keening. It's exactly how Zoë would cry when she was at her most exhausted, her most miserable. It's not just the cat this time, I know it for sure; there are even words mixed into the sobbing, an unintelligible mumbling—this is no sound a cat could make.

I look over to Steph's back, just to make sure, even though the crying sound is coming from farther away than this bed. The rhythm of her breath inflates and deflates the curve of her side in a slow, regular rhythm. It's not her.

Mireille is dead. There is nobody else here.

I close my eyes and try to sleep. I'm so bloody tired. I shove a pillow over my head, but the crying seems to follow me under the shield. I hear a word emerge out of the disconsolate mumbling: *Daddy.*

When Zoë was small, Odette would normally go to her in the night, but sometimes she'd be fast asleep and I'd rouse myself and sometimes I'd manage to comfort her. I'd feel like a hero. Sometimes, when Zoë woke and needed someone to chase away her monsters, she'd call out to me, not Odette. She'd call out to me: *Daddy.*

It's not Zoë, you idiot. Zoë's dead. You killed her.

Daddy.

I need some air. I stumble out of the bedroom, across to the window, and try to raise it, but it's jammed shut again. I'm this close to smashing the pane when I think better of it and slip on my shoes and coat instead, grab the keys, and go downstairs. Without bothering to use my phone for light, I speed down the pitch-dark stairs, trying to flee my panic, but it's inside me. Before I know it, I'm in the courtyard standing exactly where Mireille landed, craning up to the patch of sulfuric orange where the sky should be and sucking in lungfuls of air, as if they will clean me out.

It works to some extent, because at least I'm not hearing Zoë's crying anymore. I gradually become aware of myself. I'm standing in my underwear, sockless shoes, and a coat; my legs are numb with cold, and the narrow cobbled courtyard is familiar, but something's different. Then I notice it: the dim patch of light pushing through the grimy window in the courtyard.

Someone's living in there, in the storeroom. It explains the sounds—the talking, the crying. I should just leave it at that, be satisfied that I have someone or something to blame for the night's disturbances; that will make me sleep easier, won't it?

I shouldn't approach the window, go anywhere near that flaking door that looks so much like the final barricade of a slaughterhouse. I should just go back up and keep Steph company through the rest of this shattered night. But fragments of my last dream still hook in my mind: Zoë suffocating, scrabbling for my help under that smothering shroud.

My feet carry me to the window and I peer through; the decision has nothing to do with my mind. The storeroom is lit by the dim orange glow of an ancient light bulb that's absorbed into the dust-dulled surfaces of the covered furniture.

But there's nobody in there; no movement, nobody gasping their final breath.

I'm just exhausted, I tell myself as I stop and fill my lungs with air. The hush of the misty rain filtering down over the cobbles intensifies the padded silence in this courtyard, walled away from the constant city, with the sleeping windows of neighboring buildings looming over me, and the freshness revives me. I should just go back to bed; it will all be easier in the morning. I turn back toward the building, short of breath, my heart still hammering erratically, and as I do, I'm startled by a clang and a clatter at the far end of the courtyard, as a light flicks on over the entrance to the stairwell.

It strikes me that the light has never worked before, and I wonder if it's Steph, coming out to find me—it can't be anybody else—but a small shadow lurches across the wall in front of me, followed by another one. Then a preternatural wailing, but one I recognize this time—that fucking cat. It's going to give me a bloody heart attack.

I go toward the culvert where I saw it last time and crouch down to peer inside, but I can't see anything there. I spend more time than I should there, shoving my arm into the pipe and trying to extract the cat. There's a rotten smell of fish and sewage in the drain, and I try to push away thoughts of Mireille's congealing blood still lingering there as I draw my arm out, my coat sleeve rucked up to my biceps and my forearm covered with gunk.

I'm pushing myself up again when I hear the light-shod tread of someone behind me. I'm not quite sure how I'm going to explain myself, crouching half-dressed over the mouth of a drainpipe. I turn slowly.

Zoë, seven years old, smiles at me, her hands behind her back. She's wearing only jeans and a T-shirt, and her long hair is soaked and darkened by the rain.

"What are you doing out here, Zo?" I say, my mind bypassing all that is real. "You must be freezing. Come." I stand up and take off my coat and offer it to her, but I drop it when she shows me what's in her hands.

"I have something for you."

The cat is hissing and growling in her grasp. Zoë has pinned its legs remarkably efficiently in her strong hands, so that it can't lash out and scratch her. It's writhing its head around trying to nip her, a low yowl stretching from inside it.

"Put it down, Zo. Let it go."

"But why, Daddy? I know you hate it. It's been keeping you awake."

I step toward her, pleading, ignoring my shivering, my heart trying to beat itself out of my bare chest. "Sweetie, I never taught you to hurt animals. I always told you that was very bad."

She ignores me. "I hate it too. It makes me choke," she says as she shifts her grip and moves the cat's head to her right hand.

"No! Don't!"

It's too late. The cat screams as Zoë squeezes and twists. I hear the crackle of its neck as it's suddenly silent, and Zoë starts pulling handfuls of fur out of it. I hurry over and grab the animal's body from her hands as its blood sluices from its mouth onto me.

"What have you done?"

It's Steph's voice. I look up at her. "It wasn't me. It was her." I point toward where Zoë's standing, but she's gone.

"Put it down, Mark. Drop it. We're getting the fuck out of here."

I manage to stand, dazed. I look at my arms, covered with sludge and blood, then down at my stomach, my legs. "But I have to clean up. Get dressed."

"You stay here. I'll bring you a towel and our stuff. Don't you dare think of going back into that building. We are leaving this fucking place. Right now."

The tiredness and the cold must get to me then, because I'm hardly aware as Steph has returned and is rubbing me with the Petits' thin towels and is helping me into my jeans, which are still damp, and forcing me into my coat. She leaves the towels in the courtyard, on top of the cat's body, as she steers me out onto the sidewalk and closes the door behind me. I'm stumbling through the gray canyon streets, Steph huffing behind me.

I lean against a wall for a moment and open my eyes to see Steph inside a building's lobby, shouting at a man behind a desk. I know I should be doing more to help, I should be getting involved, but it's so cold. I grip my collar, and then Steph's shunting me along up a hill again.

"Hold this, Mark," Steph's saying, strapping the daypack onto my back, wrestling our two wheeled suitcases behind her. I shake my head and squeeze my eyes, trying to clear the cobwebs and help her, but I'm so tired. "Can you believe that arsehole? Said he wouldn't give us back our bags because *Serge* wasn't supposed to offer to keep them in the first place. 'What wiss all the tewwowism at the moment, madame, we should all feel lucky.' I'm so over this place."

Somehow, Steph's wrestled me and our luggage down into the Pigalle Métro station, then off again and through a change at a narrow little overground station. Although it's still dark, it's busy around us, working people starting their day. The time on the train's clock reads 5:52. The walk and then the moment to sit on the train helps to revive me enough to say, "It wasn't me, Steph."

She just shakes her head.

"Where are we going?"

"To Gare du Nord to get a train to the airport."

"But the standby flight's only at eleven tonight."

She turns to me and glares. "Does it look to you like I want to spend another minute in this city? What are you suggesting? A spot of sightseeing, maybe go up the Eiffel Tower, a three-star lunch, and then find *another fucking piece of roadkill*?"

The people in the carriage stare at us. "Shh!" I hiss. "I told you: it wasn't me. It was—"

"Shut up, Mark. Don't say another word to me." She jams her arms across her chest and looks away.

When the train stops at the Gare du Nord, at least I'm together enough to keep the daypack on and wheel my own bag. With a bitter charge of wordlessness between us, we navigate our way from the Métro station through the confusing levels of the terminal to the correct ticket machines. I stop and look around me before I take out my wallet; it's early on a Friday morning and the station is bustling with people and many of them look threatening, their hoodies and trainers dressing them as archetypal first-world criminals. I feel a little ashamed of myself, but with our colorful luggage and hesitant steps, we stand out for miles as tourists ripe for the scamming.

But it's all moot since when I take out my wallet, all I find are two euros and thirty-five cents and my impotent credit card. Steph finds another euro and forty in her pocket. We need twenty euros for the train tickets.

"Look," Steph says, pointing at the rank of turnstiles fronting the entrance to the airport-bound line. "Everyone's going through the baby carriage gate. They don't have tickets. We can just tail someone through to the other side. Everyone does it."

"No way, Steph. It's illegal to travel without a ticket. I don't care if everyone does it."

"What? What's the alternative?"

I don't say anything to her; I can't bring myself to open my mouth, but I just venture out onto the concourse with my hands like a bowl, the universal sign of need. It's shameful, but if this situation forces me to become a criminal, I'm no worse than them.

Steph doesn't try to stop me; she merely mutters, "You've got to be fucking kidding me," then shunts our bags to a railing and sits on one, slumping her chin in her hand. Right now I'd like to disappear into the earth; I wouldn't be disappointed if one of these passing gangsters or hustlers beat me to a pulp, took all I have, and just ground me into the dust.

It's a mortifying forty minutes. I don't know whose embarrassment burns me worse—my own, or Steph's as she sits by the railing, wishing she were anywhere in the world but here and associated with anyone in the world but me. As I make my absurd, meaningless, principled stand, overgrown kids laugh at me, tourists skitter away from me, and harried workers tell me to fuck myself, before a tall, dark man with a white kepi approaches me with a smile. Behind him, his wife, his son, and his daughter watch patiently. The wife wears a colorful hijab and the daughter is in a long purple one. The son wears a neat suit, a small version of his father, who speaks to me in English. "What do we ask Allah for today, my brother?"

I speak frankly. "My wife and I need sixteen euros twenty-five for train tickets to the airport."

The man produces a wallet and takes out two fives and a ten and offers them to me. I can see he has little else in there and I think I should refuse, but that suddenly seems the least honorable thing I could do today.

"Thank you," I say. "*Merci.* Let me take your address and pay you back."

"*Non,*" he says. "Think of Suleiman and his family in your prayers, *d'accord*?"

"Thank you," I say again as I watch the family move off, feeling like a fraud. I'm never going to pray for that man. I don't believe; I don't pray. I have absolutely nothing to offer him.

"You happy now?" Steph says as I join her. "Taking money from a man who probably has less than us."

"Yes, I am actually," I say.

"Nice, Mark. Very fucking nice." She stares at me for five full seconds, and I can see the spite boiling in her eyes, and she can't contain it. "I'm glad you can stand up for yourself and your own sainted morality. But you can't fucking stand up for your wife and child when they're being dragged into a bedroom by a gang of armed men." She whirls away before she can even register the hurt in my face.

Chapter 14

Steph

I started to relax only when the plane began taxiing along the rain-swept runway. Until then, I fully expected the flight attendant to tap me on the shoulder, smile apologetically, and say, "I'm sorry, ma'am, but there's been a mistake. You and your fucked-up, twitchy husband have to get the hell off the plane." Then we'd be stuck in that airport for another full day with no money, an unbearable thought after ten hours spent perching on a slippery plastic chair, sipping nasty coffee.

When we reached Charles de Gaulle, I positioned us within sight of the Air France check-in desks, a few yards from an exit. We were hit with a waft of smoke-tinged icy air every time the exit doors slid open, but I didn't care. Our flight wouldn't be open for hours, but I was so desperate to get on the plane, I couldn't relax unless I had the desks in sight.

Mark fell asleep an hour into the ordeal, head lolled back, mouth open, as motionless as a cadaver. Too anxious to doze, I managed to finish the Kate Atkinson novel that had sat at the bottom of my bag all week without retaining a word and tried not to hate the holidaymakers and businesspeople blithely queuing for the check-in machines. I used up the thirty minutes of free wi-fi doing little else but framing an email to my mom, saying that all was well and that I'd be in touch the following day. I didn't want to jinx anything by letting my folks know we'd changed our flights until I knew for sure that we'd be able to get on the plane. After that I paced, picked at a stale croissant, lugged my case back and forth to the toilets to splash water on my face and change my clothes. (Despite the chilly air blasting through the doors, as the hours dragged on I sweated through two T-shirts.) I was up and hovering by the standby desk the second it opened. We weren't the only ones hoping to squash onto the plane, but the check-in woman was kind and pretended to believe my family emergency excuse. Perhaps it was Mark who really swung it for us. I'd washed his coat in the ladies', trying not to gag as dried animal blood and a matted clump of cat hair clotted the sink, but his eyes were bloodshot and haunted. He genuinely looked like he was in mourning.

My anxiety receded further as the plane leveled out. As the woman in the window seat was determinedly reading her book, my neighbor—a thirtyish German with blond eyebrows—focused on me. He wanted to talk, and I needed distracting. He offered a hand, and I shook it limply, aware that my palm was wet. Only then did I notice that my fingernails were arced with filth. I buried them in my palms.

"You are from South Africa?" he asked.

"Yes. Cape Town."

"Ah. I am going to Johannesburg. It is my first time there."

He'd seen us in the standby queue and offered to swap seats with Mark—as the last to board, we were unable to sit together—but I told him not to worry. Now that we were safely away from Paris, I didn't trust myself with Mark. I didn't trust myself not to cause a scene, not to demand, *Just what the fuck is wrong with you?* He'd scared me, and the fear was now turning to anger. Fortunately the blond was too wrapped up in himself to question why I didn't want to sit next to my husband. He was en route to meet a South African girl he'd met online and was bubbling with loved-up happiness. *It won't last,* I wanted to say. *One day you could wake up and find her cradling a dead fucking cat.*

I mechanically ate the chicken and broccoli in-flight slop. I downed the mini-bottle of cabernet too quickly, and it turned to acid in my gullet. The lights dimmed, and my neighbor finally got tired of holding a one-sided conversation and fixed his attention to the screen in front of him, laughing unself-consciously at *22 Jump Street*. I used the corner of the in-flight magazine to dig the dirt out of my nails. It was glutinous and left a bloody smear on a duty-free advert. I knew what it was, and I tried not to think about it.

We should never have returned to that building. We were rain soaked and on edge, we didn't have a cent, and our clothes were trapped inside Carla's bloody hotel. Neither of us was cut out to sleep rough or hole up in a bus or train station for the night. But to be honest, I hadn't felt much of anything except exhaustion as we'd slogged up the apartment's familiar stairs, breathing in the familiar odor of dust and ancient cooking: no fear, no trepidation, no sadness or regret for Mireille. I was done.

I'd passed out almost immediately. I don't know what woke me—I don't remember dreaming. One minute Mark and I were wrapped around each other; the next, he was gone from the bed. I sat up and listened, but I couldn't hear him moving around elsewhere in the apartment. "Mark?" I called, my voice slurred with sleep.

I jumped up, switched on all the lights, and, still groggy, padded from the bathroom to the kitchen and back again. The only sound was the slap of my bare feet on wood, which for some reason made me think of the shadows poisoning our own home. No Mark. I don't know why, but I got it into my head that he'd gone upstairs to Mireille's room. I didn't bother to get dressed—panic was setting in by now and I was barely aware I was half-naked—nor did I check to see if Mark had left the keys behind. I left the apartment, letting the door slam shut behind me, and ran up the stairs in nothing but my underwear.

Mireille's door was half-open. "Mark?" I whispered, but I could sense the studio apartment was empty. It felt like an intrusion, but I couldn't stop myself from peering inside it and turning on the light. It still reeked of smoke and turps, but now there was an undertone of something else—something like lavender. Someone, probably one of the cops, had turned all the canvases around, and scores of big-eyed children surrounded me as I stepped farther into the room. Then it hit me that the paintings all seemed to depict the same dark-haired child in different emotional states: leering, laughing, crying, and screaming. They were too slapdash to be creepy, but there was something lonely and desperate about their expressions, which stopped them from being purely kitschy or ridiculous. I reached out a hand to touch them but then snatched it back, irrationally certain they'd infect me somehow. The laptop was gone, as were the coffeepot and the coverlet. A pair of worn corduroy trousers lay curled forlornly in the corner.

A thunking sound reverberated up from the guts of the building—the slam of the entrance door?—and I backed out of there, fleeing for our apartment, praying that Mark had returned while I was snooping in Mireille's room. Without the keys, I was locked out. I slapped the door with the flat of my hand. "Mark! You in there? Mark!"

I turned to the neighboring apartment and traced my fingers across the top of the door. The key was gone. I pressed my ear to the door but could hear nothing but the gush of blood in my veins. Mark must have gone outside for some reason.

By now the cold was really starting to bite, and my skin prickled with goosebumps. I hurried down the stairs and pushed through the door and out into the courtyard.

"Mark?"

His dark shape staggered out of the corner.

"Thank God. What are you doing down here?" His shoulders were shaking. Something was wrong. I walked toward him slowly. There was something in his arms. A dark bundle. Unable to see what it was at first, I reached out to touch it, recoiling as my fingers stroked fur, the flesh beneath it holding only a trace of warmth. It was an animal of some sort, and it must have died fairly recently. He shifted his position and I realized it was a cat. The ground beneath me tipped. I forgot about the cold and the stones piercing the soles of my bare feet. "Put it down, Mark. Drop it. We're getting the fuck out of here."

He murmured something, but I couldn't make out what he was saying. Nor could I read his eyes in the gloom.

"Give me the keys." I dug in his coat pocket, doing my best not to brush against the cat again. I breathed with relief when my fingers curled around metal. I shouldn't leave him there alone, but I doubted I'd be able to hustle him up to the apartment. "Put that fucking thing down and wait. I'll be back in two minutes."

I hurled myself up the stairs, a fresh surge of panic pushing me on. All I could think was that this was bad. Very bad. What would make him *want* to pick that dead cat up? Had he gone out onto the street to find it?

I grabbed towels, threw on my clothes—my jeans were still damp, but that was the least of my worries—gathered the rest of our stuff, and ran to rejoin him.

He was calmer when I returned and had discarded the cat in a corner of the courtyard. He didn't speak to me as I scraped the worst of the muck off his coat, gagging at the odor of spoiled meat. I asked him again what the hell he was thinking, and he murmured something about thinking it was still alive and trying to save it. I could forgive his irrational behavior at the train station—his refusal to sneak through the turnstiles like everyone else; he'd always been like that, proud of his moral compass—but I wasn't sure I could forgive him for begging from that family. Mark had scared them. He'd scared me. We were lucky they didn't call the cops. I would have handed over my wallet as well if a man with screaming eyes, an unshaven face, and matted cat hair on his sleeve had approached me. And worse, Mark had been oblivious to their fear and triumphant about what he'd done: *Look, Steph, there is kindness in the world.*

Sickened by the memory, I felt the acid in my gut turn to nausea. I slipped out of my seat and weaved my way toward the lavatory at the back of the plane. On the other side of the aisle, Mark was staring at his screen, fingers pressed to his earphones. He didn't look up as I passed him.

Safely inside the bathroom, I locked the door, sat on the metal toilet seat, and stared at the clump of dirty paper towels spilling out of the trash can. The nausea had eased, but my stomach was still churning. In less than eight hours we'd be home. Before we left, I assumed I'd be returning relaxed, confident, rejuvenated, with enough ammunition to eradicate the intruders' lingering shadows. Perhaps, I thought, I could say that I was desperate to see Hayden (which was true), then drive down to Montagu and stay at Mom and Dad's for a few days. They were scheduled to bring Hayden back on Sunday—I could easily say I wanted to fetch her myself. Could I—or more important, should I—leave Mark alone in the house so soon after we returned? No. He wasn't well. I had to face the house sometime; running off to Montagu would only be postponing the inevitable. *Unless,* a voice whispered, *you don't come back.*

The shame came then. How could I think that? Sitting in that bathroom, that stupid stinking bathroom, I came to a decision. Whatever Mark was going through was *our* problem. I still resented how he'd behaved during the home invasion, but that was my problem. I could forgive him for that. I loved him. Of course I did. And his freakish behavior—the dead cat, harassing that family—might be symptoms of a chronic lack of sleep, PTSD, and stress. I stood up and stared at myself in the warped mirror above the sink. We'd been through Hayden's difficult first months together; we'd built a life. I'd known he was damaged from the start; I'd known what I was getting myself into. You don't come back from the death of a child. *You can't run away from your history.* And I wish I could say that pride wasn't a factor, but I'd be lying. No one had thought our relationship would work, not my parents, not my friends, and especially not Carla. I needed to prove them wrong.

I left the bathroom, and this time as I made my way back to my seat I touched Mark on the shoulder. He jumped but then smiled in relief when he saw it was me. I almost mentioned that the guy next to me was willing to swap seats but decided against it. A few hours apart wouldn't hurt.

"You okay up there?" he asked.

"Fine."

The light was poor, but I searched his face, looking for any sign of irrationality. The woman sitting next to him stirred and eyed me with interest. Women liked Mark—they always had.

"Steph, I'm sorry about what happened in the airport."

"In the airport?" *Oh shit,* I thought, *has he done something else I don't know about?* "What happened in the airport, Mark?"

"You know, me falling asleep and letting you deal with everything by yourself."

"Oh. Oh right. That's okay."

"It isn't. Really." He gave me a crooked grin. "I'm sowwy, Steph." I laughed out of relief, remembering the crappy vocalist on the train ride into Paris. He was sane enough to make a joke—that was something.

"Try and get some sleep." He kissed my hand, and I returned to my seat. I felt easier, almost ready to convince myself that I'd blown the scene with the cat out of proportion. I'd just woken up, after all. I was spooked, disoriented. Maybe I *had* misremembered it. Maybe he really did think he could save it. Soothed, I fell asleep within minutes.

The blond German woke me as the plane was touching down in Joburg. At some point he must have climbed past me to get to the toilets—he was freshly shaven and was wearing a crisp white shirt. As everyone deplaned, I waited nervously outside the exit door for Mark to join me. His two-day stubble made him appear haggard and older, but he seemed calmer, less fidgety and distracted than the day before. As we queued at immigration and collected our baggage, we didn't say much, mostly just swapped inanities like polite strangers: "Did you sleep well?" "Wasn't the breakfast awful?" "Should we get coffee before the flight to Cape Town?"

A cloud of metallic balloons bounced above the crowd congregating around the arrivals-hall barrier, and my spirits began to lift. The place was packed, full of noise and color; it felt like real life again after the grayness of where we'd been. Someone screeched, making both of us jump, and then I spotted the German guy running toward a woman clutching a handful of ribbons tethered to the balloons. She outweighed him by at least forty pounds, but he swung her around effortlessly, both of them laughing. As they kissed, the people around them laughed and clapped, the balloons floating off listlessly.

I nudged Mark. "I sat next to that guy on the plane. He told me he was—"

Mark squeezed my wrist so tightly I winced. He was staring straight ahead at something—or someone—in the throng of people around us. His eyes tracked the progress of a preteen girl with mousy braids.

"What is it?"

"I thought she'd . . ." He released my arm. "Nothing," he said with a strained smile. "Nothing at all. Really. Let's go home."

Chapter 15

Mark

"Top you up, darling?"

I should get back home, but the hot afternoon sun has thawed me out and I'm lethargic. I'd like to go home and help with Hayden's bath time, but I know Steph's happy for the quality time alone with her. When Jan and Rina delivered her back home from the B and B this morning, Steph was so relieved her eyes started to well up. I made up a pretext to come and see Carla—"I should go and fetch the keys and thank her for her time"—and Steph almost bustled me physically out of the house, she was so keen to have a break from me.

When we got in yesterday afternoon, she dropped her bag and started stalking around the house. "This has been moved," she said, pointing at the dressing table that's always been under the window in our bedroom. Before I could even come over, she was across to the bookshelf. "Someone's laid these books on their sides." Perhaps it was Hayden, I said; perhaps Carla took them out while she was here, but she was off again. "Do you smell that?" "Is this where we left it?" "We closed this blind, didn't we?"

Having been through the week we just had, I know I should have been more sympathetic. Steph was right: things in the house did look different—they felt different—but I was so exhausted by our constant traumatized hyperawareness, I willfully ignored it. If I couldn't feel at home there, where on earth could I? I wanted so urgently to be lulled. So I've run out to this soul-thawing café with my comforting old friend and I'm leaning back in my chair as if I have no bones, instead of staring down this trauma by the side of my wife and child. *Good going, Mark.* I really should get back now, but rich summer light is glinting off the ocean, and a stiff breeze cools my skin. I can see half the sky from here. "Sure, thanks," I tell Carla.

She leans over and fills my glass with chardonnay from the ice bucket, and a skein of hair loosens from behind her ear and falls across her face, catching the light. Though it's hennaed with beetrooty-red highlights, there's still some of that rich bronze in it—her natural color.

I've always been a sucker for pretty hair. Odette's hair used to make her look like an American beauty queen, like the sun shone into every room she graced; it was thick, lustrous, effortless, and when we made love she'd run it across my body and I could feel the warm life stroking into me. I'd try to smother myself in its scent. At times like that, Odette embracing and covering me, shielding me from the world, I could have died happy over and over again. When Odette's hair grew back, it was strangely curly and mousy brown.

Even though Odette tried to keep up a brave face, once Zoë caught her crying at her mirror during one of the chemo courses, grasping a hank of hair in her hand. "What's wrong, Mommy?" Zoë asked. "I'm so ugly," she said. Zoë just shook her head, and five minutes later she determinedly returned, clutching all of her dolls, each of them shorn. "See, they're pretty, Mommy, just like you." Later, Zoë had gathered all of the dolls' plastic hair trimmings into a small Tupperware, "for later, when they feel better."

Perhaps it's the wine, the sun, the breeze, the distance from Steph—but I don't stop myself reaching out to feel the ends of Carla's hair. "This is nice," I say. "New color?"

She pulls back gently and frowns at me, but with a— suggestive? indulgent?—curl of the lips. "You sounded so strange when you called that day"—she does her cheeky impression of my voice—"'We need to get out of there, *now,* Carla.' What happened?"

I take a deep, slow sip of my wine—suicides, ghosts, dead cats. Where do I start? And if I start, where will I finish? I put down my glass, hoping the heat of the day will counteract the nauseating chill that's returned to my blood just thinking about that place. "Let's just say the apartment was not as advertised."

"You told me that, remember?"

"I did?"

"Mark, darling, we had a long Skype convo about it. There was hair in the closet or something." She shuddered. "Ugh. You shouldn't have made light of it. You should have moved to the hotel straightaway."

"You know how it is. You think you'll settle in, that things will be okay. Until they're not and it's too late."

But I can tell from her expression that she's aware of what I'm not saying: we didn't have enough money for a hotel, even in an emergency, even if the bloody credit card had been working. That heavy weight sits between us—that she's still sitting in a well-paid professorship on the verdant UCT campus, while I've been downgraded to my poky cubicle in an office-park college. It's an embarrassment for both of us. She's moved up, and I've moved down; I'm no longer the impressive boy with a future she once knew; I'm a pity case. For a second, I'm tempted to stand up and leave, but the waiter comes around and offers us another bottle and I settle back into my chair. Here is still better than there, my body says.

One advantage of the week is that I'm still thinking in euros, and a bottle of wine here is as cheap as a glass there. I don't express this to Carla because I don't want to seem cheap.

She takes a swig of wine. "How was the hotel in the end?"

On the flight back home I had wondered whether it was deliberate, or at least some sort of Freudian slipup—because

Carla is way too self-possessed to make mistakes like that. It's quite possible she wanted us to have a bad time, that she wanted our marriage-healing escape to fail. "We didn't stay there after all," is what I settle on. "Things worked out differently." With my dark glasses as a shield, I scan her face for any clue, but there's no admission in her features. She's always been there for me, and I don't think she'd ever want to sabotage my happiness.

"Did you hear from the apartment's owners again and find out why they never showed up at your place? Stephanie seemed so worried about them."

"Yes, she was. She wondered if they'd got lost or hijacked here in Cape Town, but as you know they at least had the decency to let us know they were alive."

"It's so weird of them not to show up, though, isn't it? Why advertise for a house swap, arrange for you to stay at their place, and then not turn up? It's a real mystery."

"It is." I fake a yawn, hoping it will dissuade Carla from probing further. Steph and I had been so fired up about getting to the bottom of the great Petit mystery, but now that we're back it seems pointless to obsess over it.

"It was nice of her to worry," Carla says. "Stephanie's a nice girl."

I ignore Carla's tone and replay our return for a moment. "You didn't happen to move things around at the house, did you?"

Carla peers at me over her sunglasses. "Huh?"

"We noticed some things were moved around a bit, as if someone had been staying there." Carla eyes me. Maybe she brought that guy—what the hell's his name?—around for a bit of off-site adventure. "You were very welcome to, you know, make yourself at home."

"I came in twice," she says, "to water the plants and check on things for you. I didn't 'move anything around.'"

Her tone is cold, and I don't want her to be angry with me—the last thing I want today is another argument. "It's fine, really. Thank you for helping. You're always so . . ."

"So what?" she says.

"Helpful."

Now she snorts with a sarcastic laugh, and she's back on form. "Yeah, right."

I grin at her for a second, then swill my wine. "It wasn't all bad, though. I had a sort of epiphany there. A sense that the world is so much bigger and fuller than it seems when you're stuck in your everyday grind." Carla leans forward and nods, encouraging me to go on, but I find I can't access that sentiment anymore; it feels like I'm grabbing at the threads of a long-ago dream. I look out over the parking lot below us, where a hipster is arguing with a car guard at the back of his Mini Cooper. "It was only a week, but it's strange to be back."

"I know exactly what you're saying. After two days in Richmond, which was so peaceful . . . the air was clean, you know. Did I tell you that Jamie Sanderson was there? You wouldn't believe the new creature she has dangling on her arm. You'd think that she was thirty years younger. So on the first evening there, we're invited to this dinner. Richmond's version of a soirée, I suppose, and all the poets are supposed to come, only Terri and Marcia and their entourage have rented a minibus in Port Elizabeth and have got lost on the road. I can only imagine that a number of . . ." I stop listening as she launches into the full story.

What *am* I doing here, really, instead of at home with my family? I know it's nothing to do with infidelity. I'd never choose Carla over Steph if it came to that—and it's nowhere near coming to that. It never will. Carla sometimes reminds me of who I was when I was still young and powerful, before everything went bad, and that's the only reason I'm sitting here. And I miss Steph right now. The trip *was* supposed to heal us, but it just ended up a mess, and now we're worse than ever. When she took Hayden in her arms this morning, she turned her back to me, shielding Hayden from me. She doesn't trust me with my own daughter. I should feel glad that somehow she's convinced herself that the cat was dead already, that I'm only deranged rather than criminally insane, standing in my underwear in a courtyard in the rain.

I have to make this right, get her to trust me and believe me again; I don't know how, but I do know that mentioning Zoë is not going to help, which is why I said nothing in the concourse at Johannesburg airport.

Sitting here with Carla might not help, but I fill my wineglass again and we call over for some snacks.

It's after nine when I get home. Someone has tipped over a trash can in my parking space and I double-park next to the neighbors' van, tripping somehow on the edge of the car as I get out to move the trash can. As I approach it, three massive rats skitter out of the mouth of the can, and I gag as I get a noseful of the putrid stench of rot emitting from it. Stumbling back to the car, I decide to park somewhere else and find a vacant spot a few houses down.

The house is quiet and all the lights are off; I fumble my keys into the locks and try not to slam the door as I finally get in, turning on the light in the living room as I pass. Upstairs, Hayden's curled up with Steph in our bed, both fast asleep. I watch them in the doorway for a minute, then head down to the kitchen and raid the cupboard for a bowlful of pretzels and peanuts and pour myself a large glass of whiskey. It's either pass out now and wake up feeling like shit at one in the morning, or keep the buzz going for a while longer.

Steph didn't want to move in here; she wanted us to buy a new place together. "Don't the memories make you sad?" she'd asked, back when she used to ask such things, back when she tried to tackle my past head-on, as if confronting and naming the ghosts was the best way to exorcize them. She was young, with a naïve, vigorous optimism. But she was no match for reality. The housing market was at an ebb, and what we'd clear for the house after taxes and fees, even if we managed to sell it in this climate, would barely get us a deposit on anything else livable. With my college wage, we'd never get a full mortgage. So we cower in this tainted house from the ghosts of Odette and Zoë and of those filthy invaders.

Perhaps I have it all wrong; perhaps we're the invaders in this house and they want us out. Perhaps we're the ghosts who need to be exorcized.

Taking another slurp of my whiskey, I turn on the TV to a repeat of an English soccer match and mute the sound. I don't know when last I had the living room to myself. By the time Hayden's asleep, Steph and I are either so exhausted we go to bed, or we sit up and talk. After all those times I've wished I had some space to myself, now that I have it, the silence is not exactly welcome.

As I settle into my usual chair, I kick off my shoes and peel off my socks, picking idly at the splinter wound in my sole. It's healing fairly well now that I've been applying disinfectant to it, but it's left a deep crack down the middle of my foot like the fissure of an earthquake. Looking back up at the game, I notice a glare on the screen—it's coming from the light fixture set into the wall behind me. I stand up, dim the light, and adjust the set, noticing that it does seem to have shifted from its normal position. The outlines of its stand are etched in dust and scratches on the tabletop. That may have happened before we left, anytime since the burglary in fact. But Steph was right about the books in the bedroom. We never pile them on their sides, and there's no reason Carla would have touched them. It might have been Hayden, I remind myself, but I'm not convinced. Hayden would have left them lying on the floor if she'd played with them, not stacked up neatly.

I glance around the room as colors from the soccer match flicker over the walls. With the alcohol beginning to sour in my blood, and without Carla to blame, I start to see the room like Steph saw it yesterday. Something *has* been moved on the bookshelf in here. There's a gap where there used to be something. I approach the shelf, aware of my own absurd timidity, but nothing leaps out at me. I crane over toward the shelf and my foot crunches on something on the floor. Crouching down, I retrieve the three photo frames from where they've fallen and line them back up on the shelf. The glass has come completely out of one that Steph's father took last year—Steph, Hayden, me, and Rina outside the B and B—and is spiderwebbed over the other two.

I put my drink down on the shelf next to the photos and go to the kitchen to fetch a dustpan. For some reason I remember Odette standing there, rolling pastry at the butcher block. This was before Zoë even. I remember those nights, my new wife standing in our new home, dusted with flour, sticky hands. I'd sneak up to her and lick her neck, knowing she wouldn't want to touch anything with her hands. She'd laugh and lean back into me.

I shake off the ghost and rummage under the sink for the dustpan, and as I come back out and pass the stairs, there's a light on up there. I could swear the house was totally dark when I came home. I creep upstairs, wincing as the wood squeaks. The light is coming from Hayden's room.

Just walk away, part of me is yelling. *Leave it alone,* that part shouts, spooling images across my mind. God, cowardice is so tempting. But there are two possibilities—someone is up there, or someone isn't. It's that simple. More likely, there's nobody there, but if there are masked bogeymen in my daughter's bedroom, I can't let them stay there and threaten my family, not again. Before I think anymore, I twist the doorknob and push into the bedroom.

My heart lurches as I scan the room and check behind the door. There's nobody there—but . . .

There's Zoë's Princess Ariel doll lying on Hayden's nightstand, hair roughly docked down to the spotted rubber scalp. It should be safely sealed away at the bottom of the pantry, taped up with all of Zoë's other toys. The princess stares up at me with injured, accusing eyes.

She's right. I killed her.

I was so tired. Odette had been in the hospital the night before and was due to take a taxi home that morning, but the doctors wanted to keep her in for another few hours and I'd made the mistake of taking an equally tired Zoë to do the grocery shopping. She'd been acting up—withdrawn and sullen and then suddenly shrieking in faked laughter about some joke she wasn't sharing. I started to get ratty with her and it ended in a meltdown in the car. I'd let her into the house, and after I'd hauled the groceries inside, I saw that she'd settled down to a game on the living room carpet. I knew none of this was her fault, and I was overwhelmed with pride in how she was coping and at the same time appalled that my seven-year-old daughter would even have to cope with something so crappy and that there was nothing I could really do about it. I gave her a box of Smarties and a bowl of chips—a Saturday treat—and we cuddled on the couch to watch *Toy Story*. She started to jiggle her leg and I snapped at her and she started to cry, so I apologized and went to find a bottle of Odette's tranquilizers, which she took on particularly bad days. I didn't want to take out my exhaustion on Zoë. I didn't think the pills were so strong as I curled back up on the couch, feeling better.

In my dream I was swimming with Odette and Zoë. We were in a pool at the seaside, at an apartment in Knysna we'd rented the year before. Zoë was lining up pebbles on the first step of the pool, Odette looking down at her. I was at the far end of the pool but I couldn't see them well because the wind was blowing leaves and dust between us, stinging my eyes. The leaves turned to crows, then to a huge black storm cloud, and I was trying to call out to them and warn them to come inside, but they couldn't hear me. There was no sound at all. The wind was silent. Then instantly the dust dropped and the sky was blue again and I zoomed in to Odette's face, smiling down blankly at Zoë as she contentedly lined up her stones, her hair dropping out in skeins, her body withering away as I watched. I tried to swim toward them, but I couldn't move. Now there was a sound of a cat beside me, puking up hairballs, and somehow it was stopping me from approaching my family. Whenever I pushed with my arm—*hack, hack, choke*—the gasping sound held me back. My kicking ankles collared with a *hack, hack, gasp.*

Odette dropped her keys when she saw me, cradling Zoë's body, her face blue, vomit frothing her lips, the bottle of bright, Smartie-colored pills empty now, killing my daughter as I failed her.

I pumped and pushed at her corpse, wanting to reverse time, wanting to take all the poison she'd swallowed and have it for myself. I wanted to die instead of her. I was still pumping, but it was way too late when Odette raised me and shoved me away.

Now I hurry back downstairs to the pantry and check Zoë's boxes. There's no reason they should have been touched, but space—seven years of meaningless things I've used to block them away—has been cleared away, and Zoë's life and all her favorite bristle-haired princesses are spilling from the worn cardboard.

It makes sense to me immediately. I can't shove her away,

out of sight. We are the ghosts in this house—Steph, Hayden, and me. Zoë wants her home back.

I know what she wants me to do. I open Hayden's closet and scratch under the piles of bedding and old clothes until I reach the sealed plastic zip-bag and drag it out. I strip Hayden's bed and work the duvet into Zoë's cover, the orange and gray chevrons she'd chosen just a few months before because she was getting too old for the Powerpuff Girls. Lilac fitted sheet and salmon pillowcases. It's only when I finally bundle Hayden's bedding together, ready to dump it in the hall, that I notice Steph's watching me from the doorway.

Chapter 16

Steph

We caught a shuttle home from the airport, and at first, the house appeared to be exactly as we'd left it. The only immediate sign of disarray was a scattering of stamens from the arrangement of stargazer lilies I'd placed on the hall table for the Petits, but otherwise the place still smelled pleasantly of furniture wax. As Mark disengaged the alarm, I waited for the anxiety that had taken root after the home invasion to flood in. It didn't. Nor was I relieved to be back in Cape Town, although the clear sky and midday heat should have cheered me after the gray pall and freezing temperatures of the past week.

It was just a house after all, nothing but bricks and mortar. Familiar and far more comfortable than the Petits' hellhole, but not loved. At least not by me.

Mark sloped off to the kitchen to make coffee, leaving me to drag the suitcases up to the bedroom. I was desperate to shower, wash my hair, and brush my teeth, and I didn't notice anything was awry until I'd dried off and started rummaging in my drawer for clean underwear. My usually carefully matched socks were separated and jumbled up with my bras. I'd almost convinced myself that I must have scrambled them up during the chaos of packing for the trip, when my eye strayed to the bookshelf next to the bureau. My Tana French and Ann Cleeves novels—the books not deemed worthy enough to be on display on the shelves downstairs—were now positioned in a horizontal pile. I was certain I hadn't done that. And the dressing table itself looked like it had shifted a

couple of inches—there were fresh scratches on the wooden
floor around it.

Panic surged. The cops had told us that thieves often return
to the scene of the crime to steal the goods replaced by insur-
ance payouts. But no. They couldn't have got in. We'd have
known about it. Nothing else was missing. The only explanation was that Carla had been through my stuff. She was the
only one with a key. How *dare* she? At the very least she could
have been less blatant about it. Something made me pull the
duvet back. A single blond hair lay curled on the white sheet
on my side of the bed. I gingerly plucked it off the fabric,
dropped it into the toilet, and washed my hands. Did it belong
to one of Carla's boy toys? Had she fucked one of her dispos-
able boyfriends in our bed? There were no other signs that
someone had slept in it—the sheets were uncreased and still
smelled of fabric softener—but I ripped them off the mattress
anyway and hurled them into the laundry basket.

Next, I checked Hayden's room. The door was shut—exactly
as I'd left it—and I didn't get the sense that anyone had been in
there. Her little army of soft toys were still lined up on the window ledge, and her clothes were neatly folded in the drawers.
I sat on the bed and waited for the internal turmoil to recede.

When I came downstairs, Mark was sitting at the kitchen
table, sorting through the junk mail, the iPad in front of him.

He glanced at me distractedly. "You feeling better after your
shower?"

"Not really, no."

"What's up?"

"Carla's been snooping through our stuff. Through my
stuff, I mean." I couldn't keep the resentment out of my voice.

"Eh?"

"She's been poking through my underwear drawer."

"You think Carla's been through your *underwear*? Why would
she do that?"

"How would I know? And it's not just that. She's been mess-
ing with my books as well. They're not as I left them."

"What exactly are you accusing her of, Steph? Are you sure
about this?"

"All I'm saying is can you ask her if she touched or moved
anything in the house while we were away? I mean, it's not
exactly kosher, is it?"

He shook his head. "Right. So, let's see. She agreed to meet
the Petits for us and hung around for hours when they were a
no-show. Then she made inquiries about them for us—which
as far as I'm concerned was going above and beyond. And *then*
when we were in dire straits she booked us a hotel—"

"For the wrong date."

"It was an honest mistake, Steph. We owe her big-time,
and all you can do is accuse her of going through your stuff?
So what if she read a couple of your books? What's wrong
with you?"

With me? With fucking me? I bit the retort back. "I didn't
mean anything by it, Mark. I'm grateful to Carla; I really am."
Lies, of course. If it weren't for her, we wouldn't have gone to
Paris in the first place.

"Are you sure you didn't just misplace your stuff? You were
really stressed just before we left."

I'm sure. "Maybe ... maybe it was just my imagination.
Sorry. You don't need this right now."

Mollified, he sighed and patted my arm—the sort of gesture someone would make to a friend, not a wife or a lover.
"And I'm sorry if I snapped at you. Listen, you mind if I catch
up on work?"

He turned his attention back to the iPad. I made myself a
cup of green tea and took it back upstairs to Hayden's room,
the only place in the house where I truly felt at ease. I took
comfort from the eggshell-blue walls I'd painted by myself, the
chest of drawers with the bumblebee handles that I'd bought

for a song from the online classifieds, and the Disney princesses nightlight a cousin had sent me from the UK.

It was the only room in the house that the invaders hadn't sullied.

When I first moved in with Mark, I'd planned to revamp the whole house and eradicate the ghost of Odette. Her personality was evident everywhere, from the retro fridge to the stripped-pine table and chairs, and even to the goddamned understated wash on the walls. I spent hours scrolling through décor websites, but time slipped away and when Mark left the university we didn't have enough spare cash to do much more than replace the essentials Odette had whisked away when she moved out. Zoë's room was a different proposition. It seems strange to me now that I didn't venture inside it until I was nearly five months pregnant and time began to run out. I knew Odette had taken most of Zoë's clothes and toys with her when she moved to the UK, but poking around inside it still seemed like an intrusion. I suspected Mark went in there sometimes, and the door was always shut—our version of Bluebeard's chamber. When I eventually got up the nerve to peer inside it, I was shocked to see how naked it was. There were no rugs on the floor, no curtains at the window. The duvet was still on the bed, rolled neatly at its foot, but the pillow was gone. Tentatively, I opened the wardrobe. It was empty except for a pile of duvet covers folded on a dusty shelf and a single pink anorak hanging forlornly from a wooden hanger.

I'd planned to sensitively broach the subject of redecorating it. But in the end I'd blurted it out one night after Mark had drunk a few glasses of red wine and seemed to be in good spirits.

It was our first real fight.

But now the room was Hayden's—and mine.

Again I considered just getting in the car and driving down to Montagu to fetch her. At the very least, I should call my folks and let them know we were home already. But I was exhausted, and why worry them? I decided to send them an email saying that I'd see them the next day, as we'd planned. Let them have one last day with their granddaughter. Then it hit me that I hadn't bought Hayden a present. I thought back to that mortifying scene in the kids' shop in Paris—I'd meant to buy her something, of course, and the urge to put this right was suddenly overwhelming.

Calling out to Mark that I was heading to the shops, I grabbed the car keys and fled.

The mall was deliciously cool after the summer heat, but everything was too bright and busy. There were too many people, too many shops; I felt self-conscious and clumsy, and colors smudged in front of my eyes. I tromped up and down the supermarket aisles, randomly throwing goods into my basket and desperately trying to remember what the hell we needed: milk, eggs, bread, bacon, yogurt, and cereal for Hayden, as well as something for supper. I ran out of energy when I reached the toy aisle, and it took me twenty minutes to choose what to get her from the display of mass-produced junk. In the end I picked out a Barbie mermaid doll, exactly the sort of sparkly girlie gift I'd vowed never to give her. Reeling from low blood sugar, at the checkout counter I added a Coke and a family-size bar of Dairy Milk chocolate. I consumed both sitting in the stifling car in the parking lot, my T-shirt sticking to my back, then hid the evidence under the passenger seat.

Mark was in the living room when I returned, staring blankly at a rugby match, although he never usually watched it. The sugar rush was making me feel trippy, and my skin was sticky with drying perspiration. I'd have to shower again. "You want something to eat, Mark? I bought eggs and bacon."

"Not hungry."

"But you haven't eaten since the plane."

Nor had he showered, but I didn't mention that. In fact, he

was still wearing the same clothes he'd worn for the last two days. I didn't want to think about his cat-blood-soiled coat—I'd give it away to the next homeless man who rang the gate buzzer. "I'm really fine. Thanks, though, Steph."

"Shall I run you a bath?"

He dragged his eyes away from the screen and yawned. "I can do it. Listen, I think I'm going to crash. You mind?"

"But it's so early." *And you stink like a fucking dead cat.*

"I know. I can stay up with you if you want."

"It's okay. Could you check the doors and windows before you go up? And set the alarm?"

I hovered while he did so, then sat in the kitchen and brooded. Bloody Carla. I wanted to take the scissors and slash a hole in her coat. Pour paraffin on it. Set it alight.

I didn't sleep that night. I streamed a film about a bunch of sex addicts with serious problems that were all magically resolved in the last ten minutes, and then sat through a grim murder mystery series set in New Zealand, keeping half an ear attuned to the house's creaks and groans. I knew they were just the sounds of an old building exhaling after a hot day, but every one of them set me on edge. I eventually fell asleep as the golden dawn light crept in, and I was woken what felt like five minutes later by Mark waving my cell phone in my face. "Text from your parents. They've just got off the N2. They're minutes away."

"What time is it?"

"Almost one thirty."

"Seriously?" Sunlight shafted through the burglar bars, stinging my eyes. My neck throbbed from falling asleep at an awkward angle. "Why didn't you wake me?" *Why didn't you bloody well come and find me last night?*

"I didn't want to disturb you."

At least he'd shaved and looked well rested and clean. My

mouth was gummy and foul. "I need to brush my teeth. Let them in and tell them I'll just be a second." I jumped up, energized at the thought of having Hayden home.

"No."

"Wait—*what*?"

"No. Look, Steph. I don't want to see them. I'll stay in the bedroom. I'm not in the mood for your father's judgment this morning."

"Hayden's coming back. Don't you want to see her?"

"Of course I do. But I can see her when your folks have gone. Please, Steph. I'm serious—I just can't take them right now."

"Where must I say you are?"

"Tell them I have jet lag."

There was no time to argue, as seconds later the gate buzzed. When I opened the door, Hayden squealed and ran into my arms and I buried my face in her hair, breathed in the scent of baby shampoo, and tried not to cry. I told my parents that Mark was still sleeping and ushered them into the kitchen. I made them tea while Hayden unwrapped the appalling doll I'd bought for her—she loved it, of course—and introduced it to the far superior Princess Elsa toy Mom had given her.

She didn't ask where Daddy was.

While my dad prowled through the ground floor, double-checking the burglar bars and griping about the cheapness of the alarm Mark had bought, I lied to Mom about our Paris trip—rhapsodizing about the scenery, the apartment, and the food—and promised to email her the photos as soon as I'd downloaded them (another lie: there were no photos of that god-awful trip, although we should have thought to take some of the Petits' shitty apartment to send to the house swap site). They couldn't stay long: they had a couple arriving at the B and B that evening. I hugged them and thanked them and tried not to get irritated at my mom for making a song and a dance about leaving—I knew she was trying to get a tear-ful reaction out of Hayden—and went onto the stoop to see them out.

Mark was coming down the stairs when we went back into the house.

"Look!" I trilled to Hayden. "Here's Daddy. Give him a kiss."

She allowed him to hug her, then wriggled free and toddled back to Barbie and Princess Elsa.

"She looks happy," Mark said.

"She had a great time."

"That's good." His eyes slid away from mine. "Look, Steph, you mind if I pop out for a bit?"

"Where to?"

"To see Carla. That okay? Better get the spare keys from her."

"But I thought we'd do something with Hayden today. She's only just got back home."

"I won't be long. I'll make it up to you, I promise."

He was looking almost like himself; did I really want to start a fight? And if he didn't go and meet Carla, there was always a chance she'd come here. I couldn't cope with that. "Fine."

"Really?"

"Sure. Go. But don't be long."

I don't know what sparked it off, but minutes after Mark left, I started to feel twitchy, and the old anxiety began to build. I sat Hayden in front of the TV, then set the alarm. I paced through the house—double-checking that both doors were shut and bolted. The heat was getting oppressive, but I couldn't bear the thought of opening a window.

I was considering having a stiff drink when the alarm whooped. The shock of it was so unexpected and sudden that it took me several seconds to process what was happening.

And Hayden was screaming.

I darted into the living room, gathered her into my arms, and just stood there, squeezing my eyes shut, holding her to me. I couldn't move. I was paralyzed; I was waiting for the cold steel of a knife against my throat. The growl of a voice demanding to know where the safe was hidden. The alarm wasn't connected to a private security company—we couldn't afford the monthly subscription. Unless a neighbor called the cops, we were alone. No one was coming. Cell phone—I needed my cell phone. I tapped my pockets but it wasn't there. Just where the fuck had I left it?

"Mumma! Mumma! Mumma!" Hayden shrieked over and over again. A fresh spurt of panic got me moving. *Get out, get out, get out!* I ran for the front door, fingers clumsily unlocking the security gate. As we reached the stoop, something clattered from Hayden's fingers. I looked down to see the panic button lying smashed on the flagstones. Shakily, and clutching Hayden to me, I bent down to pick it up. Inside the house, the alarm shrieked on, then finally died.

"Hayden?" I said as gently as I could. "Did you touch this? Did you press the red button?"

She nodded. "Yes, Mumma."

I breathed in a lungful of humid air. "You mustn't touch it again, you hear me, Hayden?"

Her lip wobbled. "Sorry, Mumma."

"It's okay. It was just a mistake." I wiped the tears from her cheeks with the palm of my hand.

"You okay?" a man's voice called. I shielded my eyes against the sun. A rangy guy about my age was standing outside the front gate. I recognized him as one of the students from next door.

My pulse was slowing. I swallowed. "Yeah. Thank you. My daughter pressed the panic button. Sorry—I hope it didn't disturb you."

"It's cool. Used to it. I'm originally from Joburg." He grinned at me. "In any case, it's been happening a lot."

"What has?"

"Your alarm. It's been going off a lot."

A cold fist punched my gut. "When?"

"The last few days."

"We've been away. We've only just got back."

"Yeah. I figured. I called the cops a couple of times, but they didn't show up. I checked your windows and doors, but they all looked cool. Reckon it's just a glitch."

"That is so good of you."

"No problemo." He shrugged. "I heard you had a break-in. It happened to my cousin and his family. Dude who broke in held them at gunpoint for . . ." His voice trailed away as he took in my dismayed expression. "I'm sorry. Not what you want to hear. I'm Karim, by the way."

"I'm Steph and this is Hayden." Hayden sniffed back the last of her tears and gave him a shy smile.

"Cool. Cute kid. That guy who lives here, is he your dad?"

Blood rushed to my cheeks, making my already hot face burn. "No. My husband."

"I can be such a dumb ass."

I laughed. It felt good to flirt. "Don't worry about it."

Someone honked a horn and called his name. "Gotta shoot. We're going to Clifton. Last-minute thing, you know."

"That'll be nice." Better than nice. A small bubble of envy surfaced: I couldn't imagine what it would be like to be so carefree. Heading off to the beach on a whim, downing beers, talking shit.

"Yeah. Going for a swim. It's so bloody hot." He slapped a hand over his mouth. "Sorry. Shouldn't swear in front of the kid."

"She's heard worse." I tickled Hayden and she squirmed and giggled.

"She is *seriously* cute."

"Thanks again for checking on us. I owe you a beer. Or six."

"Hey, no worries. You know where I am if you need anything. Laters." He gave me another grin and ambled away.

Back in the house I decided against resetting the alarm—if there was a glitch in the system, I didn't want to risk startling Hayden again if it went off accidentally. To distract myself, I threw myself into playing with her. We played pirates and dress-up and built a Duplo house, and I put on a puppet show with her new Princess Elsa doll and vile Mermaid Barbie. Little by little I felt the stress draining away. When Hayden became irritable, I settled her on the couch with a juice bottle and sat next to her while she napped.

As I sat there, listening to Hayden breathing in her sleep, I let my mind work through everything that was bothering me. The alarm might be faulty, but the house was secure. My dad had seen to that. No one was getting in. And Hayden was fine. That was all that mattered. There was no point dwelling on Paris. What had happened in France was just pure bad luck. And wasn't it possible that the aftershock of the home invasion had poisoned everything and made it seem much worse than it actually was? Sure, there was no doubt that the Petits were seriously weird, and there was no getting away from what Mireille had done, but the policewoman had said she was mentally ill. Mark and I had simply been in the wrong place at the wrong time. Carla had searched through my stuff, but so what? If her life was so unfulfilled that she got her kicks by nosing through other people's belongings, then that was her problem, not mine. And I had nothing to hide. No weird sex toys, no diary, no private love letters. Mark was a different story: he was feeling the strain; there was no doubt about that. When he got home I'd insist—for Hayden's sake—that he seek professional help.

I sent him a text—it was going on four p.m. and he'd been gone for more than two hours—but he didn't reply.

———————

It was almost nine thirty when he returned. I'd fallen asleep in my room reading Hayden a story, and the creak of footsteps on the floorboards woke me up with the usual breath-stealing lurch. But instead of leaping to my feet, I was flooded with inertia—I wanted nothing more than to just lie there: if the men were back, so be it. I remember thinking that perhaps, like Mark, I'd also reached the breaking point. I wasn't sure how much more of the endless ebb and flow of fear I could stand: the noises in the night, the paranoia.

It took a monumental effort to snatch up the panic button and tiptoe into the shadowy hallway, telling myself, *It's just Mark, it's just Mark.*

The light was on in Hayden's room, the door half-open. "You in there, Mark?"

I stepped cautiously toward it. He was hunched over her bed, pulling her duvet out of her coverlet. Another cover lay crumpled at his feet. "Mark."

He turned and looked at me blearily, like a sleepwalker who'd been rudely awoken.

"What are you doing?"

The seconds ticked by, then, "I thought this might be dirty. I thought I should change it."

"It's fine. It's clean. I washed it before we left."

"God." He gave a forced laugh. "Don't know what's got into me, Steph. Maybe I'm turning into one of those germophobes. Probably had too much sun today."

"Mark . . ."

"Really. Don't look at me like that, Steph. I'm fine."

I helped him shove Hayden's duvet back into its cover. His breath reeked of stale wine; he must have been way over the limit when he drove home.

"Mumma?" Hayden came toddling out of our bedroom.

Mark stepped toward her. "I'll put her to bed."

"It's okay. I'll do it." I swept Hayden into my arms. I didn't want him to touch her. She slipped a thumb in her mouth and buried her head in my shoulder, a sign that she was upset. She'd clearly picked up on the tension strumming through the house. "Why don't you go to bed, Mark?" I was putting on an over-cheery voice. *Look, Hayden, we're all one big happy family. Your daddy isn't going mad, oh no, no, no.* "You need your rest, Mark. Especially after . . . and you have work tomorrow, don't you?"

"Yeah. Yeah. You're right."

I gave him a spectacularly fake smile and took Hayden down to the kitchen with me. There was no sign of Mark when I carried her back to her room, but our bedroom door was shut. Good. I lay down next to Hayden and snuggled as close to her as I could get. There was no point talking to him tonight. He was drunk. Tomorrow I would insist that he go to see some kind of head doctor. That or . . . or what? Ask him to leave until he'd sorted himself out? No. We were a family. We'd been happy once, secure.

Hayden kicked the duvet off her legs, rousing me. I sat up, knocking Princess Elsa to the floor. The spare duvet cover Mark had been fiddling with was curled in a ball in the corner of the room. Patterned with garish zigzags, it wasn't something I would have chosen for Hayden. I stood, made my way over to it, and shook it out. It was bobbled and faded in places, and dust bunnies clung to it. Where had it come from?

But I knew. It was Zoë's. It had to have been Zoë's.

I bundled it into a ball and crept downstairs. In the kitchen, I shoved it into a trash bag, and for once not caring who or what could be lurking outside, I hurried out to the trash can. I hauled out the bag already inside, threw the duvet into the pool of maggoty, putrid liquid at the bottom, and shut the lid.

Chapter 17

Mark

My eyes are getting tired from avoiding Santé's gaze, so it's a relief when a cat's hiss outside sends the two massive hounds barreling off their couch and slamming out the door in a fit of deep barking, accompanied by the panicked squawk of chickens in the yard. At least I have an excuse to look away.

The therapist's room is all the way out on a smallholding in the Bottelary Hills. You'd think there'd be two therapists for every middle-class family much closer to home in the southern suburbs, but Santé Joubert is the only psychotherapist contracted with the college's homespun medical-aid scheme who had an opening. Dozens of psychiatrists could have seen me within five minutes, but I don't want to be medicated. Whatever this is, it is not something that can simply be pressed down with medication. I tried that before and it didn't work.

"I'm not delusional, Steph," I said. "I'm not psychotic. I'm not dangerous."

She clasped Hayden tighter to her and hissed over her shoulder. "So why's your daughter crying then? Why're you shouting at me?"

"I'm *not* shouting," I shouted, then stopped. What a tacky scene, played out millions of times in millions of sad, drained families. I'm nothing but a cliché. I changed my tone, turned my hands over. "What do you want me to do, Steph? What can I do to make you trust me?"

"It's not about trust, Mark. I'm worried about you; that's all. Can't you understand that?"

"Then what? What can I do?" I glanced at Hayden and lowered my voice, as if that would stop her from hearing me. "You haven't let me be with her since we came back."

"Do you blame me? Sometimes I think you have to get half-drunk just to be near her." She caught her breath. "Look, I know you're under a lot of stress. Maybe there's a whole lot of stuff you haven't processed, that you've been pushing down. It will be good for you to talk about it." I couldn't tell whether the look on her face was intensely empathetic or panicked. "We just want you to feel better."

All because I waited till I thought Steph was asleep and took Zoë's bedding out of the trash can, intending to put it back on her bed. I know what Zoë needs me to do, but I can't explain that to Steph. All I was doing was trying to settle Zoë. I'm in constant mourning, for God's sake—you don't get over it; the grief comes in waves that never end. Steph can never understand that type of grief. If she lost Hayden, she could go running naked through the streets, screaming and pulling out her hair, and everyone would indulge her. But if I want to honor my daughter's memory in some private way, all of a sudden I'm insane.

It's not fair, the voice of the bruised little child inside me wheedled, and that pathetic, plaintive appeal made me feel even more estranged. Just then, I was willing to battle it out forever, stand my ground, assert my dwindling rights, but one moment changed everything. As Steph bobbed around agitated, Hayden stopped crying and shifted her face out of the nook of Steph's shoulder; she raised her little hand and opened a chink in the curtain of her hair and peeked at me. Instinctively, I smiled and winked at her—that's what I do when I see her—and she smiled back, tentative but warm.

"I want to make this right," I said. I didn't say, *Whatever you think I've done wrong.*

"Show us that. Show us your willingness and we'll go from there." Despite her conciliatory words, her tone was ice cold and her body was a bunker wall. That was the end of the discussion, the closest we'd get to agreement that night.

I was caught behind a procession of rickety trucks along Voortrekker Road through Bellville, the slow ones overtaking the even slower ones, and even though I'd given myself plenty of time, I was late for the eleven o'clock appointment. I followed Santé's directions along a series of tributary lanes and into a rutted dirt driveway, my little Hyundai slung way too low, then pressed the button on the intercom post at the front gate. It crackled and hissed as I glanced across the property's wall of precast concrete slabs topped by razor wire and electric strands. I announced myself back to the static, and the motorized gate swung open. After I'd followed the track along a fence toward a cluster of buildings set amid a stand of cypresses, Santé Joubert, fifty-something, her indeterminate shape and size swathed in Indian silks, directed me to park against one of the tree trunks.

As I started to step out of the car I saw the two huge hounds bolting toward me from a doorway, ears flapping and a scum of drool visible against their black lips even from this distance. Perhaps a human's primitive brain is primed to detect such fine details in his last moments. I froze. Santé did nothing to stop them, watching me with a neutral face as they cantered up and then clawed to a stop in the dust a few feet away from me.

"They like you," she said in a winelands drawl, as if I'd passed some sort of test, as if the dogs could tell that I was who I said I was.

I eyed them as they snuffled around my shoes, wagging their pointy tails. I might have said something witty and collected like, "If they didn't, would they eat me?" but I was tongue-tied, on edge from the drive and shaken by the dogs, and all I managed was, "Heh," as I followed her toward one of the low outbuildings, stoking a growing bitterness. Isn't a therapist supposed to put her client at ease? Isn't that the whole fucking point?

So when she led me into the cluttered session room, any desire I'd harbored to share my secrets had been cramped up, and when she said, "I hope you don't mind if the dogs sit in with us," I really did, but who was I to say anything as the two Great Dane–mastiffs followed us in and settled themselves on a slumping couch covered by an old brown bedsheet? This wasn't my idea of a calm, minimalist therapist's room, and nothing like any doctor's office I'd ever seen. Santé's room was full of old furnishings as silk-draped and shapeless as its owner, a mismatched collection of hair- and mud-covered carpets. There was a stink of horse sweat and dog breath, and flies buzzed drowsily in the shaded light from the windows; the room was subterranean and earthy, like we were holed up in here among the roots of a vast tree.

Okay, I thought as I settled back into the armchair she had shown me, the room certainly did make me feel far away from my office park and from home and from the dreary gauntlet of Voortrekker Road with its drive-throughs and concrete government offices, transported into some stinky hobbit's burrow. I did appreciate the books double-crammed into mismatched shelves placed around the large space to create organic nooks in which you could just hide away. But then I looked at her, regarding me like some sexless matron, judging me, and I straightened my back and edged toward the front of the seat. I'm not some child who can be manipulated by cheap tricks into telling the truth. This is the therapist's classic ploy: look at you until you say something, and the first sentence you utter is the most telling, the one they'll judge you on for the entire course. I was not going to break first; she could stare at me all she liked. Of course, I have a lifetime of talk I could've just started spewing, but why now, why here? I should be speaking out my guilt to Steph and to Odette, not to this flake.

It was only thirty seconds, perhaps, but it felt like an hour as I self-consciously darted my eyes anywhere but at hers, as I realized that stubborn silence is as telling as whatever I might say first, but that now I was committed and that failing to hold my silence was perhaps the most damning possible indictment of my character, or lack thereof. Stubborn, but too weak to hold any principle. So when the cat hisses and spits outside, sending the chickens into a frenzy and the dogs barging between Santé and me and battering through the door, it's with deep relief that I can look away and say something innocuous. "Do you want to check on that?"

But it's not an innocuous question, not really. I know that the dogs are Santé's protection, along with that bristling wall around her property. I wonder what has happened here, what has provoked this level of defense, which can't simply be a precaution. There must have been some attack from the countless claimants living the desperate sprawl of poverty that extends to her doorstep. It brings those three men shoving back through my mind, makes me hear Steph's terrified whimpers all over again, when I prayed I'd never hear them again. Santé's hippie passivity strikes me as just one more layer of this protective façade.

She just draws her mouth down and shakes her head. "No, it's okay," she says, then resumes her gaze, her right hand resting on a small notepad on the arm of her chair. Not tapping her fingers, not impatient; waiting.

I don't have the energy for another round of gaze evasion, so I clear my throat. "I was wondering if we could get this over with in one go."

"Get this over with?"

"The medical aid will only pay for four sessions, so we won't be able to get into anything too deep. So perhaps we can do it all in the next couple of days, if you're available?"

"Let's see how it goes. We can always discuss rates later."

I shrug, knowing that whatever discount rates she proposes, we couldn't pay. It's now or never.

"Why did you come today, Mark?"

"To show my willingness."

The brown dog saunters back to his spot on the couch, stretches, and farts. Santé's neutral expression doesn't change, but I smile. I suppose I'm more of a dog person than a cat person. I think it's because if given the choice, I'd prefer a dog's contented life to a cat's constant neurotic preening and parading.

And for the first time since the trip, I allow myself to think of what Zoë did to that cat, to replay the scene in my mind, not the way Steph wants us to remember it, but how it really happened. Nothing about this is coincidence, I convince myself. The guard dogs, the feral cats, the barbed wire and electric fencing. This woman knows me, she sees me, perhaps better than I imagined. I might have wound up in this musty room for a reason.

"Your willingness to do what?" she says.

"Oh, it's just an in-joke. Something my wife said."

"In-jokes are important barometers in any relationship," she says. "An intricate code that excludes people outside the relationship infers intimacy, empathy—almost telepathy. But I don't know you, Mark, so . . . if you're here for my assistance . . ."

"I know," I say. "I've come here for a reason, and I suppose I'd better tell you about it. But I don't really know where to start."

She lets me think about it for a few long moments, but when I come up blank she says, "How about telling me what you thought might happen in these four sessions. You live in Woodstock, don't you? That's a long way. What did you hope as you drove here? What did you fear?"

"In general?"

She finally rewards me with a twitch of the lips. "We could start with the specifics for now. What did you hope for this session? What worried you?"

I shift my position and lean against the chair arm. I don't know when last someone asked me something about me, about what I hoped and feared. I know it's a strategy. I know it's flattery, but it's relaxing me and making me want to talk. It's far easier to try to answer her questions honestly than resist for an hour. That's why I came all this way, after all.

"I suppose I hoped the session would do its job. My wife wanted me to come here. I wanted her to be satisfied."

"She's unsatisfied now." It's not a question, so I don't answer. "She wanted you to show your willingness to . . . to do what? To see her perspective? To change your behavior?"

"Yes, and I don't think I need to change anything. There's nothing wrong with me."

"But your wife feels there is. Will it help to tell me what she feels is wrong with you?"

I consider it. "No, that's beside the point. I just want her to trust me again." I want to add *trust me with our daughter,* but it would sound bad, and I don't want to spend the rest of the session trying to convince this stranger that I've never harmed Hayden and never will. I'm not ready to bring my daughters into this conversation. "I just feel . . . when we're not talking . . . I feel alone. She's my friend, and I miss her."

"So, although you think there's nothing wrong with you, you're here to be fixed so that you're not alone anymore."

I frown; that really does about sum it up.

"I see," Santé says.

I get lost driving back home. I thought I could detour around some slow trucks by turning left on the way back though Bellville, but the road never returns and I end up winding south through Elsies River and Manenberg and Philippi. Dangerous kids with pimped cars prowl the potholed roads, but they don't give me or my uncharismatic Hyundai a second look. I get my bearings only once I've reached Baden Powell Drive almost an hour later. Normally a journey like that would have made me tense and angry, but since the session, I feel displaced, split in two, separated from myself like my body's in an impervious bubble and I'm a ghost, looking at it from the outside. And nobody can hurt a ghost.

I stop at a makeshift parking lot next to a dune, nodding at a cluster of people sharing a joint as they watch their fishing rods. I skirt behind them and stump along the dune line over the shards of glass and plastic detritus snaggling the ground and find a mound of fairly clean sand and sit on it, watching the gulls hovering over the fishing lines and the white horses capering over the rough water. The strong wind is brackish, puffing occasional drifts of human stink along with it. The scene is pretty, though: the glaring blue sky and white sand, the cold indigo of the water. I'm not sure if I've ever sat on this stretch of coast—it's not the sort of place you'd stop— and even if I willed Zoë to join me here, I'm not sure she'd find her way.

By the time I get home, it's late afternoon. Steph's bathing Hayden when I come in, so after putting my stuff away in the pantry, I stand in the doorway and greet them. Without turning around, Steph mutters, "Hi." I don't really expect a response from Hayden, since she's playing with her fish. I catch sight of myself in the cabinet mirror: my face is badly sunburned. Lifting my fingers to my hot cheeks, I notice the markings on them. I look down, turn my hands over, inspecting them: several parallel scratch marks on the backs of my hands, some of them scabbed over, dried smears of blood. Dark dirt under my fingernails.

I go to the basin and rinse my hands, the soap stinging into the cuts, the brown water eventually running clear.

"How was it?" Steph says.

"Fine," I say. "Quite good, actually. I was surprised. I think it will be—"

"Where were you this afternoon?"

"I took the whole day off." I tamp my hands on the darkest towel on the rail.

"I know. But where were you?"

"I just drove around a bit. I haven't been out that side for ages."

"You weren't with Carla, were you?"

I sigh. Defensive answer or simple answer? "No."

She fills a jug with water and leans Hayden back over her arm, gently gathering her dark curls and smoothing them back as she spills the water over them. She's so good at that; Hayden doesn't squeal—she lies back and sighs. I'm mesmerized as Steph massages the baby shampoo into the hair, rubbing and wringing and rinsing. She winds a small towel around Hayden's head and lifts her out.

"No, Mumma!" Hayden shouts. "Wanna fish!"

"Time to jump out, monkey. Get you dry and you can play a bit before supper."

Hayden carries on whining but Steph's firm and has her dry in a minute.

"Let me clean up here," I say.

"Thanks," Steph replies. She wraps Hayden in her *Frozen* bathrobe and carries her to the bedroom, and I feel ashamed of myself. If going to therapy and cleaning up after them will take this feeling away, will make her love me again, I'll do it. Santé's wrong—I'm not denying myself; I'm holding on to the last good things in my life.

I pull the plug and gather the toys and put them in the bucket at the corner of the tub. I pick out the soap and turn on the hand shower to rinse the tub. The water's draining slowly, blocked by Hayden's hair in the drain hole. I pick it out and it comes away in a satisfying mat; it shines with a blue gleam, full of life. I can't bring myself to throw it away so I squeeze the water out and take it with me.

Chapter 18

Steph

Less than an hour after I'd thrown it in the trash, I caught Mark dragging Zoë's duvet cover along the upstairs corridor. (He must have snuck out of the house and dug it out of the can when I returned to Hayden's room.) That's when I gave him the ultimatum: "Get professional help or Hayden and I are leaving." I didn't raise my voice; there was no blazing row. He simply looked down at his stinking train of fabric as if seeing it for the first time, nodded, and promised to make an appointment the next day. I didn't accompany him to the sessions, but I know for sure that he made good on his promise, as the bills from his therapist—Santé somebody (I forget her surname)—still arrive at the house. Apparently our medical aid didn't cover the whole cost of Mark's treatment. I ignore the bills, and I'll ignore the lawyers' letters that will inevitably follow. Santé somebody can take me to court. She was supposed to help Mark, and she failed. Maybe we all did.

Mark may have agreed to get help, but days after we returned from Paris, I still couldn't shift the disconcerting feeling that someone had been digging around in our stuff. I had no proof that Carla had been snuffling through my belongings, but the subtle displacement of objects seemed to be designed to make me question myself—I couldn't help but believe it was malicious. Every day I'd discover a new little oddity: the pocket of a jacket I hadn't worn for months twisted inside out; a lipstick I rarely used worn down to a stub. Each time I came across something that wasn't quite right, I'd work to convince myself that it was all in my mind, but I wasn't sleeping well, and exhaustion fed the anxiety and paranoia.

The night after Mark returned home late from his first visit to the therapist, the alarm went off at three a.m. I was lying in bed with Hayden when it shrilled, jolting me awake when for once I'd managed to snatch a few minutes of sleep, sending my book, which had been lying on my chest, skittering to the floor. This time, Hayden didn't scream. She merely sat up and blearily complained about the noise. I fought to keep calm for her sake. "It's fine, baby. I'll make it stop."

I ran to the door. "Mark!" I hissed down the dark corridor, ears straining for alien footsteps or voices. He didn't come. He didn't answer. "Mark!" Horrible scenes flashed through my mind: *they've broken in again and they've got him. They're torturing him, breaking his fingers, burning his skin on the iron, smothering him with a pillow.* And somehow worse than this, the thought that he was hiding, that he'd locked himself safely in the bathroom and was leaving me and Hayden to deal with it alone.

Hayden's voice snapped me into action. "It hurts my head, Mumma."

"It's fine, baby. It will stop soon, you'll see."

I couldn't let them get in. I couldn't let them get us. But what could I do? There was no lock on the door. I tried to move the chest of drawers toward the door, but I could only skew it away from the wall at an angle, my back muscles popping. As it jolted away from the wall, in the dim light cast by Hayden's night lamp, I spotted a dark object lying next to the baseboard behind it: an unfamiliar hairbrush, blond hair matted in its tines. Hearing footsteps, I gathered Hayden into my arms, still unsure of the best action to take. The door burst open, but it was Mark—just Mark. He hadn't left us after all. He looked calm and unruffled; he'd even taken the time to dress in jeans and a sweatshirt.

He flicked on the main light, making us blink. "You guys okay?"

"I was calling for you, Mark. I was worried—I thought . . . I didn't know . . ."

"I've been checking the house. All secure."

"You're sure?"

"Positive. Been trying to kill the alarm, but the code isn't working."

I shifted Hayden's weight on my hip. She was getting way too heavy to carry. Mark reached out for her. "Here, let Daddy carry you." After a moment's hesitation, I handed her to him. I should have been relieved at this show of concern for his daughter, but instead I felt uneasy.

"Can you see if you can turn it off?" he said to me.

"Yeah, but shouldn't we call the cops just in case?"

"I checked the house, Steph. Why waste their time?"

A vicious inner voice piped in that if I had a job—if I hadn't chosen to stay at home with Hayden—then maybe we'd be able to afford the five hundred rand a month to hook the alarm up to a security company. And it could just be a glitch, couldn't it? "Apparently it went off a lot while we were away."

"Who says?"

"One of the neighbors—a student—told me."

"Why didn't you tell me?"

"I meant to. You've been distracted lately, Mark." *Not to mention borderline insane.*

"Noisy, Daddy!" Hayden cried.

"Can you try and switch it off, Steph?" he said again.

I ran down to fiddle with the alarm. It died the second I touched the control pad. I didn't rearm it, rationalizing that even if someone did break in, it was useless. Instead I scurried through the house, double-checking the windows and doors, jumping at every sound.

When I returned to Hayden's room, Mark was moving the

chest of drawers back into place. The hairbrush behind it had gone out of my mind. Hayden was tucked into bed, and her eyelids were drooping.

Mark smiled at me. "Well done. I'll get someone to come and look at it tomorrow. Probably just a loose wire."

He turned off the main light. His elongated shadow drifted across Hayden's duvet—an eerie Nosferatu shape. I shivered. Hayden was now breathing steadily.

"She's out, Steph. Come on. Come to bed."

I couldn't bear the thought of leaving Hayden alone in the room. Or maybe I couldn't bear the thought of being alone in bed with Mark. "No. I'm going to stay in here with Hayden."

"Why don't we bring her in with us?"

I stared at him. He'd been against letting her sleep in our bed from the start. We'd never discussed why, but I'd assumed it was a habit that Zoë had got into and it was the kind of clingy behavior he was reluctant to encourage in Hayden. "Seems a shame to move her now."

"Okay. Sleep well." He kissed me chastely on the cheek and left the room. I crawled into bed with Hayden, convinced that sleep wouldn't come, but it crept up on me almost immediately.

Hayden woke me up by stroking my hair. Bright sunlight filtered through the crack in the curtains. "Mumma! Mumma, get up. Mumma. Look." She was pointing under the bed.

"What?"

"Look, silly! Look at the funny lady."

"What funny lady?"

"Look!"

I swung my legs off the bed and got groggily down on my hands and knees. All that was under there was one of Hayden's socks and the Mermaid Barbie. I dragged it out and handed it to her. "This funny lady?"

Hayden put her hand on her hip in a perfect imitation of

my mom when she's exasperated at Dad. "No, Mumma!" She clucked her tongue and took Mermaid Barbie from me.

"Where's Daddy?" And what time was it? When I tracked down my cell phone—I'd left it on the nightstand in Hayden's room but stupidly hadn't thought to use it last night—I saw it was almost nine. Hayden was usually up at six. Jesus. Had she been unsupervised for three hours? I carried her downstairs and saw with relief that Mark had left a note on the kitchen table, saying that he'd tried to wake me earlier but couldn't rouse me and had left only when he heard I was awake. Why didn't he call out to me? He must have crept out of the house; I didn't hear the creak of the front door or the jangle of the gate slamming shut.

"Did Daddy make you breakfast, Hayden?"

She nodded. "Yucky cereal."

"Did you eat it?"

"No, Mumma. I want eggs with faces."

"*Please* can I have eggs with faces."

"Please, Mumma," she said, sweetly.

I made Hayden a boiled egg, drawing a smiling face on the shell as I always did, and cut a piece of toast into narrow slices for her to dip into the yolk. I didn't feel like eating; I wasn't sure if I could even stomach coffee that morning.

"Spoony, Mumma!" Hayden said.

"Please," I snapped back.

"Please, Mumma."

I opened the drawer, looking for one of the special novelty spoons she liked, but most of them were in the dishwasher, which I'd forgotten to turn on last night. I dug through the knives and forks, metal rasping against metal, until I found one, although it was covered in a fine patina of black mold. I dropped the spoon straight into the trash, then yanked out the drawer and heaved it onto the counter. The plastic tray was spotless, as was the rest of the cutlery. It didn't make any sense. Maybe Mark or I had accidentally put a dirty spoon into the drawer without noticing.

Hayden called for a spoon again, so I distractedly grabbed one from the dishwasher, rinsed it, and plonked it in front of her. Then I went through the rest of the kitchen. Nothing else appeared to have been touched, but it didn't *feel* right. Paranoia nibbled: maybe it was all an elaborate ruse, like in one of my crime books, engineered to drive me mad. To split up Mark and me.

Maybe I was the one who needed a psychiatrist. No. That was bullshit. I wasn't crazy.

"Mumma! Look!" Hayden grinned at me and chucked a piece of buttery toast on the tiles.

"Don't do that, Hayden."

She did it again.

"Hayden. I'm warning you."

She giggled, and then, making sure I was watching her, picked up the last piece and dropped it. She wasn't doing it to irritate me; she was simply playing a game, but I wasn't thinking at that moment. Rage surged, and I grabbed her bowl and flung it into the sink, where it shattered, screaming, "I *said,* fucking *no!*" I had never raised my voice to Hayden before, and for a second we both stared at each other in mutual shock.

Then Hayden gasped and burst into tears. I picked her out of her tight seat and cuddled her to me. "Sorry, Mumma," she stuttered between sobs.

"No. Mumma's sorry, baby."

Then we were both crying. The scene is etched in my mind, as clearly as if it's a still from a movie. Me holding Hayden in my arms in the center of the kitchen, both of us howling, the tiles littered with squished eggy toast.

"Don't cry, Mumma." Hayden leaned back and stroked my face. "I will let you play with Princess Elsa."

When we'd both calmed down, I dressed Hayden and then let her play with the iPad while I cleaned up the mess and the broken bowl, fighting the guilt that kept surging up. Not showing any signs of being affected by my appalling behavior, she continued to shout, "Mumma! Look!" whenever she managed to get to the next level of the game she was playing. Another jab of guilt: I'd been using the iPad and its store of addictive kids' games as a babysitter since we'd returned from Paris.

When the mess was cleaned up, I was hit with the urge to confess what I'd done. I called Mark, but his phone was off. I thought about calling my mother, then changed my mind. I mourned the fact that they were my only two real choices when it came down to it. I scrambled in my handbag for an emergency Urbanol, but the packet was empty. I was supposed to take them for only two weeks: the meds were a short-term solution for the anxiety I'd felt after the home invasion. If I needed more—and I was fairly sure I did—that would mean another trip to the doctor, an expense that probably wouldn't be covered by Mark's medical aid. I'd have to go without. And considering how Zoë had died and his current fragile state of mind, I could hardly tell Mark I was in the market for tranquilizers. Instead I practiced the breathing exercises the police counselor had taught me until the anxiety stopped frothing in my gut.

Getting out of the house might help. Perhaps I should do what I'd thought of doing the other day and head off to the beach. Afterward, Hayden and I could kill time shopping for groceries. She loved going to Pick n Pay and being wheeled around in the shopping cart. But since she was absorbed in her game, I decided to wait until she got bored before I suggested an outing, and checked my emails instead. There was nothing from the literary agent, but I didn't allow myself to indulge in a spiral of doubt about that. I clicked onto Facebook and scrolled through the random boastful updates about other people's lives, relieved that I hadn't posted a message letting everyone know about our plans for the Paris trip.

I was about to log off when a message from the Petits zinged into my Gmail in-box:

> *We are sorry for the trouble about the woman who it seemed was dead there in the apartment courtyard. And we are sorry that we could not arrive at your house there in Africa. Can you tell us, did you have any other experiences during your time in the apartment or now? It would be good if you would leave a good review for the other guest who might like to stay there.*
>
> *Wishing you good cheer.*

I barked out a laugh, startling Hayden. Leave a review? Leave a fucking *good review*? Desperate to share this nugget, I tried Mark's phone once more. This time it went straight to voice mail. I forwarded the email to him, then sent him a text message urging him to check his email.

Hayden was thankfully entranced by the iPad once more, so I amused myself by making up a review for the Petits' place:

> *Not only did the Petits—if that is even their real name—not show up to our house or let us know that they had changed their arrangements, but their apartment was a fucking mausoleum and nothing like they described it on the site. Think the Overlook Hotel but with less charm and more creepiness. The building was empty except for a mad squatter, who invited herself to our apartment and then threw herself out of the window. It's an awesome spot for anyone who likes being traumatized and enjoys the*

ambiance of creepy empty concrete buildings that
stink of old food and shit.

I didn't send it to them; instead I wrote:

ARE YOU SERIOUS?????? A GOOD REVIEW? Go
fuck yourselves. Also, why are there no other people
living in your goddamned building????

I didn't send that either (it's still in my drafts folder). Instead, I wrote a furious email complaining about our treatment and sent it to the house swap site, copying in the Petits. Now bubbling over with righteous indignation, I stared at the computer screen. It was definitely time to get out of the house and blow off some steam. I gathered up the sunscreen, Hayden's beach toys, and a towel, shoved them into a bag, and headed out. I strapped her into the car seat, and she babbled away happily to herself as I tried the engine. It just ticked over. The battery was dead. The alternator had been playing up for ages, and I knew it was only a matter of time before it died. I tried it again and again, despite knowing it was useless, while sweat stuck my dress to my back. Without the air-con, Hayden and I had to get out of the hot car as soon as possible. I hit the steering wheel with my fists, mouthing, "Fuck, fuck, fuck," so that Hayden wouldn't hear me cursing out loud. She'd already witnessed enough out-of-control behavior from her mother for one day.

I'd promised her the beach, and now what? With no car, the day stretched ahead interminably. Hayden and I could walk to the park, but it would be steaming at this time of day. And we couldn't take a minibus taxi to the beach: Mark had made me promise that I'd never use one with Hayden because he saw them as unsafe, and I couldn't disagree.

I climbed out of the car and unstrapped her. Oddly for her, she didn't question or whine about the change of plans.

"Hey."

I turned to see the guy from next door. "Hi, Karim." I tried to smile at him but could only manage a grimace.

"Car trouble?"

"Mm-hmm. My own fault. Needs a new alternator, but I've been putting it off and now the battery's dead."

"I'd offer to give you a jump start, but I only have a scooter."

"Thanks. We were only heading to the beach anyway." Hayden gave him a shy wave. "Do you want to come in for coffee?" It popped out before I could stop it.

He was taken aback. "Now?"

"Yeah. Look, it was just an idea. It's fine if you don't have time."

He checked the time on his cell. "Sure. Why not? I have to get to work, but I've got time for a coffee."

"Great!" This time my smile was genuine. I didn't care that he was only being kind, that he might have read the desperation in my eyes.

He was good enough to play *Frozen* with Hayden and Mermaid Barbie while I made the coffee. I felt fluttery and excited, like I was on a date. I know how that sounds, but it had been weeks since I'd hung out with anyone my age.

"I'm sorry about last night," I said, when Hayden was absorbed with Princess Elsa and her Duplo castle (fuck knows where Mermaid Barbie had got to), and he sat with me at the kitchen counter.

He was looking at me in confusion. "Sorry about what now?"

"Our alarm. It went off last night again. We'll get someone in to fix it soon, I promise." Thinking, *Before or after we buy a new alternator?*

"Oh. I didn't hear it."

"Were you out late?"

"Nah. I was in all night. Strange that it didn't wake me—I'm a light sleeper. Hey, I meant to ask, where did you go?"

"When?"

"You told me last time you went on holiday."

I took a sip of scalding coffee. "Paris."

"Oh, cool."

"Not really."

And then I found myself telling him everything. Well, almost everything: I left out the part where I discovered my husband clutching a dead cat. Karim was an excellent listener, interrupting only once when I told him about Mark discovering the hair in the closet.

"Hang on . . . *Hair?* What kind of hair?"

"Hair trimmings or something. Mark said there were buckets of the stuff." I didn't mention Mark's twitchy behavior after he'd returned from disposing of it, nor did I dwell on the fact that I hadn't actually seen it for myself.

"Ew."

I told him about the peculiar noises we'd heard in the night, the oddity of a building in a desirable area being empty. And then I came to Mireille's suicide. Verbalizing it really underscored the bizarreness and the horror of what we'd been through. I was also aware that it didn't sound plausible.

"That's hectic," he said when I wrapped up the story, adding a footnote about the Petits sending me a message asking for a review.

I didn't know him well enough to gauge if he believed the story or not.

He drained his mug. "Listen, thanks for the coffee, but I'd better get going."

"Really? I can make you another." I knew I sounded desperate, and again I didn't care. I didn't want to be alone. I didn't want Hayden and me to be alone, counting the hours until Mark got home.

"Sorry." He started heading for the door. "I'm going to be late. Great coffee, though."

He waved at Hayden, and I followed him to the front door. I reached around him to let him out, my bare arm brushing his. "Thanks for listening," I said.

"It was quite a story. And thanks for the coffee."

"Karim . . . what I told you about Paris. It was all true. I know how it must sound. Sorry for unloading on you; we hardly know each other and you must think I'm some kind of—"

He waved me into silence. "I didn't think you were bull-shitting me. Thanks for telling me about it. And sorry you had to go through that." He paused. "We should do this again."

I felt a momentary charge between us—I'm sure I wasn't imagining it or searching for an ego boost—then he left.

Still fluttery, but feeling strangely lighter and less unsettled than earlier, I called Mark again, left a message about the car, and asked him to have the alternator replaced. Fuck the cost. I cleaned the house, thankfully not discovering any more displaced belongings, then rooted through the freezer looking for something to cook for supper.

The hours crept by.

By six that night, Mark still hadn't returned home. I fed and bathed Hayden. I tried his cell phone over and over again. I lost count of how many times I tried it. His last lecture was at three, so unless they'd asked him to fill in for the evening classes—and he would always let me know if this happened—he should have been home hours ago.

Seven p.m. dragged into seven thirty. I put Hayden to bed and she fell asleep almost immediately. I paced, wondering if I should call the hospitals, alert the cops. But he'd done a similar thing last night after his therapy session. The area's usual dusky sounds—the bark of a neighbor's dog, the screech of tires—had an eerie, threatening edge.

In the end I caved and called Carla. "Is Mark with you?" I barked at her the second she picked up.

"No. Why would he be with me? Wasn't he supposed to go to his therapist again today?"

Was he? And why hadn't he told me that? "He's not back yet."

"Have you tried his cell?"

"Many times. He's not picking up." I was past caring if she thought our marriage was in trouble or not.

"You sound stressed, Steph."

"That's an understatement."

"Shame, Steph, it's been hard, I know. And I'm sorry about what happened in Paris. On top of everything else . . ." I could hear the faint sound of voices and laughter in the background; she was at a party, a restaurant maybe. "Listen. Mark told me that you think some of your things have been moved. I've been thinking, and it's possible that *maybe* I brushed up against a few items when I went in to check the house. But I certainly didn't rearrange anything on purpose. Didn't even make myself a coffee."

I didn't quite know what to say to that. Perhaps it *was* all in my mind. Could I have rearranged the books in the bedroom during the hectic spring cleaning session just before we left for Paris and forgotten about it? I suppose I should have apologized for accusing her—even by proxy—of riffling through my things, but the fact was I still suspected her of doing more than just innocently brushing up against the furniture. In the end I settled for, "The house feels weird."

"Of course it does, Steph. You were brutalized in it. That's completely understandable. And then your lousy experience in Paris. Well, it's a wonder you can even bear to stay in there for five minutes. And now Mark isn't home. Do you want me to come over?"

"No! I mean, thank you, but I couldn't ask you to do that. It sounds like you're out somewhere."

"It's nothing important. It's no trouble; I'm in the area. I'll be there in ten."

She hung up before I could dissuade her. But to be honest, part of me was relieved that I wouldn't be alone. I watched *MasterChef Australia* for a few minutes, jumping when the gate buzzer sounded despite steeling myself for it. Carla arrived dressed in some kind of Tibetan-monkish robe laced with gold thread, a waft of booze trailing behind her. Perhaps, I thought, this was why she was being so kind: she was drunk. She gave me her usual air-kiss treatment. "I tried Mark as well," she said the second I let her in. "No answer."

She gripped my wrist with her cold fingers and pulled me into the kitchen. "Come on. You need a drink."

Before I could stop her, she pulled out one of Mark's bottles of Meerlust, a present from an old university friend, and dug in the drawer for the bottle opener. She poured us both a glass, moving around the kitchen with more possessiveness and confidence than I'd ever felt in it.

She leaned against the counter and took a slug of wine. "You know, I've been thinking about what you've been saying about the house. About the bad vibes."

I took a sip from my own glass. The wine was smooth and woody—delicious. Mark had been saving it for a special occasion, and now I knew why. "It's probably just my—"

She flapped a hand to cut me off. "I know how it sounds. Bad vibes, blah blah. Mumbo jumbo, sure, but just hear me out." She took a dramatic swig of wine. "God, that's good. What about getting someone in to erase them?"

"Erase what?"

"The bad vibes."

"You mean like an exorcist?"

"Like a sangoma, a healer."

I laughed. Carla didn't. *"Seriously?"*

Carla nodded. "Seriously."

"Carla, Mark and I are atheists. We're not even slightly spiritual."

"Yes, I know. But what can it hurt? Maybe it's all in your head. Maybe it is just your imagination. But then again, maybe you picked up some bad energy in Paris, brought it back with you. You guys had a tough time there. Why not keep an open mind to these things?"

I thought back to what Mireille had said just before she killed herself, which seemed less like gibberish now and more like a warning: *I think maybe it will go with the last people . . . Now I must take it with me, or it is with you.* "A sangoma, though. How would I even get hold of one?" The sangomas I knew of were charlatans, guys who advertised their trade via fliers in Cape Town station, offering a cure for everything from TB to erectile dysfunction.

"I know one. She came over from Holland ten years ago when she had the calling."

"Wait . . . she's white?"

She shook her head sadly. "Not all Dutch people are white, Steph." But even Carla could see that I was in no mood to be patronized and she changed her tone. "But, yes. She does happen to be white. So what?"

"Have you ever used her?" *And if so, for what?*

"No, but I met her at a friend's book launch and we hit it off."

Well, that's okay, then. I wanted to laugh in her face. I thought about asking how someone from Amsterdam went about getting "the calling," but I didn't want to get into a discussion about cultural appropriation. Instead I merely said, "Sure, why not?" Thinking next we could try a priest, a rabbi, and, finally, if all else failed, a divorce lawyer.

But Carla was already tapping a message into her phone.

The answer pinged straight back, almost as if the whole thing had been prearranged. "She can come the day after tomorrow."

I was about to respond when I heard Hayden calling me. "I'll just be a minute."

Carla waved me away and grabbed the wine bottle to pour herself another glass.

Hayden was sitting up in bed, hair mussed, her night-light casting princess-shaped shadows on the wall. "What is it, monkey?"

"Mumma. It's under there. I heard it."

"Under where?"

"The bed, Mumma." Now she was whispering. She didn't looked scared, simply tired.

"What is? The lady again?"

"I don't know, Mumma."

"There's nothing under there, Hayden, but Mumma will look-see, okay?"

"Okay, Mumma."

I got down on my hands and knees again and peered into the gloom under the bed. And just for an instant, a skittering, shadowy thing, flat and blank-faced and multi-limbed, darted for me like a trapdoor spider lunging for a fly. I jumped, knocking my head on the edge of the bed, blinked, and looked again. There was nothing there except for the lone sock I'd seen before.

Chapter 19

Mark

"So what Poe's really dealing with is somatized desire, the physiological and psychological expression of illicit yearnings that have no other way out. Their doppelgängers allow them to act out desires that polite society would never allow. It's the same in *Jekyll and Hyde,* of course. And we know from Stephenson, Stoker, Gilman, that the construct of polite society is the flimsiest veneer that covers a cesspool of abuse and corruption."

I'm scared to look up at the class. For some reason, this lecture is suddenly flowing from a place of genuine interest; today it's feeling less forced, less labored and dutiful than it has for years. Something's clicked in me, and I feel engaged with my subject matter like I was when I first studied it. But if I look up, I know I'll be met by that same depressing wall of twenty-three blank, bored faces. I suppose I can understand students at first-year level finding themselves marooned in a module they hate—expecting an easy, rote credit, they'll find they made the wrong choice. But the apathy and disinterest of third-year undergrads who've made the informed decision to take this module—one that's all about sex and death and dreams and blood—bewilders me. Why do they bother? Why are they here?

I glance across at my notes and rub my temples. I've become used to this constant exhaustion, but that doesn't stop me from wishing I could sleep. The bloody alarm went off again last night—this morning, whenever—and Steph went crazy, setting Hayden off. Of course the little girl will react like that when she sees her mother in a flat panic. For my part, I felt surprisingly calm as I scouted for the cause of the malfunction. It's another symptom of my improvement, I think. I'm able to remove myself from a situation; I'm starting to trust that the worst has happened and we'll be okay. That they're not coming back. The monsters threw their worst at us in Paris and we made it out alive. We'll be okay.

I feel all right; I really do. The therapy session was fun as an intellectual exercise. I can see how all those psychodynamic themes play out in the stories I'm teaching this semester, but Steph's really the one who should seek help. She's always alone in that house with Hayden—she could do with someone to talk to—and after last night I'm starting to wonder whether there isn't some sort of Munchausen thing going on, Steph feeding Hayden's fear, terrifying her just so that she can come and rescue her. If that's the case, I can't let it go on.

When I hear a giggle from in front of me, I realize that I've paused for rather too long. "Sorry, where was I?"

"They're just kids," Lindi reminds me whenever I stand in the office kitchen, complaining to her about the students' apathy. "They're tired. They've been working night shifts to pay for their fees or their drugs, they've been having panic attacks and nightmares, they've had breakups. Their lives are dramatic and consuming. Try not to take it personally."

So I continue, keeping my head down: "We can never be sure whether the situations Poe presents in the tales are merely symptoms in his narrators' hysterized imaginations or whether they really happened. You see—"

"Excuse me."

I almost don't hear and trundle out a few more words before a shifting and creaking bring me to a stop and I finally raise my eyes from the invisible audience of rapt acolytes embedded in my desktop and up to the real youngsters in front of me, who're craning around in their desks to the back of the classroom to see who's spoken. At first I can't see her, my eyes taking a while to focus farther than a couple of feet. Bright sunlight's glaring in between the blinds of the broad window along the side of the classroom and the kids' faces are sliced into two halves of shade and light.

I glance myopically toward the origin of the voice and she continues her question in a round, exotic accent. "What do you mean 'really happened'? It's fiction, *n'est-ce pas?*" She's at the back of the class, completely obscured by a trio of students in the row ahead who have shifted their desks together. I don't recognize her voice as I do some of her classmates'—it's the beginning of the semester and she may have swapped in from another stream—but at the same time there's something familiar, something warm and resonant about it.

"Well, yes, it is fiction, but depending on the structure of the story, there are several levels of reality between the author, the narrator, the protagonist, and the reader," I say, taking refuge behind a wall of theoretical discussion. "In this case, I'm speaking about reality on the narrative level; the disjuncture between what the narrator is describing and what—"

Then one of the boys in the row ahead of her turns in his seat, revealing the student in a glow of slatted light, and I'm struck silent. I know this girl; I place her immediately. She's been in my thoughts every day; I've thought about her every night as I've tried to sleep. It's the girl from the museum. It's Zoë, glowing golden in the sunlight. Zoë, alive and fourteen years old. I drag my eyes away and down.

I don't know how I get through the rest of the class, but twenty minutes later, chairs scrape and desks clatter. I've barely risked another glance upward in that time, and as the students file out, I suspect I've imagined her since no Odette-rasped blond angel trails the rest of them out.

As I watch them go, the last couple of kids turn back. "*Ooh la la,*" one mutters, and the other chortles. They're looking over my shoulder.

I turn too, and see her standing silent behind me, twisting a strand of her long hair in her fingers and scuffing one toe of her Scooby-Doo sneakers, just like the pair I bought for Zoë during her last winter, against the gray carpet tile.

"*Viens, Papa. Regardes,*" she says.

I turn away, scanning the classroom—half to make sure that the place is now empty apart from us, and half hoping that the girl will be gone when I turn back. But she isn't, so I pocket my wallet and keys and follow her out into the corridor and then through the stairwell door. Wordlessly and without looking back, she leads me up to the sixth floor of the block. I struggle to keep up with her young body as she rounds the final half flight up to the rooftop exit, and by the time I push through the heavy emergency-only door that's always wedged open by smokers with a mangled paint can, adjust my eyes to the silvered glare, and catch my breath, she's sitting on a ledge, languidly swinging her legs.

Finally she turns to look at me as I approach. In the sunlight, I get a good look at her at last. She's not Zoë—she's a good facsimile, but her face is a mask. Despite her easy smile, there's something effortful in her eyes, like she's concentrating hard on playing a part. At least that's what I tell myself, because Zoë is dead.

"Come and see," she says again, and again I catch the edge of an accent in her rich voice.

I push myself up to sit next to her, the tacky silvering burning my hands as I press on it. The ledge overlooks a lower roof across a narrow alley, where a grubby flock of pigeons is bobbing and jostling over the remnants of a pie, all watched over unseen by a dusty gray cat in the shadow of a stack of crates. Table Mountain looms over the cluster of boxy buildings scattered in its shadow as a pungent mélange of restaurant smells, trash, and exhaust presses on the stiff breeze into our faces. It flips a skein of the girl's hair into her eyes and she brushes it away before latching on to a hank and twisting it around her finger like she did in the classroom.

When she stops twisting her hair, several strands blow off her fingers and onto my shirt, into my face. I move to sweep them off, but she's looking out in the other direction, a vague smile on her face, and I find myself gathering the hairs together, winding them up, and putting them in my pocket.

"What did you want me to see?" I say.

She frowns, as if disappointed that I'm keeping up the pretense that brought us up here.

The gray cat has been looking up at us with its yellow eyes, flicking its tail in annoyance at our presence. Now it turns back to stalking the birds, jiggling its butt.

"Look at that," she says.

"At what?"

"That disgusting thing."

"What?"

"The *cat*, Papa. I hate cats," she says, something cold grating in her voice. "They make me choke."

My heart spasms. "Who are you?" I say. "Why are you here?"

Her only answer is a shrug.

"What have you done with her?"

Now she turns. "With who?" *Wiss oo?*

"With my daughter. With Zoë. When she was small."

"She grew up." Her green eyes lock into mine and I'm afraid she's going to push into me, kiss me, bite me, like she did at the museum. My thighs are burning on the hot ledge now and I'm lifting myself off it when there's a clash and a noisy plosion on the rooftop opposite. The cat has launched itself at the pigeons and they panic and shatter into the air, making directly toward us. Instinctively, I raise my arms to defend my face and my head, and I'll swear that I feel the birds' wings and claws scratching against me as they wheel and right themselves and swarm away.

When I've calmed myself enough, I see the girl at the edge of the rooftop, now flipping her legs over. I hurry toward her as she sits, lifts both her hands, and gathers her hair away from her face, twisting it behind her in a loose knot.

"Stop!" I say. "Be careful!"

She turns to me. *"Pourquoi, Papa?"*

"Because I . . ."

"I'm always here." She leans forward and tips herself over the edge.

Of course when I run and look over, there's nobody on the sidewalk below.

I'm still shaken by the time I get back to my office. Luckily, Lindi's door is closed, so I manage to avoid her well-meaning inquiries. Even though it's my consultation time, I lock my own door behind me and sit at the desk. It was only in my imagination, I tell myself, but my mind is at an uncanny distance from my viscera. What just happened—part of it, at least—was real, but I can't say where or when the reality changed to imagination. I'm trying to recall the order of events directly, but there's a blank spot over them that evades my grasp.

I can't explain it to myself, so I pick up the phone and call Carla. I end up telling her about seeing Zoë in the waxworks museum and how she has somehow followed me here.

"It's understandable, Mark, sweetie. You have such a rich mind—it's trying to help you out of your trauma, into a world where none of the bad stuff ever happened, into a world where Zoë survived. Of course there are layers of guilt associated with that thought—you blame yourself, though heaven knows we've told you it's not your fault. We'll—your friends will—just have to keep repeating that until it's played out."

"But it's not just my mind, Carla. I've never experienced anything like this before. I'm not someone who goes wandering around in the grip of vivid hallucinations."

Carla doesn't respond, and I read something judgmental in her silence. I need to prove—to her, to myself—that I didn't just cook this up. Then I remember: I push my hand into my trouser pocket, and, yes, there it is. I pull out the knot of blond hair I gathered. It's quite a big skein, more than I remember brushing off my clothes, but there it is—proof that something happened, that I didn't completely imagine a windy conversation with a long-haired girl.

"Anyway, it's high time I called Marlies."

"Marlies?"

"I've told you a hundred times, Mark. My Dutch friend. The sangoma. She calls herself Gogo Thembi now."

I remember now. Ever since the burglary, Carla's been threatening to have someone over to our house to cleanse it of the evil spirits. I thought she meant just a regular woo-woo spiritualist, but it's Marlies the Dutch witch doctor. "What's she going to do? Chase away our trauma with chicken bones and a hunk of Gouda?"

"You should open your mind a bit." Her voice is cold; my flippant remark seems to have offended her. "That's your problem right there. Eighty percent of this country uses sangomas for all manner of problems. You don't have to be so fucking superior. This is a legitimate form of therapy. She can cleanse your house. Cleanse you."

The liberal offense she's taken provokes me. "Since when are you the champion of African traditional medicine? Last I heard, high-fat low-carb was going to save your life, make you a better you."

"Oh, fuck off, Mark. I'm trying to help. You have darkness in you—legitimate darkness, I know—but wouldn't you like relief? Since the attack everything's just become worse for you—and your family. Wouldn't you want to try *anything* to help alleviate your situation?"

"Christ, Carla. We don't need a fucking cleansing. I need some sleep."

"You never ask for help. That's another of your problems, while we're on the subject." She laughs. "But there are many people and many structures out there to help us when we're in need. The human family is vast. And it's good, Mark. Can you bring yourself to believe that?"

I don't say anything.

"Anyway, despite what you might think, African healing is not magic; it's not witchcraft. It's a philosophy, just as valid as any other religion or secular philosophy. Just like them, it's a therapeutic system, offering us solutions when times are hard. Nobody believes in real ghosts, but just like your priest or your therapist or your secular European atheist philosophers, sangomas can help you to chase down and understand your dreams, offer you life advice, help to exorcize your psychic ghosts."

Her argument is convincing, if only because it relativizes everything into a mash of inoffensive spiritual comfort food. "What suddenly makes you the expert?"

"I saw a documentary the other night."

I snort out a laugh. "Even if I did agree, we can't afford it." My refrain. "I've just taken out another overdraft to pay for Jan's bloody alarm system. Anyway, Steph'd never agree to having someone like that in our house."

"Don't you worry. I'll convince her. I'm very persuasive, you know. Especially when it comes to what's best for you, my friend."

————

When I get home later, it's to find Carla in my living room, drinking the Meerlust Geoff gave me at my UCT send-off, watching my TV.

She looks me up and down, as if I'm the unexpected intruder. "What have you done to yourself?" she says.

"Where's Steph?"

She looks at what I'm holding in my hand. "Why don't you put that away and clean yourself up?"

I go through to the kitchen, turn on the kettle, and put my parcel in the box in the pantry, then come through to wash my hands and arms in the bathroom. In our bedroom, I dump my shirt in the hamper, put on a clean tee, and go to rejoin Carla in the living room. But as I step into the hallway, I see Steph backing carefully out of Hayden's room. She turns and startles when she sees me. For an unguarded moment her face is blanched and her eyes wide; then she gathers herself, frowns, and beckons me into the kitchen.

She folds her arms, stands ten feet away from me—as far as possible in this room. "Where've you been?" she says.

"Who invited *her* over?" I hiss.

"She invited herself over, of course." She doesn't bother to lower her voice. "Where have you been?"

"Therapy. Traffic was bad."

I can see her clenching her jaw, forcing herself not to respond, not to accuse me of anything, not to start anything while Carla's here, but she can't help glancing at the clock on the wall. It is after nine.

"Is Hayden okay?" I ask, trying to deflect her.

"Jesus, Mark. No, she's not okay. She's completely unsettled. She can't get into a deep sleep, and I think she's becoming sick again."

Not for the first time today, I worry that Steph might be making Hayden sick, or at least that her anxiety is having a bad effect on her.

"Listen, Steph," I say as Carla comes through from the living room and stands in the kitchen doorway. "Maybe you've been here in this house by yourself too much. We could put Hayden in day care. Maybe it's time we should think about finding a job for you."

When Marlies the sangoma rattles up to our house just before noon two days later, I'm not in the mood. And she does rattle—her beaded bracelets and dangly necklaces and the cloth bag draped over her shoulder hammer against her drum as she locks up her Kia on the roadside and crosses, ignoring the shout of a couple of stoned homeless people who're leaned up against the neighbor's wall.

I watch her through the front window as she opens the gate and then stops. She puts down the drum and her bag and frowns up at the house. Under her beaded headband and her long skirt, she seems to be about my age—late forties maybe—squat body, a clutch of drained and unkempt pale hair scraped out of the back of the headdress. She seems to sniff the air for a minute, wobbling slightly on her legs as if standing in a gentle tide; then she picks up the drum and bag and turns away, back to the gate, where she stops again, undecided.

I help her choose. Now that she's here, there's no point in her leaving, is there? I open the door and call out: "Hi. Marlies?" I can't bring myself to call her "Gogo Thembi."

She looks at me and scans me with the same hesitant eyes as she's used on the house.

"Everything okay?" I step down from the porch toward her. "Can I give you a hand?"

"No," she says.

"Are you going to come in?"

She takes a deep breath in and follows me, muttering something low under her breath—whether in Dutch or isiXhosa or Elvish, I can't tell. I let her in the front door, and she closes it behind her, as if she's the one who's ashamed of this transaction. She puts her things down in the hallway and puts her hands on her hips and tracks her eyes around the entrance.

"Your wife and child are out, yes?"

"Yes," I say. One of the rare things Steph and I have agreed on lately is that Hayden definitely doesn't need to be involved in this.

"Good," she says. "It's better for the small one not to be here." For a moment I'm lulled into a sense of normality. I looked at the documentary Carla recommended on YouTube, and apart from some sensible comments from a professor of anthropology—where Carla picked up her semi-convincing arguments about philosophies and therapeutic systems— nothing about the suburban sangomas themselves inspired any confidence. It all looked like a ridiculous act to me, aging hippies indulging their need for drama and ululation, sprinkling their middle-class diction with explosions of *Eish!* and *Wena!* and *Aikhona!*, phrases they picked up from the *Madam & Eve* cartoons they read with their herbal tea when they're off duty. And of course the rural elders who trained them just did it for the easy money. Why wouldn't they? There's an ex-postman from Liverpool who's now a sangoma; his British pounds must have done his trainer's village a lot of good. There was a vegetarian sangoma from Sandton on the show, who had the trainer slaughter the goat and the chickens for her.

So far, though, apart from the getup, Marlies is behaving like a normal person, not putting on an act. She seems convinced about herself, which helps me ease into this charade. Let this be an experience I can open myself to; it's like listening to somebody else's story for a while; that's all.

She's now started to wander off, and I trail her into the living room. "But your other girl," she says, staring at the photos on the bookshelf and at the beading around the ceiling. "She's still here."

My mood turns immediately. Fucking Carla. She must have told this woman my whole bloody history. When will she understand that it's nobody's business? "No, there's no other girl."

Marlies doesn't bother to turn to me as she says, "She's the one you need me to take away."

No. No. There's a pull inside me, like a hook going in and ripping out.

"Hang on," I start to say, but she's opening her cloth shoulder bag, muttering under her breath.

"We need to appeal to the ancestors, ask them what is their plan."

I don't want Zoë erased. I never want her to leave me. That is not what I want. I hurry up to her, trying to ward her back into the hallway without touching her. "Let's leave it, you know. It's fine. It was just something my wife wanted. You can go. Let's do this another time." I'm battling to keep my voice calm.

Finally she looks up at me, just for a moment, and says, "It's out of your hands." Then she moves over to the far corner of the room, whispering gently under her breath as if trying to seduce the shadows.

My body tenses and my mind starts to focus in animal instinct. She's become a direct threat to my child. The hook goes in again, rips out more of me. But still, somehow, I can't bring myself to touch her, to wrestle her up and throw her out of the house. It feels somehow as if she's protected.

So I stand in the doorway and talk, my fucking solution to everything. I try to raise my voice, try to sound authoritative. "Listen," I say, "this is our home and you must leave."

But Marlies is not listening. She's squatted down and has

started burning something, her voice now beginning to rise into an unintelligible gibber. "Did you hear me? You need to go." I approach her, but the smoke she's making is thick and acrid, shit smelling, and somehow I can't find my way through it.

At the same time the witch stands and waves the burning leaves under my face, now yelling something, her eyes rolling back, the vibration from her lips and chin rippling down her whole body. The sound from her chest is too low, too loud, and I need to back away. I gasp, sucking in a lungful of smoke, which causes me to gasp again. I have to breathe it out but my chest is ground into a spasm and the smoke has broken into my body. I can feel it invading every cell.

And now there's something wrong with my eyes, because I see flashing lights against gray fog and shapes forming out of the mist. There's the shambling shape of a hunchback, a man in ancient clothing grasping at a stab wound in his chest. A metal face lurches at me, clanking open to reveal only a skull. The waxen skin of a Nazi soldier comes too close to my face, the smell of rot trailing it as it passes. A broken man swings a hatchet at a small, cowering figure. Three large men in balaclavas shout orders as they thunder down the wooden hallway.

This is not real. I've seen this before. It's just a memory.

And as if I've willed it away with my affirmation, the fog clears to reveal my living room, almost as it was, but now dark, when the morning sun was just shining in. As the last drapes of fog clear, one shape remains standing. A small girl. She looks at me, cocking her head.

It can't be, but it is.

I look behind me. The witch doctor is gone, but I can still hear her sobbing gasps. The smoke is still in the air, but now it smells sweet, like incense.

Zoë is staring at me, angry, deep blue rings around her eyes, a smear of vomit over her chin. And now she winces and starts to cry, as if something she loves has been crushed in front of her. The hook pulls inside me again, and I know she's feeling the same thing.

I go to her. "It's all right, sweetie. I won't let her take you away from me."

But she's looking through me, to where I was standing before, talking over me as if she can't hear me. "I must show you something," she says, in a voice that's not hers, the sound of it grating through pain-clenched teeth. I hear a knocking sound coming from behind my ear.

I follow her as she leads me through to the kitchen, pushes the swollen door into the pantry.

She opens the cardboard box I've been using, the one I've stashed behind the gas bottles for winter. "What have you done, Mark?" she says.

I look down, into the box. "I wanted to make you better. I wanted to bring you back, love."

"No," she says. "It has to be alive."

Chapter 20

Steph

"Mumma, everything smells bad." Hayden scrunched up her nose the second we walked through the front door. Mark and I had decided that it was best for her not to be present while Carla's sangoma did her thing, and now that the car was fixed, I'd taken her to the beach and then to Pick n Pay for the afternoon. I wished now that we'd been able to stay out longer, but she'd become testy in the supermarket, the day's heat making her irritable. And she was right: the whole house reeked of burned sage or whatever crap the sangoma had used to "cleanse" it.

Mark emerged from the kitchen, mumbled a greeting, and dutifully helped me with the plastic grocery bags. He looked furtive, as if I'd just caught him watching porn.

"So?" I said, hefting Hayden into a more comfortable position on my hip. "How did it go?"

He shook his head. "Exactly as you'd expect. I have no idea why I agreed to it."

"*We* agreed to it."

"Yeah."

"The place stinks. What did that woman use in here?" *And why did you let her?*

He shrugged. "I don't know."

I slid Hayden into her chair, promised to make her cheesy pasta, and started to unpack the groceries. I pulled at the fridge door, but it wouldn't open—it did that sometimes. I gave it an almighty tug that almost caused it to fall on top of me, and this time the door flew open, exhaling a foul whiff of vinegar and spoiled meat. The source of the rotten meat stench seemed to be a half-finished packet of bacon, which shouldn't have gone off so quickly, and the vinegar stench clearly emanated from an opened tub of pickled herring I didn't remember buying. And that wasn't all. A bottle of tomato sauce had spattered its contents over the vegetable drawer, already drying to a sickly crust.

"Did you do this, Mark?"

"Huh?" He was miles away again, frozen mid-move as he packed spaghetti into the cupboard.

"Did you move stuff around in the fridge?"

"No. Of course I didn't." He sounded irritable, annoyed that I'd jolted him out of his thoughts. "Why would I?"

"Well, someone did." I stepped aside so that he could look at the damage himself. Fucking Carla. It had to be her. It would be like her to show up when the sangoma was doing her thing. She wasn't one to miss the action.

He showed no surprise at the mess. "I'll clean it up."

"How did it happen, though? Did Carla—"

"Not now, Steph." He looked meaningfully at Hayden.

"Mark—"

"Someone must have knocked against the fridge during the"—he flapped a hand above his head—"the cleansing."

"It looks deliberate to me."

He didn't answer, merely rooted the bleach and a clutch of rags out from under the sink.

While I made Hayden's food, he doggedly picked through the fridge, pulling out the trays and rinsing them under the tap. It seemed to me that he was deliberately avoiding looking at me. I had to ask him twice if he wanted something to eat, and he mumbled something about eating earlier. The smoky stench had erased my appetite.

Hayden picked halfheartedly at her pasta and yawned. "My tummy feels funny, Mumma."

Mark chucked the cloth he was using in the sink and approached her. "You want to come watch a movie with Daddy?"

I couldn't tell if he genuinely wanted to spend time with her or if he was looking for an excuse to get away from me. She nodded and yawned again, and stretched out her arms to him. Somehow I stopped myself from snatching her from him, and instead leaned against the kitchen counter and listened to the opening track of *The Lego Movie*. I couldn't face clearing up. I wanted to convince myself that the sangoma's juju, or whatever it was, had worked, that the house was now free of its taints, but the mess in the fridge had shaken me. It had to have been Carla, but I couldn't quite believe that of her. The smoky odor wasn't receding; if anything, it was getting stronger. And I still couldn't bring myself to open a window.

I peered into the living room to check on Mark and Hayden—they were both staring blank-faced at the screen and didn't notice me spying—then returned to the kitchen and opened my laptop, hoping that the house swap site would have finally responded to my furious email about the Petits' behavior. It hadn't. Nor had the book agent got back to me, although that was understandable, as she'd had the full manuscript for only a week. I daydreamed idly about book launches, picturing (to my shame now) Carla seething jealously in the back of a crowded bookstore. *Maybe,* I thought, *I should use the time to join a temping agency. Mark had mentioned something about me returning to work in front of Carla two days ago—he could've at least waited until she was out of earshot.* Restless, I made myself a cup of tea, then surfed around on the internet for a while, telling myself that I'd hunt for a job in the morning. The spectacularly handsome real estate agent we'd spoken to in Paris had said his boss wouldn't be able to help us with our inquiries about the Petits for another week at least, but I couldn't see the harm in sending him an email. I dug in my bag for the business card and sent him a message explaining who I was, that I was looking into the history of the Petits' building and was curious about why it was empty.

I logged on to Facebook, feeling a rush of guilty joy when I saw that Karim had sent me a friend request. Seconds after I accepted it, a message from him blipped onto the screen:

<Hey. Been thinking about your story. You checked out other sites????>

<hey! What sites?>

<like airbnb, couchsurfer.com, stuff like that. Your owners might have advertised on those too>

He had a point. I couldn't forget that Mireille had mentioned that other people had stayed in the apartment—it was entirely feasible that the Petits had lured other people into their place via other means. I should have thought of it myself.

<thanks>

<no worries>

I paused for a second, then wrote:

<Coffee tomorrow?>

There was no answer for a couple of minutes, then:

<cool. What time, lectures till 1 then got to be in work at 5>

A shiver of anticipation: Mark would be at work from ten until four.

<3?>

<see you then>

Next, I typed in the building's address and "accommodation to rent in Paris." Bingo: I couldn't be sure, but it looked like it had once been listed on another house swap website. But when I clicked on the link, nothing came up. I scrolled through link after link until I came to Parisdreaming.com, which catered to American travelers seeking budget accommodation. Below the same picture of the bathroom that the Petits had posted on our house swap site there was a single review:

> *Don't stay here. It smells bad & has no air-con. Don't be fooled into thinking your getting a bargain because it is not worth it. We left after 2 days.*

The review was posted last July, but there wasn't a place for me to leave a comment, and when I clicked through to the site's contact details I hit a "page not found" wall. Frustrated, I pressed the go-back key, but after half an hour of fruitless searching, I couldn't seem to locate the page again. I was about to give up when I came across a link to an accommodation forum for ex-pat Brits. A thread had been started by a Mrbaker9981 in September last year, entitled *DON'T STAY HERE*. The poster had written the Petits' address in caps, followed by: *came across this hellhole on a cheap accommodation site that conveniently is no longer active. Worst place I have ever stayed in. Hot, smelly, and owners didn't show up and refused to give us a refund after we left early. It was haunted as well and not in a good way. YOU HAVE BEEN WARNED.*

Two other posters had responded with messages along the lines of *thanks for the heads-up* and *is there a good way to be haunted?* but Mrbaker9981 hadn't replied to them.

Heart beating harder, I signed up to the site, left a message saying that I'd stayed at the same "hellhole," and shamelessly begged Mrbaker9981 to contact me. I included my email address—I didn't care if I got spammed because of it.

On a whim, I googled the username in case he was signed up to other forums under the same moniker. And I struck gold. He appeared to be active on two other sites: *The Guardian*'s Comment Is Free, and loveulots.co.uk, a "discreet" hookup site for married people. Without hesitating, I joined the dating site (I had to pay two hundred rand to do so and fill in a questionnaire) and went to his profile. I scrolled straight to the "leave a message" button and left a slightly more desperate plea, asking if he was the same man who'd posted on the accommodation forum and entreating him to get hold of me to share information. The site's rules stated that I couldn't leave my email address unless he messaged me back.

I'd been so absorbed in my detective work I hadn't noticed that the house was now quiet and the movie had ended. In the living room, Mark and Hayden were asleep on the couch. She was lying on his chest, one of his arms loosely draped over her. Here's where I'm supposed to say that I was overwhelmed by a feeling of love, but I just felt that same uneasiness, as if his gesture was possessive rather than caring. I uncurled his arm— he didn't wake, and his skin was slimed with sweat—and picked Hayden up. She protested blearily, then flung her arms around my neck and her legs around my waist, monkey-style.

As usual, I turned on her nightlight and lay down next to her on the bed. The sense that we weren't alone in the room didn't creep up this time; it flashed through me. I turned my head to the side and saw that something dark was lurking in the corner of the room next to the chest of drawers. A scream locked in my throat as I watched the blank-faced thing writh-ing in place on its multi-limbed form. I blinked, and it was gone. Frozen with fear, I didn't move for at least a minute. Gradually, I sat up, then scurried in a panicked burst to turn on the main light. The room felt empty again. It didn't take a rocket scientist to figure out what my mind was trying to conjure up: a monstrous amalgam of the men who'd broken into the house and terrorized us. And again, when I checked under the bed, there was nothing but Hayden's lonely sock. After taking ages to muster up the courage, as if I half expected it to bite me, I reached under and grabbed it. There was some-thing else a few feet from it. Zoë's hairbrush. The one that had fallen behind the chest of drawers. Or maybe it wasn't Zoë's. No matter: what the hell was it doing there? I wrapped it up in the sock, intending to put it in the trash can.

I couldn't leave Hayden alone, but nor could I sleep. Lights blazing, I read my way through her shelf full of picture books, determined to stay awake until the morning light came. I sup-pose I must have dozed off as the hours passed, because the next thing I was aware of was the sound of the shower run-ning. Hayden was still in dreamland, her fists curled into her chest, her hair sticking to her forehead. Careful not to wake her, I got up and tiptoed down the hallway to the bathroom. I could make out the murmur of Mark's voice through the half-open door. Was he on the phone? Ridiculous—he was in the shower. I gently pushed the door open and listened. I couldn't make out any individual words through the spit-spattering of the water; then came: "I did it for you. I *said* I did it for you." His voice rose with every word.

I ripped the shower curtain back, and he jumped and turned to face me.

"Why are you talking to yourself, Mark?"

"I wasn't . . . Hey, how about some privacy here?" He tried to chuckle, but it sounded like a death rattle. He wasn't the man I'd married, whom I'd once felt such desire for. What-ever mental battles he was waging were taking their toll on his body. He'd lost weight; I could discern every rib. His skin was corpse white and, despite the steam and hot water, rid-dled with gooseflesh, and there was a scribble of scratches and nicks over his arms. A bright blue network of varicose veins bulged beneath the skin of his calf. *Old,* I thought, *you're old.* He turned off the water and bent down to grab a towel. "Is Hayden up yet?"

"No, Mark. What's going on with you?"

"I don't know what you mean."

"You've been distancing yourself from me and Hayden ever since we got back from Paris." That wasn't true. It had started before then. Way before then. Since the night the men broke into the house.

He dried himself hurriedly. He'd lost too much weight. I tried to remember that firm body I'd lusted after, but all I could see were these stringy arms, this concave chest. His cheeks sagged. "I'm getting help, Steph. That's what you wanted me to do, wasn't it? I'm seeing someone like you asked."

"Mark, *please* talk to me."

"Go make us some coffee and we'll talk."

"Really?"

He smiled. "Really."

Had I just seen a flicker of the old Mark? But as desperate as I was not to let things slide even further out of my control, I knew that was just wishful thinking.

I looked in on Hayden on my way down to the kitchen. Unusually for her, she was still asleep. I hesitated and then peered under her bed. Nothing. Of course there was nothing. I dropped the hairbrush into Hayden's trash can, reminding myself to dispose of it later.

The kitchen still held a trace of that foul burned smell,

the dishwasher needed unstacking, the stove was spattered with grease, and the microwave door was peppered with melted cheese bits from Hayden's supper. I dug through the cupboards, hunting for clean mugs. We were nearly out of the good coffee. Mindful that Karim was coming over later, I spooned the emergency blend into the coffeemaker, not caring if Mark noticed.

When he joined me a few minutes later, he was dressed in a suit—the one he'd worn at our wedding and his father's funeral. He read my dubious look. "All of my other clothes are dirty."

I searched his face for a sign that he was pissed off at me for not bothering to do the washing. It would almost have been a relief to see such a normal emotion. "I've been busy."

"Doing *what* exactly?"

Since Hayden was born, we'd both avoided arguing about domestic niggles. He told me he'd had his fill of them with Odette; it was too easy to allow them to slide into fighting and resentment: *What do you mean we don't have any milk? Haven't you been at home all fucking day while I've been working? The least you could have done was empty the dishwasher before you left the house, blah blah.* I knew I should have let his sideswipe go, but instead I snapped: "Looking after your fucking daughter."

"My daughter is . . . my daughter is . . ."

"Your daughter is what, Mark?" Seconds passed without him responding. The coffee machine blipped and sizzled. "Mark? Hayden is *what*?"

"She's just sleeping, isn't she, Steph?" His voice was high and whiny, as if he was pleading with me.

Oh Jesus. "Yes." I cleared my throat. "You want some coffee?"

"No. I have to go."

"I thought we were going to talk."

"We will. Just not now."

It was five to seven. His classes didn't start before ten most days. With a small nod, he turned and walked into the hallway, grabbing his car keys from the hall table. He hesitated, returned to the kitchen, and pushed past me to enter the pantry. I didn't ask him what he was doing, nor did I ask what was in the battered shoe box he was now carrying under his arm. Without acknowledging me, he left the house, slamming the door behind him.

Refusing to allow myself to get upset, I went to rouse Hayden. She was groggy and complained of a sore throat. Her forehead was warm, but I wasn't too concerned—she often had colds. I settled her on the couch and let her play with the iPad. I filled time by taking a shower and spring-cleaning the kitchen with disinfectant. Its sharp odor made me think of sickness and hospitals, but at least it erased the stale, smoky stench. Next, I gathered up our dirty clothes and used the washer's sanitize cycle. I didn't want to dwell on Mark. More than one line had been crossed since we'd returned from Paris. Everything was out of synch. Instead, I thought about Karim. I thought about his skin, his hair, the small black tattoo that emerged out of the sleeve of his T-shirt (I didn't know what it was—I still don't know). He was everything that Mark wasn't. I admit it: I'd been thinking about him more than I should. It didn't occur to me then that maybe he'd been thinking about me too.

At two thirty I raced upstairs to get changed and hastily slapped on a layer of foundation, which wouldn't last in the heat. My fingers trembled as I tried to apply eyeliner. I wiped it off and started again.

The door buzzed at exactly three. Karim smelled of soap and shaving foam, as if he'd showered minutes earlier. The second Hayden saw him, she stretched out her arms for a hug, and he was forced to get to his knees next to the couch to greet her. I put *Frozen* on for her, which I knew would distract her for at least an hour, and Karim followed me into the kitchen. I was sweaty and self-conscious. Neither of us spoke while I readied the coffee things. Impulsively I said, "It's too hot for coffee. How about a beer?"

"Seriously?"

"Yeah. Why not?" I said, regretting the suggestion—what if he thought I was an alcoholic?

Then he smiled. "Yeah. Why not? One won't hurt."

This time the fridge door behaved. I dug out a couple of bottles left over from the night Carla and her friend came over for supper, and handed one to Karim. As we clinked, glancing into each other's eyes, I said, "Can I ask you a question? It's going to sound stupid."

"Go for it."

"Do you believe in ghosts?"

"Why?"

"It's just . . ." And then I told him about the thing under Hayden's bed. It all tumbled out: the sense I'd had in the Paris apartment that we weren't alone; the feeling that Mireille was there when I was back in the apartment after our night at the police station.

He listened carefully, like he had last time. I expected him to say something about trauma and imagination—he was a psychology student, after all—but instead he said, "There're lots of rational reasons people see ghosts. You know, stuff like infrasound, carbon monoxide poisoning. There's even a mold that people think might be the cause of hallucinations."

"A mold?" I looked down at my beer. It was empty. I didn't remember drinking it, but I didn't feel even slightly tipsy.

"Look here." He pulled out his phone and tapped something into it. He passed it to me. He'd downloaded an article about a group of scientists who'd discovered a link between hallucinations and toxic spores from mold found in old buildings. There was no concrete proof of their theory, and I didn't miss that the article was published in a British tabloid not known for its fact-checking.

I handed his phone back to him. "Interesting." *Could* we have brought something back from Paris? I shuddered at the thought of mold spores growing in my brain, infecting the neural pathways or whatever they're called. Perhaps that explained Mark's bizarre behavior as well. And that Mrbaker9981 review had mentioned something about the place being haunted. The theory was far-fetched and unproven, but it was better than the alternative: that Mark and I were basically going insane.

"Was there any mold in that apartment where you guys stayed?"

"Actually, yes. And it stank. What was that other thing you mentioned? Infrasound?"

"Yes. It causes a vibration that can make some people feel uneasy, or something like that." He grinned at me again and held up his phone. "Let me look for you."

I moved closer to him so that I could read what he'd called up on the screen. My shoulder brushed his arm. I don't know who started it—I'm being honest about this—but suddenly, I was in his arms, kissing him. I could taste the malty beer on his tongue and feel the solid weight of his muscled back under the shirt, so different from Mark's. His hands snuck under my shirt, and then I heard Hayden calling me. I jumped away from him. "Shit. You'd better go."

"Yeah." He shoved his phone into his pocket and followed me to the front door. We were both avoiding each other's eyes, and there was a moment of supreme awkwardness as I unlocked the gate and let him out of Alcatraz. My face was burning, not with shame exactly, but mortification at the thought that Hayden could have walked in on us. I hurried into the living room.

"Mumma, I'm hurty."

She was still warm, but not terribly, and I gave her some cold medicine just in case. I settled her back on the couch where I could keep an eye on her and returned to the kitchen. I stashed the beer evidence in the recycling bin, and while Hayden dozed, I turned back to the computer, intending to google the article about the ghost-inducing mold to distract myself from the guilt of what had just happened with Karim. I couldn't blame it on the booze.

My spam folder was heaving with messages from the dating site. I'd written only the sketchiest of profiles and hadn't uploaded a pic, but this hadn't deterred the site's members. I was about to delete the messages unread when I realized that one was from Mrbaker9981:

Dear Stephanie,

My name is Ellie Baker. You left a message on this site for my dad. I am ashamed that my dad was part of this site but he had a lot of troubles in his life on account of an abusive childhood and other things that I won't go into so I know he was looking for outlets & it's not his fault. I keep an eye on his emails & I forgot to cancel the debit order for the subscription which is how I was alerted to your message. Usually I would have ignored it but you seem like a nice lady so I thought I would reply to you. I have to tell you that he cannot help you with your inquiries about the apartment he stayed at with my mum in August last year in

France. He and my mum died in October in an accident.

Regards,

Ellie

At the bottom of the email there was a link to an article. I didn't need to click on it to make out the headline: "Two Die in Possible Murder/Suicide Crash."

Chapter 21

Mark

The wind hisses through the pines in Plumstead Cemetery, and the children's graves are making me cry again. The cracked-faced dolls and dead flowers, the yellowed cellophane around limp balloons, make this section look like a birthday party abandoned because of sudden tragedy. I know the pain of those families as they've laid their angels to rest. Nothing will make them feel better; they will never be whole again. I look over at the overblown Barney mausoleum and it reminds me of the excesses of grief; it makes me self-conscious; it stops my tears. You could paint the whole earth purple, you could tear it all up in your despair, but nothing will bring her back to you.

I wouldn't know how to explain to Steph what I've been doing here. Why now, why after all this time. She'd just imply that I should have got over it and that I should worry about Hayden instead. She's done with my grief.

I can't really explain it to myself. Sure, Zoë's always been with me in one way or another, but since Paris, she's with me much more viscerally. I can't explain that to Steph, or why I'm making my collection for Zoë—she'll just think I'm mad. She already does.

A flurry of guinea fowls traipse across the row of graves, absurd and precise in their spotted suits. I briefly consider them, but, no, feathers won't do.

Why should death provoke a normal response? Why should I be sane and measured, coldhearted in reaction to my loss? That's why Zoë's haunting me now: because I've tried so hard to tamp her down, to carry on with my life as if it could ever

be normal again. I must not allow my scars to heal; I must
not allow Steph to pressure me into forgetting her. My life is
defined by my scars, and to deny that is to deny that I ever
loved Zoë. I've been depriving Zoë of her voice, of an effect
on me; I've been depriving myself of my scars. More than anything, the home invasion brought that into focus for me: I am
nothing without my pain; I am nothing without my rage and
my fear.

I squat down by her gravestone, squeezed into Odette's
father's family plot, between her grandmother and an uncle.

ZOË SEBASTIAN

the stone says, and the seven years, three months, and one day
she lived with us.

MOURNED BY MARK AND ODETTE
WE WILL MISS YOU FOREVER

Those words are not enough to honor her, I know now, and
what we wrote there, Odette and I, is a promise never to forget.

I didn't plan it, but that afternoon when I left my first session with Santé, I spotted something dark on the side of the
dirt road, knotted into the veldtgrass and rubble mounded
along the drainage ditch. I knew it was some sort of animal
and I stopped the car in case it had been run over and was still
alive. Perhaps I could do something for it. I got out, approached
slowly, careful not to frighten it. It was fairly large—bigger
than a rat and smaller than a dog. Perhaps a ferret or an otter
or something wild. I can't say how, but it *felt* wild—I had a
distinct sense of its life-force and its desperation to live.

But when I got there, I saw that it was a domestic cat, and
it was dead, ripped open. It must have been hit by a car going
very fast. It must have died instantly. Fascinated by its body, I

squatted down to take a closer look. The skin on one side of
the wound was peeled back off the muscle, just like I've seen
rabbits skinned on a cooking show.

My mind turned to those buckets of hair in the Petits' apartment, and suddenly I understood. I felt a sense of clear direction that I haven't felt for as long as I can remember. Hair is
an archetypal symbol of vitality, sexual vigor, life-force. Think
of Samson and Delilah, Rapunzel, Ophelia, the hair-cutting
shame rituals practiced the world over. That's what they were
doing: it wasn't just filth, a sign of their perverse degradation;
the Petits (or whoever they were) were collecting life, distilling
vitality, a talisman against the cold, life-sucking mood in that
building. I felt guided; I finally felt some compelling purpose
in my drifting life. Zoë knew the answer all along. Her hair
collection succeeded—she healed Odette, after all. Perhaps it
was too late, but Zoë was asking me to try. When I decided
what to do, the raw-burned Zoë-shaped hole in me soothed,
the hook in my heart eased for just a moment, and I knew that
she'd approve.

I know it's not normal to remove a dead cat's pelt and keep
it, unless you're a biologist or taxidermist, but that's what I did.
It made complete sense to me at that time. Hair was life-force
distilled, even after death—it never rots away with the body. A
little collection of hair would be my talisman against the death
all around me. It might even help me start to live again.

Now I stand up from my daughter's graveside and turn my
hands over, run my finger over the cuts and bites and gashes
from the last few days. They sting, even though I've been dis-
infecting them. I must have scraped my hands on the weeds or
perhaps there was some barbed wire hidden in the grass.

I only intended it as a memorial for her; I didn't expect Zoë
to get involved. But when she came to me in class the next day
and gave me some of her own hair, I knew I had done the right
thing. After my session with Santé that next afternoon, I found

more roadkill. I thought I was doing the right thing, but now I'm unsure. Yesterday, when the sangoma came, Zoë told me it had to be alive to work.

Along the peripheral road, a funeral cortège arrives. I brace myself to leave in case they come this way, but the cars move on up to the far corner of the cemetery where the newer plots are laid. A scattered group of mourners walks up behind the cars, carrying bouquets and gaudy framed pictures of the deceased, some glancing over at me as they pass, and I see myself as I am: a sad, folded man in a suit, squatting over a weathered grave with an old shoe box.

What's wrong with me? I should have brought flowers for Zoë's grave, not a box of hair.

I sit on the grave's edge and lift the lid of the box. Here's the twist of blond hair to one side. I've tried to keep it separate from the pelts, which are starting to smell.

It has to be alive, she said to me.

I know it was just a message from my own mind. I know as well as Steph knows that Zoë doesn't exist in a physical sense—she's dead. All I'm experiencing is a particularly vivid set of symbolic images that's finally helping me process Zoë's death. It's been brought on by the psychotherapy, I'm sure, dislodging the symbolic patterns of my thought and rendering them concrete. But that doesn't mean I should discount what my unconscious is telling me.

Squirrels scurry up and down the pines and dart between the headstones. Zoë used to call them squillos; Odette and I didn't have the heart to correct her—it was just too cute. I take out the bag of peanuts, rip it open, and toss one on the pathway a few yards ahead of me. It's not long before a squirrel approaches, grabs up the nut, and stands staring at me, quivering on its back legs, sniffing for more. They're obviously used to being fed here and are almost as tame as the brazen squirrel gangs in the gardens in the city.

I chuck another peanut, halfway between it and me. The squirrel darts closer. Then another, only a foot away. Now I glance around me to see that nobody's watching, place a nut in my palm, and wait.

The squirrel hesitates to come within an arm's length; it's jittery, keeps darting looks back toward its cohorts. But it can't resist. It goes for the nut and I close my left hand over its shoulders. It squirms and scratches and tries to bite, but I have it in a tight hold, pinning its legs to its body.

The creature's heart is rattling so fast I think it'll pop. Its fur is warm and soft; a second ago, it trusted me.

"Sorry, squillo," I say, and let it go, tossing a handful of nuts far down the path for it to collect. The real Zoë, my living daughter who died irretrievably seven years ago, would never want me to kill an animal for her. I look back down at the box, the brown blood and shiny bits of flesh blooming damply against the cardboard. She wouldn't want this either. I pick out the skein of blond hair from the box and put it in my pocket. On my way out, I find a trash can and throw the stinky box away. It's too late to save her, I realize at last. I was never going to save her.

As I drive away, southward, not back home, I think of that headstone, the only place in the world that our names are set in stone together: Zoë, Odette, me. I park outside a little shopping center in Bergvliet, halfway to the sea, and dial.

"Hi, Odette."

A silence, a bracing, a gathering, the whole length from Bristol to Cape Town. "Mark. Hello."

"I'm disturbing you, aren't I?"

"No, not really. Same old." Sounds of children in the background. She has two, I think. She never got remarried. The last I heard, she was living with another guy, not their father. "Saturday morning, you know. Football, shopping."

"How are you?"

"Okay. And you?"

"Okay, thanks." Then I realize I didn't call Odette to swap pleasant lies. "I've been going to therapy."

"Oh?" Instantly wary.

"Yes. It's been bringing back a lot of"—*ghosts?*—"memories."

"Sure. I suppose it would." I can hear the effort she's making to sound civil.

"I didn't want to disturb you. I was trying to remember. It's horrible how things get blurred. Funny question, I suppose, but was Zoë a cat person or a dog person?"

"You called to ask me that?"

"I don't know. Something's come up. She always hated cats, didn't she?"

"Hated cats? No. She loved them. Remember—you even got her those Hello Kitty sneakers for her seventh birthday."

"Hello Kitty? I don't think so."

"You *did*, Mark."

"Nah. I got her those little black high-tops with Scooby-Doo on them."

"Uh-uh. Why on earth would she want those? She hated that cartoon. It freaked her out. She got scared easily. You seriously don't remember?"

Her tone is fraying around the edges. She's still angry with me. She'll never forgive me, and I don't see any reason why she should. "Okay, thanks. Sorry to disturb you."

Hearing my discomfort, she relents and babbles on a little to comfort me. "It was definitely Hello Kitty. I remember thinking it was odd of you to go in for something so gendered. In fact, I've got the picture on my computer; I'm sure of it. I'm going to find it and email it to you." She was always kind like that. We loved each other.

"Thanks." I hang up and notice the sign for a little pub in

the center: one of those cheap steel signs sponsored by Castle Lager, WALTER'S BARREL. Why not? Steph only expects me back at four.

Locking the car, it strikes me that my suit is going to look odd in a place like this. But I have no choice; there's blood on my shirt. I check myself in the side mirror, button my jacket tightly, and push my way inside. It's only noon, but the bar's pretty full and stinks of yesterday's sweat and smoke and grease and today's beer. The front window is completely painted over by an advertisement, so I can barely make out anything in the gloom apart from clusters of men, maybe a couple of women, staring up at the TV screens, which are showing a rugby match.

I sit down at the bar, as the man behind the counter eyes me as if I'm taking a regular's seat. Normally this would be enough to send me back outside and home to my local, famil-iar, safe café, but not today. I sit up straight and order a draft. The barman gets pouring without a word.

"Getting married?" A man, two seats away, has turned to me with a friendly, toothless smile. He's eyeing my suit, wearing tracksuit trousers and a stained T-shirt himself. "A last dop as a free man?"

"Uh, no. Meeting," I say. "That sort of client."

"Sure," he says, looking back up at the screen above the bar.

"Who's playing?" I say.

"Stormers and Force."

"It's a bit early for rugby, isn't it?"

"It's in Perth," he says. "Australia." He shifts his body away from me, turning his face back to the screen. "Ja, you know. Super-rugby what-what."

I can't help feeling like I've disappointed him. For a minute, I wish I could have come in here with an interesting story— a story of altar shirking or last-night prostitutes—one that would help him escape for a minute.

I take a deep pull from my tasteless beer and look around the space. Now that my eyes are accustomed to the gloom, I notice the mismatched, stained, and scratched dark-wood furnishings, the quiet drinkers looking up at the screens as if they're portals away from their lives and they've just closed forever. It's not the time of day for jolly drunks, and it's too early in the season for anyone to get excited about the game. There's a step up to a room with a few pool tables, where music is playing from a fake jukebox, a molded plastic front with a satellite station playing obligatory radio pop from a speaker inside. A couple of young women move listlessly to the music. I can't tell if they're drunk or stoned or just tired, but it's wrong to see people moving like that at noon.

I stare up at the TV and it seems just a couple of moments later when my phone buzzes, but when I look in front of me, my glass is empty and the first half of the game is done and there's an advert for a car playing. My phone's beeping in my jacket pocket. The barman juts his chin at my beer glass and I nod and check the message on my phone.

Nice, if a bit weird, to hear from you. You sounded strange. Hope all's okay with you?

Here's the picture.

x

I push back from the bar, vaguely aware of the patrons looking at me as I stumble over the worn wooden floor, following my instinct to the bathroom, through the pool room, through the arched hallway toward the smell of piss and pink freshener blocks and finally get to slam a door behind me and gasp at the pain of my shock.

When I've gathered myself, I splash water on my face, trying to ignore the grime on the basin glaring clearly in the daylight that streams through the high-level windows. I flick the phone on again, trying to immunize myself. I've seen this picture before. I had a copy of it myself, but it was on my old computer and I just backed all those photos up onto a drive and never looked at them again. Zoë with her birthday shoes. And her smile that shreds me all over again.

It's a while before I hear the knocking.

Someone says something. A woman's voice, gentle.

I stand up, try to straighten myself, wet my face again. In the mirror I see blood on my shirt.

Knocking again. The voice. I can't make out what it's saying.

The door's opening.

"*Qu'est-ce qu'il y a, Papa?*"

It's her, the girl. She's got a star on her pink T-shirt today, green jeans. On her feet are dopey Great Danes.

"You're not her, are you?" I say.

"Not who?" *Naut oo.*

"My daughter. She's dead."

She comes closer, until she stands an inch from me. I can feel the electricity coursing through her body, charging every follicle in my skin. A shadow covers the light from the windows, but she glows with a Kirlian aura crackling purple and luminous black. I feel the energy reaching to me and sparking off me, burning as it invades. She opens her lips and tells me, "I am yours. I am your anything. I am what you want."

Her breath is sweet and rotten, like fruit that's too ripe. She licks my mouth with her tongue, then bites my lip.

"What do you want from me?" I say.

"I want you to keep me alive." And now she touches my face, runs her fingers into the thin hair at my temple, and I'm blinded by an image that seems like mist, but I put my hands out and feel: it's hair. I part it, push through it, and still there's more; I'm cocooned in it. Soft, smelling of apple shampoo and fruity perfume. It's life.

How I used to hold Zoë to my chest and breathe her scent; her sweat, her dirt, the natural oils, the apple shampoo. It was love; I loved her too much and she couldn't breathe. I have her in me, her molecules still in my lungs.

A bang, a slam, the girl is gone, and there is blood running down my chin.

"Hey! Hey! What the fuck you think you doing with Dierdra?"

The man's first swipe is slow and I duck under it, and behind him, in the corridor, there's a woman staring at me with a mixture of fear and curiosity, like I'm an animal on exhibit. She's thirtysomething and ugly and dark haired, and she's wearing green jeans and a pink T-shirt with a star on it.

I turn away and get the man's second punch at the back of my skull. I'm down on the floor, mopping up the piss with my suit, heavy weight on me, some muffled pummeling in my back before the weight is pulled off and I'm dragged out of the bar and pushed to my car. The barman hands me my keys and wallet. "Thanks for the tip, friend. Hope you don't mind, I helped myself."

It's late when I get home. I've been thinking. About how I'm afraid of Hayden, of loving her so much that I suck away her life with my need. I killed Zoë, and even though I know there's no way to bring her back, I can keep her spirit alive.

Steph is passed out on the couch when I come in, an empty bottle of wine on the coffee table; Hayden's asleep in the armchair. When I go through to the kitchen, I find beer bottles dumped in the recycling bin, the good coffee mugs, the ones we keep for guests, in the sink.

I brush my jealousy aside. Steph's entitled to guests, after all, and I need to get started; she could wake up any minute, though the fact that Steph's drunk will help me. I throw my stinking jacket on the bathroom floor, take the scissors from the drawer, and approach Hayden. She's fast asleep as only a toddler can be. I sit down next to her and smooth the hair back from her face.

When I start, I only mean to take a little.

Chapter 22

Steph

Snick, snick.

Brain muggy from the wine I knocked back after Karim left the house, I sat up, neck stiff from sleeping awkwardly on the couch.

Snick.

The only light came from the television, which was silently tuned to a home-shopping channel. A figure was hunched over the armchair where Hayden slept. I didn't make a sound: I couldn't. I couldn't breathe. For a split second I was certain it was the slippery multi-limbed monster—*the thing that lived under the bed*—then it shifted its position and I realized it was Mark. Of course it was Mark.

Snick.

My voice came out in a whisper: "What are you doing?"

He froze, then looked over his shoulder at me. It was too dark to see his eyes, but he was gripping something metallic in his right hand—the light from the television bounced off it. *Oh shit, he's got a knife.* Dismissing me, he turned back to Hayden.

Snick.

A dark curl drifted onto the wooden floor. Hayden's hair. *He was cutting her hair while she lay sleeping.*

"Get away from her, Mark. Get away from her right now." I spoke coldly and calmly. I couldn't afford to panic: if I lunged for him or if Hayden woke suddenly, she could get seriously hurt. The clearheaded version of me, the person who'd taken over in the moments after Mireille jumped, was back when I needed her.

Mark jerked his head in my direction and then stepped away from the couch. Muttering a vacant "Sorry," he placed the scissors on the coffee table and left the room.

I rushed to Hayden, who was mercifully still asleep, and brushed the shorn locks away from her face. The room was too dark for me to fully assess the damage, but a scribble of hair came loose as I ran my fingers through it. She stirred.

"Mumma. Haydie tired now."

"I know, monkey."

Willing the icy calm to stay with me a few minutes more, I gathered the hot and sleepy Hayden to me and ran upstairs. Balancing her one-handed on my hip while she protested blearily, I pulled out a bag, shoved a bunch of my clothes and underwear into it, then dragged it into Hayden's room and packed a random selection of T-shirts, shorts, and toys. At the last minute I dove into the bathroom for my toiletry bag.

Then, as it had before in Paris, the calm receded, leaving me feverish with fear. *Get out, get out.*

My back muscles screaming from the combined weight of Hayden and the bag, I crept downstairs, half expecting Mark to lunge out of the gloom, or for the multi-limbed thing to skitter out of the shadows toward us—*wearing Mark's face this time, it would be wearing his face*—but we were alone. I fumbled in my bag for the car keys, slammed out of the security gate, and lurched toward the car. Hayden was now wide-awake and crying in mucusy gasps, but I didn't dare risk taking the time to comfort her. I forced her body into the car seat, trying to ignore her sobs, and hurriedly strapped her in. I screeched away from the curb.

It's a miracle I didn't crash the car that night. My anger at Mark pulsed through me, so hot and raw it was all I could focus on. In retrospect, bolting out of the house with Hayden like that was not only stupid but dangerous. After the beers I'd shared with Karim and downing half a bottle of wine on an empty stomach, I was way over the limit. Somewhere around Worcester sense took over, and I eased my foot off the accelerator and slid into the slow lane. For the first time since I'd strapped her into her car seat, I peered into the rearview to check on her. She'd fallen asleep, head drooping. The hair on the left side of her head stood up in a clump of ragged tufts.

It was only when I pulled off the highway and onto the lonely country roads that I began to regret my decision to flee to my folks' place. I considered driving back and finding a hotel, but I needed to be around people who were on my side. I couldn't let them see Hayden like that, her scalp showing through the shorn hair. Checking that there was no one dodgy around, I stopped outside a deserted farmers' market near Ashbury and woke Hayden. Using the nail scissors I'd shoved into my bag, I neatened her hair as best I could. Hayden hardly protested at all—perhaps she'd picked up on my desperation. After a limp "What you doing, Mumma?" she stopped wriggling in the seat and submitted to the ad hoc haircut. Her numb acceptance of the situation made my anger spike again. A part of me wanted to gather the hair and carry it with me—for some reason it felt wrong and dangerous just to leave it behind—but I buried it under a rock and drove on.

It was past one a.m. when I crunched the car into my parents' driveway. The B and B was dark and silent, and I hesitated before I rang the gate buzzer. I had to get my story straight, but what could I say? The truth wasn't an option. It would set them against Mark once and for all.

"Yes?" my dad's voice barked through the intercom.

"It's me. Can I come in?"

"*Stephanie?* That you, doll?"

I could hear my mother's voice behind him. "Please let me in, Dad."

"Hold on, doll, I'm coming."

The sobs came then, and I fought to calm myself down,

scrubbing at my eyes. I had to appear calm. The gate creaked open. I drove through, stalling the engine as I jerked to a stop and fell out of the car and into my dad's arms. My mother fussed and buzzed around me.

"Can you get Hayden, Mom?" I managed.

"Of course. But, Stephanie, what's happened? Has something happened? Why didn't you call? Did you drive from Cape Town now, at this time? Where's Mark?"

"Everything's fine. We had a fight, Mom. Don't worry, it's nothing serious. I just had to get out of the house." I made a stab at a rueful grin. "I overreacted. We've both been under a lot of stress lately."

They didn't buy it, but I caught Dad giving Mom a look, silently entreating her not to pry right then. I loved him for that.

She settled on an exasperated "Oh, Steffie. Dad would have driven down to get you."

Hayden was breathing easier as my mom carried her up to one of the guest rooms. She dropped off the second Mom tucked her in. I kicked off my shoes and, without removing the rest of my clothes, crawled in next to her, reassuring my mom that all I needed was a good night's sleep. My parents finally crept back to their own room, leaving me in darkness.

I slept until almost two p.m. the next day, waking disoriented and without Hayden next to me. I jumped up, irrationally panicking that Mark had crept in during the night and stolen her, but then I heard a ribbon of laughter trailing in from the garden. I peered out of the window. Hayden was helping Mom weed the flower beds that ringed the B and B's lawn. Now that the fear had abated, the anger was back baking inside me. Fuck Mark. *Fuck* him.

I brushed my teeth too roughly, drawing blood from my gums, pulled on a clean T-shirt, and headed downstairs and into the garden to face the music. Hayden waved at me distractedly and returned to her digging. She was looking much better, and her sniffles appeared to be lessening.

Mom hurried over to me. "Did you sleep well?"

"Yes, thanks," I said automatically, but it hit me then that I'd slept right through for the first time in almost a week. Longer than that. I had the trace of a hangover, but otherwise my brain felt sharper, as if it had been sluiced with ice water.

"What happened to Hayden's hair?"

Here we go. "She got some chewing gum caught in it. I tried to cut it out and made a bit of a mess."

My mother gave me a look. "Really? Where did she get the chewing gum from?"

I gave her my brightest smile. "I'm not sure."

Hayden laughed and held up a bunch of weeds and flowers. Mom handed her an empty flowerpot and then shuffled over to me, dropping her voice. "Your father says I shouldn't ask you this, but will you tell me why you came here last night? I'm worried about you, sweetheart. Has something happened with Mark? Has Mark—"

"Not now, Mom." She winced and I softened my voice. "Okay if I make myself something to eat?"

She brushed dirt from her hands. "I'll get you something."

"It's fine, Mom. You stay with Hayden."

"You know you can stay as long as you like. We don't have anyone booked in until next week, and even then there will be plenty of room. It's your home."

Is it? I thought. My home was supposed to be in Cape Town, with Mark. This wasn't how my life was supposed to go: running to Mom and Dad whenever I had a problem. But I had more than just a problem. It was more than just a marital spat. A glimmer of last night's anger surfaced.

I kissed her cheek and went back into the familiar cluttered kitchen with its clunky tan tiles, flouncy floral curtains, and my mom's collection of gewgaws. It was comforting being there. It was safe, and I hadn't felt safe for a long time. I grabbed the bacon from the fridge and mechanically placed the rashers in the pan.

I knew I'd have to figure out my next move. Was my marriage over? Self-pity flooded in. I had no job, no cash of my own. Bacon fat hissed and spat, searing the back of my hand. I barely noticed. I tipped the rashers onto two thick pieces of white bread and squashed them into a makeshift sandwich. I was no longer hungry, but I made myself choke it down, standing over the sink and staring blindly out of the window.

The weight of a hand on my shoulder made me jump—my dad. "Don't eat too fast, doll." He joined me at the window. "Your mother loves having Hayden here." He cleared his throat. "I told her not to bother you, but I need to know. Did Mark do something to you or Hayden?" My dad's face was carefully blank, but his eyes were hard.

"No, Dad. We just needed time apart; that's all. Hayden and I will be out of here soon as we can."

"Doll, this is your home."

It's not my home. "I know you didn't approve of Mark, Dad." I'd used the past tense unconsciously, as if the relationship really was over.

"That's true. I won't deny it, doll, but he's your husband. It's your choice. Whatever you decide, we're here for you." For some reason I thought back to my low-key wedding day. We'd got married at the Cape Town Magistrate's Court, followed by a small lunch with my parents, Carla, and a few of Mark's closest friends at the Five Flies Restaurant. The food had been good, but the atmosphere was stilted, the guests divided into two camps: my parents perched stiffly at one end of the table, Carla and the rest of them at the other. Someone, possibly Carla, maliciously suggested my dad make a speech. It had been mortifying for him—he loathed being the center of attention—but he struggled gamely through it, reaching for something positive to say about my new husband ("Cape Town University, where Mark works, has a good reputation, or so I've heard").

"Thanks, Dad."

He hovered for a while, then drifted out of the kitchen to resume whatever DIY project he had going.

With Hayden still happily occupied, I cleaned the kitchen, then slogged upstairs to my laptop—my refuge. Ignoring my emails, I applied for jobs online in a feverish spurt and joined three temping agencies. This manic practical behavior, doing something I should have done months ago, helped. The way ahead no longer seemed so murky. *And just think,* I told myself hollowly, *you're on your way to being a published author.* I decided that tomorrow, when I hoped the anger would have faded, I would contact Mark, tell him to check himself into a government-funded clinic or something to get the help he needed. I would insist that he move out of the house until he was well—the night before it hadn't occurred to me that he should be the one to leave. Only ... did I really want to go back to the house? It dawned on me then that the shadowy twitching thing hadn't visited last night. I looked around the room, at the flouncy curtains and pastel walls decorated with benign watercolors my mom had bought wholesale at a furniture warehouse. Whatever it was, it hadn't followed us here.

I didn't call Mark that day, and he didn't call me. I checked my phone regularly, but the only messages were spam from 419 scammers.

My mom tried digging for more details that evening, but I brushed her off, placating her with bullshit about Mark being stressed-out at work and needing some alone time. I watched the rugby in silence with Dad while Mom bathed and fed Hayden, hiding my irritation when she made her a typically unhealthy plate of fish fingers and processed sugary sauce. I turned in early.

Again, I woke late after a dreamless night. My body felt loose and relaxed, as if I'd been soaking in a hot bath for hours. One of my parents had placed a small pot of coffee and a plate of toast next to the bed. The toast was cold and the coffee luke-warm, but it was still drinkable. I stretched and padded over to the window. Down below, Hayden was helping my mother hang out the washing, giggling and chasing the birds that pecked at the breakfast crumbs scattered over the sun-dappled lawn. I dove back under the covers with my laptop.

My heart gave a sideways skip when I saw I had an email from the Canadian book agent. Expecting a rejection, I had to read the message twice before it sank in: she was offering to represent me. My first instinct was to tell Mark the good news. I wanted to share it with him, see the pride on his face, hear it in his voice.

You can't. You left him. You left him in the house and ran away.

I had a right to be angry after what he'd done to Hayden, of course I did, but he wasn't well. For all I knew he was in the midst of a full-on nervous breakdown. And instead of getting help for him, I fled.

I left him alone in that house.

Flushed with shame, I grabbed for my phone, almost knock-ing the coffeepot flying, and dialed his cell. It went straight to voice mail. I sent him a text, asking him to call me.

More out of twitchiness than hunger, I ate the toast, which was limp and chewy, and read the agent's note again. I man-aged to formulate a reply, accepting her offer, that I hoped didn't sound overeager and toadying.

I forwarded it to Mark and scanned the rest of the in-box. Karim had sent me a Facebook message, which didn't help with my growing shame. I deleted it unread. There was also a message from an Olivier. It took me a second to place the name before it clicked: the French real estate agent, responding to my inquiries about the Petits' building. I didn't feel any trepidation as I opened it; I was too distracted by the news from the book agent and my conflicting feelings about Mark.

Mme. Sebastian,

I am writing to give you the information you request, but please understand that after this I cannot help you anymore, and I respectfully ask that you do not contact me again.

I first encountered the building in question nearly twenty years ago when I was approached by M. Philippe Guérin to act as the agent for it. After many years during which it had remained derelict, M. Guérin had bought the building and renovated the apartments, and I was instructed to advertise for tenants.

At first I thought it would be easy. Many people were interested because the area was desirable and the apartments were spacious. But time and time again people would view the apartments and then decline to live there. Some of the people said they experienced une mauvaise ambiance, *but most could not describe why it was exactly they were uncomfortable in the building. I myself could not understand it, as I did not experience this thing. We made the rent lower and lower, so of course we did attract the tenants, but anyone who did move in did not stay for long or renew the lease, and the building was never more than half-occupied. It was not enough. This went on for many years. Eventually, M. Guérin, who was in poor health, wanted to sell the building but could not, as he had overcapitalized on it and he would have lost even more money. At this time, France was in a recession also.*

I was frustrated that I could not secure tenants and I know that later M. Guérin engaged many other agents in the hope that they would have more luck. As far as I know, they did not. A structural survey was done, but no source of what could be creating such a bad atmosphere could be found. Confused and also fascinated as to why so many people found the accommodation odious, I decided to explore the building's history.

I must say now that I did not believe in les fantômes. *I still do not. I must also say again that I myself have never experienced bad things or feelings there in the years I acted as M. Guérin's representative.*

The building had changed hands many times over the years, so I was having much difficulty obtaining reliable information. I decided to speak to the businesspeople in the neighborhood, and heard a rumor that something terrible had indeed happened in the building during the 1970s. No one knew all the details, but it was suggested to me that I speak to the proprietor of a nearby tabac *who had been in the area for many, many years. I was also warned that he did not like to speak of it. I began to use the* tabac *as a regular place to drink at night, and soon the proprietor—who is now deceased—began to trust me. I am lucky, as I can be charming, and one night I used all of this charm and a bottle of good pastis to help loosen the man's tongue, as you say.*

He said that during the 1970s the building fell into disrepair, but still many families lived there. One of them was the building's concierge, who lived in an apartment (I do not know which one) with his wife and two daughters. The proprietor of the tabac did not know this man well, but said he was a veteran of la Guerre d'Algérie and had been injured and very much traumatized there by the atrocities he had witnessed. He had returned to France with his wife, an Algerian, and found a job as a concierge. After several years, they began a family and had two daughters. The proprietor said that the concierge was a quiet man who depended on his wife for his strength and that the family was poor but seemed to be very happy. Then, the concierge's wife became very sick. It was a long illness. For many months she lingered between life and death. Thereafter, she died.

The concierge turned to drinking as solace and began neglecting his job and his daughters. He had many warnings from the patron of the building, but did not change his ways. The tabac proprietor said to me that it was as if he was a changed man. His wife and he had shared a grand passion. His spirit was broken. His heart was broken. He gathered much debt and was then told to leave. He had nowhere to go.

His body was discovered lying on the courtyard of the building by his oldest daughter when she returned from school. It is believed that he threw himself from one of the high windows.

The coffee turned to bile in my throat. *Mireille*, I thought. I continued reading:

This was not the most tragic part of the situation. The oldest daughter found the body of her younger sister in the cellar of the building. Her father had done things, terrible things, to the child before she died. Mutilations.

The proprietor did not know what happened to the surviving daughter after she made this discovery.

Mireille? Was Mireille the missing daughter? I did the math—it was possible she was born in the sixties. And after reading this, how could I not think of Mireille's attic room and her paintings of the sad-eyed child? Then there was the scrap of paper I'd found in the kitchen drawer in the Petits' apartment. The child who'd written it—Mireille's younger sister perhaps?—had implied that her father blamed her for her mother's illness. Could this be a possible motivation for why the concierge had murdered his youngest child?

At the bottom of the email the real estate agent had written, *As I say before, I cannot help you more. It is possible that you can verify this tragic story by exploring the records of the Paris newspapers. Also, I do not know if the building is still owned by M. Guérin nor do I have information about* la famille Petit. He signed off with, *This is the last telephone number that I have for M. Guérin. Perhaps he can help you more.* The number signed off the email. I googled the prefix code 02. It covered the area on the outskirts of Paris.

The B and B's wi-fi wasn't strong enough for me to use Skype, so I snuck downstairs, grabbed the cordless house phone from the kitchen, and slipped back up to my room. Without planning what I was going to say, I dialed. It rang and rang, and I let it ring, not sure whether or not I really wanted anyone to answer it. My hand grew sweaty on the receiver.

I counted twenty rings, twenty-five; then came a click, the sound of a throat clearing, and, *"Oui?"*

I jumped, flustered. "Oh, hi . . . hello, *parlez-vous anglais?*"

A long pause. *"Oui.* A little." A cough. "Who are you?" A man's voice, elderly, interspersed with a hissing sound as if he was breathing through an oxygen mask. *Darth Vader. You're talking to Darth Vader.*

I bit back the humorless giggle. "My name is Stephanie. Stephanie Sebastian. Is this Monsieur Guérin?"

"Oui." Pause, *hiss. "C'est moi."*

"Monsieur, I am sorry to disturb you, but could you tell me, do you still own property in Paris?" I rattled off the address.

"Oui. Pourquoi?"

"I stayed in one of the apartments in your building recently and I was hoping you could—"

"No, madame. This is not possible."

"Excuse me?"

"The building is empty. No one stays there." *Hiss,* pause, then, "Ah . . . *un moment."* Another pause, longer this time, followed by a flurry of mumbled voices in the background—I made out the words "Papa?" and *"anglais"*—and then a crackle and a fumbling sound. A younger male voice came on the line: *"Allo? Qui est-ce?* Who is this?"

I repeated my name.

"My father does not know people from England. You have the wrong number."

"Wait! I'm not from England. I'm South African. *Afrique du Sud."*

"This telephone number. How it is that you have it?" The voice had become guarded, less irritable.

"It was given to me by Monsieur le Croix. He used to be Monsieur Guérin's"—I searched for the word—*"immobilier.* I was hoping to talk to Monsieur Guérin about—"

"This is not possible. My father, he is very sick."

"I understand, but . . . monsieur, please, it's important. Will you help me then?"

"Help you? *Non.* I cannot help you, and now I must go—"

I jumped in, praying that he wouldn't hang up. "Please. *Please.* Five minutes, that's all I ask. I need answers."

A sigh hissed down the line. I took this as encouragement. "One of the apartments in your father's building near Pigalle was advertised on a website by a couple who called themselves the Petits. My husband and I stayed in their apartment and they were supposed to come to South Africa and stay in my house but they never showed up."

Silence. Now I couldn't even hear him breathing. "Hello? Monsieur? Hello?"

"I am here."

"It seems the Petits don't exist. I know the police have probably been in contact with you or your father, but while we were staying there, a woman, Mireille, died. She killed herself. Monsieur Petit, I . . ."

A sharp indrawn breath. I hadn't meant to call him that; it slipped out.

"I cannot talk to you, madame. I cannot help you."

"*Please.*"

"I am sorry."

"I know about the building's history. I know that something bad happened there. I know . . ." *I know that after we stayed in your building, my husband—my already fractured husband— has gone completely fucking mad, and there's something vile, something dangerous, lurking in my house.* "Were you the one who contacted us? Are you Monsieur Petit?"

"That is not my name."

The voice was cold, but he hadn't yet hung up on me. "Why did you want us to stay in the apartment? Please, Monsieur Petit—Monsieur Guérin—tell me why. Help me. You don't understand, my husband, he's . . . he's . . ." *Mad. He's gone mad. We brought something back, we brought something back from your building.*

"I am sorry." He was whispering now.

"What are you sorry for, Monsieur Petit?"

Another long pause. "I am sorry it had to be you. *Merci,* and goodbye."

A click, followed by dead air. I tapped in the number again, but it wouldn't connect.

Merci. What was he thanking me for?

Je suis désolée.

What was Mireille sorry for?

Mark. I have to talk to Mark.

Once more, his phone went straight to voice mail. I tried him again. And again. Still no answer. I sent another text. Then, in desperation, I called Carla. She didn't answer either—perhaps she was with him. For once, the thought of them together didn't make me anxious; this time it was reassuring. I left a message saying that I was worried about Mark as he wasn't answering his phone, asking her if she'd mind checking on Mark and letting me know how he was. I didn't tell her exactly why I was worried about him—*you might want to hide the scissors if you go round there*—although now I wonder if things would have turned out differently if I had.

Should I blame myself for this? I still don't know.

All I could do then was wait and think about what had come before.

Chapter 23

Mark

A car's lights scan into the living room, over my books, the TV, across the glaze of the photographs on the shelf, over the masks and wire sculptures Steph brought here. I realize I've been sitting in the dark for several hours. The German shepherd next door starts blaring, but I'm not afraid when Steph and Hayden aren't here.

The stamp of the men's boots, the sharp ooze of their voices. I wasn't afraid for myself—the only point of my focus was Steph and Hayden. I directed all my psychic energy to protect them. It sounds stupid, I know, but when the men left, and Steph and Hayden were unharmed, I felt I had done my job. That was all that mattered; it's still all that matters.

But now it's just me. I haven't set the alarm. They can come in; I have nothing left to take.

On another night like this, I might have a drink beside me, but tonight I don't. I can't swallow because the darkness is heavy enough to crush my windpipe. I think idly about killing myself, but I don't have the fortitude. I can't even get up; I wouldn't know where to start. Perhaps if I sit here for long enough, the darkness will snuff me out. I smell the acrid tang of old smoke. I am decamped.

The students next door laugh on the sidewalk as they return from their Saturday night out. Later, the gate across the road squeals as the nurse leaves for her predawn shift. Birds cackle at one another. I am finally provoked enough by this reminder of time to stand. I piss, avoiding my face in the bathroom mirror, then make for the pantry. In the kitchen, even though my eyes are accustomed to the blackness, I crack my hip bone on the corner of the butcher block as if it has deliberately been moved into my way.

When I was about five years old, I was terrified of going into our pantry at home. There was a banshee who lived there, and, my eight-year-old cousin James told me, banshees suck out your soul as they scream. I could hear the banshee some nights as I lay in bed, an interminable low drone. I told my mother once and she said there was no banshee; my father laughed. *You want to get a tin of fruit from the pantry, Markie, you're going to have to brave the banshee.*

James and his parents came for lunch one Sunday. He locked me in the pantry and didn't come back. It felt like hours, trying not to move in case I woke it. I tried not to cry, knowing that banshees loved fear and sadness more than anything. *They can smell your fear,* James had told me. I could smell the roast chicken coming in from the kitchen, Mom and Aunt Petra chatting, James outside, playing with the dog. They had forgotten me, and the banshee would wake if I moved. Finally, about to sneeze, about to wet myself, my legs cramping, I needed to escape. Eyeing the small window above the top shelf, I pushed up to the first rack, not looking back because if you don't look back what's breathing down your neck doesn't exist, it can't hurt you. I couldn't breathe, trying to keep in my body's noise.

Don't think of the fear, close your eyes, climb.

I darted my short arm up, just reaching the next shelf. A bag of rice flopped over, rattling over two bottles of orange soda—a little intrusion of noise, settled as quickly as it started. A final roll of something; then I heard it. The banshee, it's drone louder than I'd ever heard it.

It's awake.

It's right behind me.

Cupping my hands over my ears, I fell, curling fetal.

I probably screamed. I probably cried. I remember Dad coming in and yelling at me, "Would you calm down? It's only a bloody toy."

The banshee was a plastic battery-operated keyboard with a stuck E. The banshee didn't exist. I don't remember eating roast chicken with James and Aunt Petra and Uncle Leon.

Now I close the door behind me and will her to emerge from the enveloping void.

Waiting, I run my tongue over my lip where it's split. I press my fingernail into the cut, use my thumb to pare it open, concentrate on the ragged sting. But she doesn't come.

Later, the sun shines in, so I close the curtains. But in Hayden's room, the Disney princesses still glow too brightly and I tear them down.

I crawl on the living room carpet, gathering up the hair where we all left it.

This bed is Odette's. She owned it first. When we were young and amorous and could still express desire without pain or guilt and before Zoë was born, she made it hers in countless ways. Steph insisted on a new mattress and new sheets, but this bed is Odette's.

I sit at the edge of Steph's side and open the drawer in her nightstand, like an intruder, careful not to disturb anything. A forgotten paperback, the sort she prefers to hide from me, a notepad scrawled with plotlines for her children's book, a tangle of necklaces and bracelets she hasn't bothered to unknot after Hayden played with them, balled tissues, a cracked lip-stick with the lid missing. I'm looking for clues to her that don't exist.

I close the drawer and stare around the room, trying to feel something other than this. So much has happened in this bed-room, but it's all dust-caked now. Just me now; it's all led to this. None of the love or joy or anguish or impassioned argu-ment I've wasted my life on can counteract the fact that I am here, alone. It all seemed so important, life.

I sit awhile and wish for her to come, and for a moment I think she has because I see something moving under the dresser. But it is not her. I go toward the shadow and crouch down, but there's nothing there but dander.

Then there is a crash of glass to rouse me. I want them to come in, finish the job, take away the nothingness. When they don't, I push myself up and limp through to the living room, my hands aching, the skin on my knees grazed, a bruise on my forehead. It is dark again and all that has happened is that the photos have been pushed off the bookshelf again.

I sit down, bare foot bleeding from the glass.

The dog barks; I have a pain in my stomach. The gate across the road shears on its hinges. Birds shout. Someone swears. It is light. I stand up to close the curtain. Nobody comes. Some-thing dark looks at me with many red eyes from the vacant shelf. I curl up around the ache.

Bang, bang, bang. Tap, tap. Tap, tap, tap. That annoying sound of a chunky ring smacking against the window. It's going to crack.

"Open the bloody door, Mark! I know you're there."

I force myself up to sitting, my spine crackling. For a moment I don't know where I am; the drawn curtains across the bay window seep tepid light and I feel like I'm in a cave.

Carla rattles and calls again and I get myself up and shuffle to the front door.

As soon as I open it a crack, she shoulders through. "God, it's rank in here, sweetie," she says, bustling down the hall, dumping bags on the kitchen counter. "And you look like shit. Go and take a shower."

"What are you doing here?" I drag my hand through my hair and over my face, trying to wake myself up.

"Your wife called me. She was worried about you. Said you hadn't answered your phone for more than a day. I tried too."

"My phone?" I don't even know where it is. It must be dead, I don't know.

Carla hustles into the living room and opens the curtains and windows, flaps them pointedly as if to draw out the stink in here. As I approach and smell the freshish evening air coming in from outside, I realize she's right—I could do with a shower.

"Okay," I say, grabbing a clean pair of jeans and a shirt from my room and heading toward the bathroom.

The water does improve my mood. I feel more than sticky sweat washing off me. I have been acting crazy. I don't really know what I was thinking, trying to cut Hayden's hair, and Steph was right to react like that. And if she's been trying to get in touch with me, it means she's willing to work it out. I can stop all this nonsense and start being her husband and Hayden's father again.

A short knock and Carla ducks inside the bathroom and picks up my dirty clothes, then darts out again.

The odd thing is I really can't remember what seemed so urgent a few days ago. Picking up dead animals, drifting around town chasing ghosts. Maybe this long, dark night of the soul is just what I've needed to gain some perspective again, sweating out my horrors.

I soap myself all over, scrubbing until I'm red and tingling. Until I'm almost new. I dry myself off and get into my fresh clothes and find Carla wiping down the counters in the kitchen, clean dishes aligned on the drying rack, the washing machine going.

"This isn't just a weekend's worth of mess," Carla comments, not turning to face me. She's wearing jeans and a hooded jacket over a casual silk blouse—obviously she hurried over, but I can't help thinking that she looks good. "She's not looking after you very well."

I click my tongue. "I don't need looking after, and that's not her job."

Carla shrugs, as if what I've said doesn't make any difference. "I'm not trying to stir, but you're out at work all day, and she stays here, doing what? The laundry's piled up; the dishes aren't done."

"Christ, Carla, that's a bit old-fashioned of you."

"Don't be absurd, darling. You know it's got nothing to do with gender roles—it's about sharing the workload. If she were out working all day and you were here, you know you'd keep the dishes clean."

I suppose I would, but I say, "She's been busy with Hayden. It's draining, looking after a kid, especially a two-year-old. You're constantly walking after them, keeping them out of danger . . ."

I stop talking as the air ices over. I don't want to discuss this, but Carla doesn't let it go. She finally turns to face me, color in her cheeks. "Yes, I'm quite aware that I haven't had the *privilege* of motherhood, but from what I can see, looking after a two-year-old without working for a living involves a lot of sleeping." She slaps the cleaning cloth into the sink, surprising herself, I think, because then she composes herself again, takes a tumbler off the dryer, and reaches for one of the bottles of wine next to the window.

I know it pains her to be vulnerable, and I go and take a glass for myself. "Some for me too."

She pulls out a stool at the kitchen counter and sighs as she sits. "It's not my business, I know. But you're my friend, and I don't like the way she undermines you."

I join her at the table, soothed to have someone on my side. I can't tell her what I did to Hayden to make Steph take her and leave. "She doesn't. I owe her a lot. You know Hayden was quite difficult when she was small—she had colic, she was really uncomfortable, she hardly slept—and I didn't help Steph with her."

"Did she let you?" Carla snaps. "No, hang on, let me answer that. No, she didn't let you. I see how she is with her, so possessive, of course you can't find your way in."

"It's not like that. I feel so guilty about—"

"What you need to do, Mark," she interrupts, "is *stop* feeling guilty and start asserting your place in this family. Hayden's *your* daughter, and you need to stop living here—in your own bloody house—like you're an unwelcome lodger. For Christ's sake, you're the sole breadwinner; you're the man of the household. Start acting like it."

I could choose to be offended or inspired or enraged, but I'm simply embarrassed. I sip my wine and slump my forehead into my hand. "Acting like a man. Jesus, there's a fraught topic."

Carla pauses long enough to let the air settle. "As I say, it's none of my business."

"When those men broke into our house, I was immobilized. I just sat there while they took Steph away from me. I couldn't even look at the guy who stayed with me, just stared at my feet while he rooted through our stuff. If I had owned a gun, would I have shot them?"

"Mark," Carla starts, trying to steer me onto another course, regretful of having spoken her mind. But then she recognizes that my tone is meditative, not angry or defensive. I'm really wondering aloud here, telling things to my oldest friend that I can't share with anyone else.

"I don't think I would have," I continue. Now I look into Carla's eyes. "My only role, I think, the only thing I know how to do, is mourn."

Carla puts her hand on mine.

"I miss Hayden," I say.

"They'll come back soon," she says. "Then you can start again."

I know I'm out of chances to start again, so I say nothing.

We go to the couch and Carla puts on a soothing cooking channel, an elegant woman in her dream house with a fragile, seductive smile and sad eyes, then two life-weathered and time-sweetened old men driving around Italy. At some point, Carla puts her head on my shoulder and I let it stay, smelling the fresh shampoo and salty grass of her hair. My hand's on her hip, just for comfort's sake. I have the sense that things are going to work out just fine. None of this is a matter of life or death—it will all come out in the wash.

Her hand's on my chest, under my shirt, because it's getting cool in this room, her foot brought up to nestle under my calf. Her lips on mine, my fingers along her back. I turn onto my back and Carla covers me, her hair draped into my face, and it's then I see her, Zoë, standing in the corner of the living room, watching.

A slant of light from the hallway falls into the angle where she stands, slicing across her face so that I can see her chin and her mouth, and half of that yellow hair, a languid finger curling a skein of it. Her jeans and T-shirt could do with a wash, I notice, and there's a rancid smell in the air. I'm about to say something to her, but then she smiles and glides her tongue over her lips, still twisting, twisting the hair around her finger.

Carla pulls back. "What's the matter?"

"Nothing. It's just . . ."

But now the girl's smile is becoming too wide, her lips stretching unnaturally over teeth I can see are blackened and broken. The smell comes at me like a solid object and I shuffle backward on the couch, but Carla's weight is keeping me there.

"It's okay, sweetie," Carla says, her breath fast. "It's all gone. Nothing can hurt you again. It will all be okay."

The girl twists, twists, twists her hair around her finger until a thick drape of it comes free from her scalp. She steps forward and her whole face comes into the light. The gray skin is mottled with bruises, one eye swollen shut, the other burst red. She licks her cracked lips, and her tongue grows longer, stretching away from her mouth, a smear of bloody spittle following it around her face.

Pulls another hunk of hair, drops it to the floor. Rips at her scalp and at her face, still smiling, ingratiating. Pleading.

"*Papa? Pourquoi tu ne m'aime pas?*"

The skin melts off her face, revealing blackened flesh.

"*Papa. Pourquoi?*"

I try to force my eyes shut, but she wants me to see. She's dissolving into a pile of darkened carrion on the floor, reforming now into something with too many thin, bristly legs, something with red eyes, shimmering like a wraith along the baseboard.

"Mark? Mark?" Carla comes in close, her warm, living hands to the sides of my face, her hot, sweet breath in my mouth, and finally I can stop seeing. She's kissing my tears and I'm grasping at her like she'll keep me alive.

Carla is living. She blocks my view of everything I don't want to see. She protects my eyes from myself. I give in. Decades fall from me, and for a moment I feel liberated, as if none of it ever happened. I'm back in college, back when life was light, making out with my girlfriend as if joy was never tinged with sin or guilt.

We spend the night like that, curled together, and everything is forgiven. But when dawn rises in the room, I smell it first, then feel the sticky gore all over my skin. Then, against every screaming instinct, I open my eyes.

Chapter 24

Steph

I sit in the car, hunkered down in the driver's seat like a private detective, a cup of shitty McDonald's coffee cooling on the dash. I have a clear view of the house from here, but so far there's been no sign of life.

I haven't been back here for two months, not since the night Hayden and I fled to Montagu. I haven't dared return, convinced that being in the vicinity of the scene of the crime will unblock the toxic buildup of emotion kept in check by the tranquilizers my folks' prescription-happy doctor has been feeding me. Tranquilizers I won't have to hide from Mark. But now, as I stare at the new front door—an incongruously modern hardwood thing my dad picked out when he came down here to clean up—I'm not feeling much of anything at all. No sadness, regret, pity, or the old standby, anger.

Without pulling my eyes away from the door, I take a sip of coffee, ignoring the jitter of the cup in my trembling fingers—a side effect of the drugs. Karim's cousin and his wife have been in there for a week now. *Is that long enough?* I don't know much about them (I don't want to know), just that they decided to move to the Cape and needed a place to stay. I mailed the keys to Karim and asked him to take care of the details. They're his family, after all. My dad offered to collect our personal belongings, and I rented the house partially furnished to save on moving costs, although most of the living room furniture was beyond saving. The first month's rent and the deposit have been eaten by the mortgage, minus the percentage the real estate agency is skimming off the top.

Karim's relatives jumped at the chance, and why not? They're getting a good deal. It's at least two grand cheaper than anything else in the neighborhood. Zainab, the leasing agent, was aghast when I told her the price I was willing to let it go for. I could hardly tell her that I needed a particular kind of tenant, and Karim's family fitted the bill.

I double-check the time. I have three hours until I have to fetch Hayden from playgroup. The drive back to Montagu takes two and a half, so I'm pushing it. I open my door and splatter the cold coffee onto the sidewalk. I toy with the ignition key.

I shouldn't be here.

I jump as the door opens and a man steps out. He's short, dumpy, his Lions T-shirt pulled out from his shorts—nothing like Karim. He shivers and screws a cigarette into his mouth. He stares straight ahead and smokes. I'm right in his line of sight, but his eyes skate over me.

How much has Karim told him about what happened here? It made the national papers and news sites, after all, IOL.com leading with the headline CAPE TOWN'S NEW HOUSE OF HORRORS. Carla got a small obit in the *Mail & Guardian*. She would have appreciated that.

I don't know what possessed me, but I went to her memorial service, deciding to drive down on a whim. It took place two weeks after her murder in the cavernous chapel at the exclusive Bishops Diocesan College (one of her brothers was on the board there), although I'd heard her railing against the Bishops old boys' network many times. Arriving late, I found a pew at the back. The chapel was only a quarter full, the empty seats adding a tawdriness to the whole affair. One by one, her colleagues and members of the South African literati tried to outdo one another with their overblown eulogies and readings. I tuned them out and stared at the backs of the mourners' heads, hoping no one would recognize me and imagining what they would say if they did.

Don't look now, but that's the wife. You know, his *wife.*

Do you think she knew he was crazy all along?

She wasn't there when he did it, so who knows?

Where is he now?

You haven't heard? Valkenberg. Locked up in the secure wing. Electroshock treatment, the works. When they found him he was a gibbering wreck.

Yes. That I knew.

Still, the wife was lucky she wasn't in the house when he did it. It could have been her.

Oh yes. And they have a young daughter, don't they? What could make someone do something like that?

Well, I heard he says he didn't do it. Said a gang broke in.

Didn't the DNA evidence prove it was him?

You're joking. DNA evidence? In this country? You think they'd bother? The backlog in the labs is a joke.

You know, it's so tragic. He had another daughter once. She died.

Did he kill her too?

No. They say it was an accident.

Shame. It's a terrible thing.

And what he did to Carla . . .

Pieces. She was in pieces.

Toward the end of the service, a middle-aged white woman sitting a few pews in front of me whipped her head around and stared at me intensely. She was dressed conservatively in black, but on her wrist she wore a bracelet made of goat-skin: the sangoma. I stared right back at her without blinking, then mouthed, "Fuck you." Shaking, I got up and left. I half expected her to follow me out—I half wanted her to. I still don't know why I focused my rage at her. Perhaps because like me, she hadn't been able to save Mark.

After what Mark did hit the headlines, old friends tried to reach out to me, but I ignored most of them, choosing to cut myself off and cocoon myself and Hayden in Montagu. I couldn't tell who gave a shit about us or who simply wanted to hear the gory details, eager for a chance to trot out the old South African "you're so lucky you weren't there" line. Then Karim messaged me a month ago to see how I was doing. I wrote back. Perhaps some part of me knew he'd be useful. We chatted every day, and then he mentioned that his cousin was moving down from Joburg and needed a place to stay. I recalled him telling me the family had endured their own brutal home invasion, and I offered to rent the house to them. Of course I did.

Mireille's voice ghosts in: *I thought it had left with the last people. They had pain, but not enough.*

Now it is with you.

I reach for my coffee and take a sip and get a dismaying ghost-mouthful of nothing before remembering I've poured it on the sidewalk. Karim's cousin sucks at the cigarette furiously, eyes squinting, like a gangster in a movie. He chucks the butt at the skeletal sticks of Odette's long-dead wisteria, then lights another. He looks like he can handle himself. A strong character. Stronger than Mark, or is this just fanciful thinking? Again, he seems to look straight through me. To him, I'm just a dumpy white girl in a secondhand Mini, which I'll pay off after the advance for the book comes through. Five thousand dollars: not enough to set Hayden and me free, but the plummeting rand is on my side, and it'll keep us going until I find a full-time job.

It will keep us going until we can return home.

Most of Carla was found crammed into the pantry.

I didn't see the aftermath firsthand, but my imagination filled in the blanks. The superintendent who came to Montagu to question me after the incident was kind. She advised me not to return to the house "until it was cleaned up." Mark didn't ask to see me when he was arrested, and he still hasn't. The cut-price attorney my parents hired is adamant that due to Mark's actions and state of mind I don't have a duty of care to pay for his legal representation. I am going to fight to keep the house, and refuse to give into the bank's demands to sell. It's Hayden's. It's not the bank's. It's not Odette's. It's not Zoë's. It's Hayden's. It's all she will ever have of her father.

But I can't risk bringing her back here until . . .

How long will it take? We were in the apartment for only— what was it, five, six days? I haven't been back in touch with Monsieur le Croix, but I don't need to get in touch with him. I've been online. After we left Paris, all the apartments in that building, including the one we stayed in, were rented out in less than two weeks and the building itself is back on the market. Whatever was poisoning the bricks and mortar—bad juju, infrasound, dead children, fucking mold, whatever—left with us. Or with Mireille when she threw herself out of the window.

Or maybe the Paris real estate market just picked up.

The man on the stoop scratches his belly. A small hand clutching a Barbie appears through the bars of the security gate. I grip the steering wheel and lean forward in my seat. A little girl. Not much older than Hayden. I suck breath through my teeth. Did Karim tell me that his cousin had children?

Yes. You know he did.

I lean across and roll down the passenger-side window. The little girl is saying something to the man—I can't make out her words from here—and he ignores her. He's blank-faced, focused in on himself.

Like Mark was just before he . . .

We went to the apartment. We brought something back. Now I have to get someone else to take it away.

Now it is with you.

You don't really believe that, do you?

I could cancel the lease and throw them out of the house before it's too late. I could shout a warning right now, right this second, tell them who I am, try to convince them the house isn't safe.

Maybe the damage has already been done.

Maybe it hasn't.

I roll up the window. The man still shows no interest in me. The small hand disappears back through the bars and into the gloom beyond the door. *Merci,* I think as I turn the key in the ignition and drive away. *I'm sorry it had to be you.*

Acknowledgments

S. L. Grey thanks:

Lauren Beukes, Rob Bloom, Wayne Brooks, Louise
Buckley, Eileen Chetti, Jennifer Custer, Hélène Ferey,
Claire Gatzen, Adam Greenberg, Sam Greenberg,
Bronwyn Harris, Savannah Lotz, Charlie Martins,
Oli Munson, Alex Saunders, and Carol Walters.

THE BLUMHOUSE BOOK OF NIGHTMARES
The Haunted City

Original and terrifying fiction presented by Jason Blum,
the award-winning producer behind the groundbreaking
Paranormal Activity, *The Purge*, *Insidious*, and *Sinister*
franchises. Jason Blum invited sixteen cutting-edge collab-
orators, filmmakers, and writers to envision a city of their
choosing and let their demons run wild. *The Blumhouse
Book of Nightmares: The Haunted City* brings together all-
new, boundary-breaking stories from such artists as Ethan
Hawke (*Boyhood*), Eli Roth (*Hostel*), Scott Derrickson
(*Sinister*), C. Robert Cargill (*Sinister*), James DeMonaco
(*The Purge*), and many others.

Horror